MURDER IN THE TOMB

For
Gladys Carlisle
in appreciation of a
lovely lady,

Lucian Austin Osgood

13 October 1937
M. S. Co. W.

From an inscribed copy of *Murder in the Tomb*

MURDER IN THE TOMB

LUCIAN AUSTIN OSGOOD

COACHWHIP PUBLICATIONS
Greenville, Ohio

ISBN 1-61646-398-8
ISBN-13 978-1-61646-398-4

CoachwhipBooks.com

THE UNIVERSITY HIGH SCHOOL

Lucian A. Osgood, A.B.

The University High School offers courses leading to high school graduation and to entrance in the University. The high school also provides a means of making up pre-collegiate credits of conditional freshmen, and serves as a highly developed field for practice teaching for seniors in the Department of Education.

U. H. S. is represented each year by athletic teams in all major sports. The "Coyote Pups" played through a complete football and basketball schedule during the 1922 and 1923 seasons with a creditable record. Literary societies and other organizations have also been formed within the student body.

The steady increase in enrollment may be taken as indicative of the success of the sub-freshman courses. The University High faculty, which is headed by Principle Lucian A. Osgood, is composed of four other instructors: Marian Hopkins Sweeney, A.B., Edith Mathilda Swanson, A.B., Robert Fawell, A.B., and Susan Olive Norwood, B.S. in Ed.

1924, in Vermillion, SD

MARGIE C. MORRIS
A.B., A.M.
Assistant Professor of Modern
Foreign Languages

LUCIAN AUSTIN H. OSGOOD
A.B., A.M.
Assistant Professor of English

WEENONAH POINDEXTER
Assistant Professor of Music.

1938, during Lucian Osgood's time in Columbus, MS

Lucian Austin Harden Osgood (1888/9-1951) was an English professor who gave the mystery oeuvre a single volume of detective fiction. It is a strange mystery, with many moving parts and exotic angles, but one that should keep the average "locked room" enthusiast on their toes as they sort through the clues.

Lucian Osgood was born in California, received his teaching degree at the University of South Dakota (producing a thesis, 'Spiritual Mysticism in the Poetry of Tennyson'), then went on to join the University of Minnesota English faculty before moving to the West Texas State Teachers College (now West Texas A&M). Lucian had married Evangeline Manning, a minister's daughter from Kansas, and they had one son, Robert Manning Osgood. In 1926, young Robert died at the age of 12 and was buried in Canyon, Texas. (A memorial was provided in the college library.) The Osgoods had no more children, but seem to have thrown themselves into mentoring roles with students, being actively involved in many aspects of college life. Lucian was a popular speaker, and the Canyon, TX, newspaper has numerous mentions of the couple in local society in the college town. They also managed to travel to Europe and Canada when school was out.

Lucian and Evangeline moved to Mississippi in 1933 as Lucian joined the faculty of the Mississippi State College for Women in Columbus. He taught English and journalism and coached the debate team. It was here, in 1937, that Lucian published *Murder in the Tomb*. He apparently sent copies back to Texas, as the *Canyon News* noted that

the book "combines a logically complicated plot with weird atmosphere, distinctive characters, and an ingenious solution."

The Osgoods later moved to California, where Lucian joined the
faculty at Loyola Marymount University (approx. 1944). In 1951, apparently before he could retire, Lucian suffered a stroke and died at
their home in Playa del Rey. Evangeline and a widowed sister moved to
a cottage in Inglewood, CA.

More mysterious than *Murder in the Tomb* itself, is its publishing company, the appropriately named "Unique Mystery Novels" of Columbus,
Mississippi. This is the only title the publisher seems to have produced,
though the back cover of *Murder in the Tomb* suggests there were several others to come: *The Ghost of Dr. Arnette* and *Death by Candle
Light*, both by Osgood, and *I Wish You Glad Tomorrow* and *Heloise*, by
Robert Grayle. Grayle is a complete mystery. "Unique Mystery Novels"
may very well have been a self-publishing venture by Osgood. *Murder
in the Tomb* is the only one of these titles to have been published; perhaps from a college or historical society archive further details on this
"unique" mystery may someday emerge . . .

DOROTHY O'MALLEY, B.A.
Librarian

LUCIAN A. OSGOOD, M.A.
English

DANIEL O'SULLIVAN, S.J.
Philosophy

1950, while at Loyola Marymount

(Thanks to Curt Evans for providing images.)

MURDER IN THE TOMB

CRIME COMMITTED AT WINDERMERE BAFFLES POLICE
Howard Ralston Murdered Under Strange Circumstances
Murder Done in Tightly Barred Tomb
Police Unable to Uncover Motive

The headlines stream their story across the front page of the *Minneapolis Clarion,* under date of August 16, 1932, where it lies spread before me on the top of my desk in the big room at *Windermere.* Two weeks have passed since the night of that bizarre crime, and I am only now sufficiently readjusted to set myself the task of recording the truth about the murder in the tomb.

I suppose that this account of what the newspaper elected to designate *The Mystery of the Murder in the Tomb* logically begins the night of August 15, although it actually had its origin in the unusual events of the night of June 15. I shall therefore begin at the former date, and weave in as best I can the happenings of the intervening two months.

THE EVENING OF THE FIRST DAY

1

August 15, 1932. Overhead the ominous roar of thunder; against window panes, intermittent dashes of rain. In the distance, sonorous booming bells; on the mantel, a French clock tinkling the hour of six. On the Spanish divan, feet stretched toward flickering gas-logs, sat my boss—Mr. Howard Fredrick Ralston—and M. Cornier.

Small, the boss was; five-eight, thin—weighing one hundred thirty-five, handsome and distinguished in appearance—despite his beaked nose, strong—notwithstanding his fifty years.

M. Cornier, five years Howard Ralston's senior, was a slightly larger man, but not so good looking as the boss. The item in his personal appearance that invited the passerby's second glance was the *imperial:* an affectation that caused him to resemble portraits of Napoleon III. I figure that is the reason why he was universally addressed as "Monsieur Cornier."

Like ourselves, M. Cornier had just returned home. I had been with Ralston on a sixty-day circling of the globe; M. Cornier had been on leisurely expedition to New Orleans and Havana, seeking relics of Columbus and Jean Lafitte.

As Howard Ralston's private secretary, I was supposed to be translating an old volume on the love-life of Napoleon and his Josephine. The translation was part of the research Ralston was making for information upon the Josephine diamonds, jewels recently come into his possession. Endeavoring to be consistent and thus justify my presence in the room, I translated with one eye and two hands. The other eye, and both ears, I concentrated upon the partners sitting on that old Spanish divan.

Windermere!

That is the name Ralston had given his residence on Park Avenue. The boss and M. Cornier owned an entire city block, and occupied twin houses. Cornier called his mansion *Fontainebleau.* The establishments were connected by a *porte-cochere,* above which was a glassed-in hall-way that permitted easy communication between the partners.

It was through this passage over the *porte-cochere* that Cornier had come this stormy night to hear the story Howard Ralston had to tell.

Exactly two months before, in that same room, on just such a stormy night, Ralston had told his friend of three antiques he wanted: a Borgia poison ring, a Chinese vengeance dagger, and the mummy of Serapion. The boss declared that he was going to have all three of them. Cornier laughed, declaring that to attain possession of the coveted articles was impossible.

The outcome of the argument had been a wager—a bet of fifty thousand dollars against fifty thousand dollars—that Ralston could not secure the three treasures and have them in that room within two months.

It looked to me as if Ralston were tossing fifty thousand bucks to the wind; but I knew that he was not one to surrender that much money without a struggle.

The Lord knows the room in which we sat contained enough of the world's rare, beautiful, and exotic creations without adding to the "conglomeration," as Paul Ralston was wont to describe the heaped-up accumulations of his father. Surveying the big room, I could understand why Ralston's friends called it "the tomb."

In dimension, the place was twenty-eight by forty-two, with high, beautifully beamed ceiling and with walls that were leather-paneled and hand-tooled in blue and gold. The dominating style of the interior decorator had been that of the Italian Renaissance. Shelves and cases were everywhere, stored with priceless relics out of the dead past; for Ralston loved the remnants of ancient days. Even the furniture recalled the dead past. The only modern pieces were the Chinese cabinet, the desk at which I sat working, and a few chairs.

With the boss hell-bent on making his reckless wager, I scanned the horde of stuff that was already his, wondering why he could not rest satisfied. But not he. He could never hear mention of a rare antique without becoming obsessed of burning desire to own it.

I speculated then on his chances of getting the Borgia poison ring, the vengeance dagger, and the mummy of Serapion.

Had Henri Cornier not scoffed, the wager had never been made that night of June 15, 1932, and I had not been dragged through two hectic months of intrigue and terror. Had the wager not been made, I had not sat in "the tomb" the night of August 15, two months later, with a storm raging over *Windermere* and fear clutching at my heart.

As on the night of June 15, so now a hurricane swept over the city, rocking houses upon their foundations and shouting alarm in the ears of the inhabitants. As on the night of June 15, so now the partners sat in comfort, apparently unmindful of the storm. Now, as then, the partners sat before the grate fire, the night grown suddenly chilly.

"Well, I've got them!" Ralston exclaimed, after easeful draft on his pipe.

"Let's have the story," was the calm rejoinder of M. Cornier, although he stood to lose fifty thousand dollars.

"Pietro and I did it."

"Pietro?"

"Pietro," the boss replied, "is an expert artificer I acquired the day you left Minneapolis, feeling cock-sure that I couldn't win the wager."

At that moment a door, on the side of the room opposite my desk, opened, and the Italian stood silhouetted against the light of the room behind him.

"I have just returned home, Master," Pietro said, tone silkily smooth.

"How is it outside?" Ralston asked him.

"Unusually gloomy. The storm is rolling up heavily."

"H'm. . . . Well, if you must employ yourself, you might brighten that Romanov pendant."

The door was closing, when Ralston called, "*Vien qui*, Pietro. I want you to meet my partner."

Pietro advanced into the room to be introduced to Cornier, who had risen. The Italian gave his hand, glancing up at the Frenchman with an unusually charming smile illuminating his faun-like face. Cornier returned the smile, but his eyes were unfriendly.

Pietro was no sooner gone back to his shop than Cornier said, "I don't like your artificer."

"If you knew him, you would not say that, Henri. He is a wonderful boy. I would trust him with my life."

"You may some day regret your confidence in him." Cornier's remark was brittle. I knew that his dislike would be something that the Italian would never be able to overcome.

"I am willing to take my chances with Pietro," Ralston said, puffing lazily at his pipe. "But for Pietro, I should not now possess the Borgia poison ring. Without that, I had not won my wager with you."

Cornier smiled, saying, "I have not conceded you victory." Again the cloud of smoke from Ralston's pipe curled ceiling-ward, and the tale began.

"You were no sooner out of Minneapolis than I cast about for an artificer in precious metals."

"Why?"

"Necessity. The mummy of Serapion and the vengeance dagger, I was certain to obtain; for Reni's cablegram was reassuring. The poison ring, however—"

"I understand," Cornier caught him up. "You knew that you could not get that, so you decided to counterfeit it."

Nasty color darkened Ralston's face—a flush as sometimes comes to a person whose heart is over-strained.

"Don't misjudge me, Henri. Recall, if you please, that I said I would have the three antiques in this room tonight, and that I would secure them by fair means or foul."

"It is not like you to have recourse to anything dishonorable."

Ralston's features softened when his friend said that.

Resuming his narrative, he said, "Quartermann of the Art Institute told me about this boy, Pietro Martini. Pietro is nephew and former employee of the Chicago Martini Brothers. He learned his craft under old Raphael Martini himself. Give him any metal, and he can fashion it into anything you demand. He made me a perfect duplicate of the Borgia poison ring."

"Howard, you ask too much in expecting me to believe this."

"Within his craft, Pietro epitomizes the art of generations of skilled artificers. But, as I said, Quartermann introduced Pietro to me. The boy and I liked each other at once. I took him to Italy with me. There we contacted the Duke of Vedena, who generously permitted us to examine his Borgia. Because of his photographic memory and his skill, Pietro easily duplicated the poison ring."

"Surely he needed more than one look at the original. Didn't the Duke become suspicious?"

"You must know that while I kept the Duke intrigued with poker, Pietro courted the Duke's daughter—the flaming Francesca."

"I see." Cornier's lip curled. "Through her he gained opportunities to study the original Borgia."

"All's fair in love and war, Henri."

"But was it fair to the Duke? Or to the 'flaming Francesca'?"

"I had to win that fifty thousand, Henri."

"And you exchanged your artificer's duplicate for the original ring?"

"That was not so difficult."

"What if the exchange is detected?" Cornier queried, after a pause.

"I had to gamble on that; but I do not believe detection likely, as the Duke's attention is at present given to dinosaur eggs. By the time he gets around to thinking again of his Borgia, I shall have returned it."

"You mean to return it?"

"After I have collected from you."

"When I made the wager, I had in mind permanent possession of the ring."

"You failed to specify that."

Cornier bit his lip. His eyes looked tired. I did not know then that a pile of his investments had collapsed.

"How am I to know," he demanded, "that the ring you have is not the counterfeit?"

Ralston passed the ring to his friend, saying, "You are a connoisseur. Examine it."

From a vest pocket Cornier drew a watchmaker's lens and critically studied the ring.

"It bears every mark of old craftsmanship," he reluctantly admitted. "A modern goldsmith might imitate that craftsmanship, but his imitation would easily be detected by an expert. . . . Still, I may be deceived at that—if your artificer be as clever as you say."

"You are not deceived." Receiving back the ring and holding it up, he exclaimed, "Isn't it a beauty? The Borgia poison ring—the damnable ring of death!"

As if by way of melodramatic emphasis, the storm's lightning shot its silver flame athwart the room—illuminating Ralston's hand and the cursed Borgia.

"See," the boss pointed out, "the ring bears the date, 1503. Also the motto of Cesare Borgia, engraved in Old French. The bezel, you notice, is wrought in the form of a lion. When Cesare Borgia presented this ring to the red-robed ancestor of the Duke of Vedena, he filled the body of the lion with slow-working poison—a subtle life-stealer that worked unsuspected upon the victim."

As he spoke, the red glow from a Moorish lamp, hanging from the ornamental beam above his head, bathed Ralston's hand and the ring in crimson light. I thought of blood. A terrific peal of thunder rolled over the roofs of *Windermere*. Ralston slipped the ring upon his finger.

"Now," Ralston laughed, "when you shake hands with me, it is an easy trick to bring pressure to bear upon the bezel of the ring. That pressure turns the bezel of the ring inward and the claw of the lion produces a slight puncture of my skin. At the same time, the poison in the bezel is released; it flows down through the claw of the lion and into my blood. Death slowly, painlessly follows."

Ralston extended his hand, his lips smiling invitation to a hand clasp.

"Howard!" Cornier fell back. "You haven't poison in the bezel now?"

"No. Shake."

Cornier reached for the hand of his friend, touched it, recoiled.

"I can't," he faltered. "I don't want to chance being your murderer."

"You and I have nothing to fear from the Borgia, Henri. Thank God, we live in the twentieth century when poisoners and poison rings are out of vogue."

"And it's yours," Cornier said, as if convinced. "The famous Borgia death ring!"

His eyes widened and then narrowed as he gazed intently upon the jewel, while his fingers worked, nervously.

Then he uttered words that I later had cause to remember. "I would give twenty years of my life in exchange for that ring. . . . Provided, of course, that it were the genuine Borgia."

"You still doubt?"

The boss watched Cornier as he went to the mantel, where he filled his pipe from Ralston's tobacco jar.

"It is an unbelievable story that you relate, Howard."

His pipe loaded, Cornier took up the Chinese vengeance dagger that had lain on a tabouret at the right end of the fireplace. The weapon was an oddly wrought thing with a triangular blade and a dragon twisted handle, red-tasseled.

"Admire it?" Ralston asked. "Two months ago I told you that I was going after three prizes. Well, that is the second one of them. Older than historic time, that sword—legend avers—served as vengeance dagger of the formidable Scarlet Dragons, an organization said still to function in China."

"Howard, you are the devil himself! By what means did you obtain it?"

"A Shanghai agent procured it for me, and delivered it to me just before I sailed for San Francisco on my return journey. Not wishing to carry it in my luggage, I expressed it to Lao Wong, who brought it here to me only this afternoon."

"Can you trust Lao Wong?"

"Why not?"

"There isn't a shrewder man in Minneapolis than Lao Wong. Who knows what conspiracies he engineers behind his profession as herbalist down there on Third Avenue? His avocation in antiques may in itself be only a blind. Why, Lao Wong himself may be a Scarlet Dragon!"

"But he isn't."

"I wish that I had as childlike a confidence as yours, Howard." Cornier examined the dagger quite as meticulously as he had examined the Borgia ring.

"Nasty hole this blade would make in a man's carcass," he said. "And what are these blotchings—rust? or dried blood of hapless victims?"

"Blood, let us hope," grinned Ralston.

Cornier replaced the vengeance dagger upon the tabouret. He said, "The Scarlet Dragons will never rest until they have recovered that sword."

"So I suspect," Ralston replied.

As he drew a handkerchief from his pocket and unfolded it, a card fluttered from its folds to the floor.

"*Mon Dieu!*" ejaculated Cornier.

My glance followed his to the card. Upon its surface was engraved a writhing dragon—etched in scarlet.

"A silly trick," was Ralston's comment, as he retrieved the card. "They are not frightening me this way. Why, ever since I purchased the dagger, I have been receiving these missives at regular intervals—always with warning that so many days remain in which I am permitted to return the dagger and live."

"But how did that card get between the folds of your handkerchief?" Cornier demanded.

"Wah Sing does my laundry, you know. But I do not believe that he is affiliated with the Scarlet Dragons. Some renegade Chinese probably sought employment with him to pull this pretty stunt. I shall put Ben Bailey* on the fellow's trail."

Thrusting handkerchief and dragon card into a pocket, the boss drew Cornier's attention to the third prize—a sarcophagus, which had been placed upright against the wall of "the tomb"—the wall beyond which Pietro Martini polished the Romanov pendant.

"Again I win!" the boss exclaimed, swinging open the lid of the sarcophagus (which he had been to the pains of having hinged). "Behold, the mummy of old Serapion!"

Did you ever hear the cry of a rabbit as the racing hounds pounce upon it? Well, such was the sound that escaped the throat of M. Cornier when he beheld the shrunken corpse in that painted grave box.

Ralston chuckled.

"I never believed you'd get it!" Cornier muttered, dropping weakly upon the Spanish divan. "The mummy of Serapion, terrible founder of the still more terrible Brothers of Karnak—"

"Powerful masters of the black arts, eh?" Ralston completed, interrogatively. "*Oui,* Henri, here is danger indeed. Already they have

---

*Ben Bailey was a young private investigator—a fraternity brother of Paul Ralston, the boss' son. Ben was often at *Windermere.* Howard Ralston liked Ben, and would spend whole evenings—now and then—discussing Dr. Bertillion and the methods of the Paris *Surete* with him. Ben was sold on French police-detective routines, and always itching to try them out. He was also interested in the occult, but not in the same way that Howard Ralston was.

threatened me. If they follow their embalmed Imperator here to 'the tomb',—well, there is no telling what may happen."

The storm rumbled threateningly; then crackled fearfully. The foundations of the house seemed to tremble; the windows rattled, harrowingly—one of them in particular.

"Listen," whispered Cornier, pointing to that window. "It's talking. . . . It's rattling out the letter *D!*"

I heard it—Morse code, as sure as fate.

Ralston laughed aloud.

Then a greater crash of thunder, and with ghastly emphasis that apparently bewitched window rattled—dash and two dots!

"*D!*" cried Cornier. "Howard, the Brothers of Karnak are warning you through the medium of the storm. *D* is for death!"

He implored the boss to heed the warning and ship the fateful corpse back to Egypt.

"Remember what befell the despoilers of the tomb of Tutenkhamon!" he wailed.

Ralston affectionately patted the bandage-bound remains of Serapion.

"I am fond of the old *stiff*," he chuckled. "In fact, I am quite possessed of the idea that I am a reincarnation of the diabolical mentor of the Brothers of Karnak. Never will I surrender this shell that may once have housed my ego."

He carefully closed the lid upon his dead self.

Filling his own pipe from the tobacco jar on the mantel, he leaned an elbow on that mantel and puffed indolently, speculatively contemplating the beams of "the tomb's" ceiling.

"Serapion, modern skeptics to the contrary," said Cornier, "was a master of the black arts. He undoubtedly vitalized his *ka,* the astral double of his physical body, so that it might remain with his mummy through the centuries to protect it from despoilation."

"Rot!"

"Say *rot* if you want to, Howard, but you know as well as I that the Brothers of Karnak might summon the *ka* out of that mummy to punish you with horrible death."

"You old aunty," Ralston mocked, "do you suppose that because I am a Theosophist I believe all the horror tales Madame Blavatsky spun from the flax of her imagination?"

"Beg pardon, sir," murmured Brookes, Ralston's butler, who had entered unnoticed and now stood respectfully extending the card salver toward his master.

Ralston read the two cards twice; then passed them to his friend,

"You will see them?" Cornier asked, lifting startled eyes from a rapid glance at the names.

"Show them in, Brookes," was Ralston's indirect reply.

When Brookes had passed into the hall, Cornier stepped quickly to his partner's side.

"The Borgia! It is still on your finger," he warned.

"Yes," Ralston said, "it is on my finger—the genuine Borgia death ring. But there is no poison in it, my friend."

2

Mrs. Lucretia Lansing, looking as violent as the storm through which she had come, sailed into the room, followed by the dapper Duke of Vedena. She was a towering woman; quite a mountain of flesh, but not at all obese. There was something majestic about her hugeness. She was Amazonic, perhaps—if you will permit the word. There was about her, too, an air of commercial masculinity, engendered, doubtless, by hard dealings with business men; for she was one of the most efficient agents for antiquarians in America. Knowing the tricks of her trade from A to *Zed* and maintaining in Minneapolis a clearing house for collectors residing east and west of the Mississippi, she had earned an enviable reputation and was proud of it.

"Ah, *madame*," Ralston murmured, advancing to greet the lady and offering her the hand upon which he wore the Borgia ring.

Mrs. Lansing and the Duke saw the ring in the same instant; both gasped astonishment.

"Do you think that I would shake hands with a common thief?" demanded the lady, head high.

Howard Ralston, appreciative of the lady's quick observation, smiled down upon the ring.

"It is a beauty," he murmured, moving his hand to display the jewel advantageously. "But," and he lifted his eyes to those of Lucretia Lansing, "you shouldn't call me a common thief, *madame*."

"By what other name shall I call you?" she demanded, eyes hard. "You deliberately robbed the Duke."

"Are you sure that I robbed the Duke?"

"Hear the man!" she cried, addressing the Duke. And to the boss, "My word, haven't you the ring upon your finger?"

"*Si, si,*" snarled the Duke, bristling like a feisty poodle.

"Ah, good evening, Duke," said Ralston, for the first time taking cognizance of his one-time opponent in friendly games of poker. "We must have a few bouts at our game before you return to Venice."

The diminutive nobleman, eyes popped and fists clenched as if to control the rage that trembled his small body, glared helplessly at his *aide-de-camp,* the stately Lansing.

"We have come," Mrs. Lansing announced, "to demand return of the Borgia."

"But, *madame,* this ring is mine."

Ralston spoke in matter-of-fact tone, just as if he were telling the truth. He again held out his hand, as though for better scrutiny of the jewel, while the aggravated Duke and Mrs. Lansing gulped, helplessly. I noted, too, the almost imperceptible flicker of M. Cornier's lids as his partner denied the Duke of Vedena's ownership of that ring.

"You have the temerity to stand there and say that ring is yours?" demanded the irate lady.

"Mine," murmured Ralston, complacently.

"Mr. Howard Ralston, you amaze me!" And as the boss lifted his brows, "Why, every evidence points to you as the thief who stole the Borgia from the collection of the Duke. Do you suppose that Marco was asleep those days you and your minions spent in Venice?"

She did not glance my way, but I felt infinitesimally small when she rasped out the word *minions.* I envisioned prison walls closing in upon me.

Ralston yielded me quick glance, to which I responded with lift of the brow, as much as to say, "We never suspected that bird."

"Who is Marco?" the boss inquired, eyes bent upon the ring.

"You know well enough!"

"Oh!" The boss whistled his sudden enlightenment. "You mean the Duke's *major-domo.*"

"The supposed *major-domo* of the ducal palace!" came Mrs. Lansing's crisp affirmative. "A man as clever as yourself should have recognized Marco as a member of the Venetian secret police."

"Indeed!"

Only mildest surprise crept into Ralston's tone.

"Well?" demanded the lady.

"Well?"

Slipping hands into trouser pockets, the boss stood regarding her.

"Are you returning the ring now?"

"I am not returning it now. Why all this fuss about a copy I had made of the original?"

"Copy!"

The meticulously lined brows of the Lansing went up in surprise.

"My daughter Francesca, she told me how Martini often look upon the ring," the Duke chimed in. "My Francesca is angry because he steal the Borgia from under her eyes. And all the time he make love to her. Bah!"

"You are caught red-handed!" asserted the angry Lansing. "I gave you credit for greater shrewdness."

Had I been Ralston, I should have withered under the blast of her scorn; but he kept smiling throughout her arraignment of him.

"I still maintain, my dear lady, that this ring is mine," he said. "If the Duke's Borgia has disappeared, I am sorry."

"Why do you quibble, Howard Ralston? Of course you know that the Duke has been robbed; and you know as well as we by whom the theft was committed. If you will deliver the ring to us, we will depart without calling the police."

"You will do as you think best, *madame*," the boss said, bowing. "But let me tell you, in presence of these witnesses, that the police shall not take this ring from my finger until it is proved beyond dispute to be the property of the Duke."

"It *is* mine!" cried the impassioned Duke. "Over four hundred year she has been in my family! Ah, it is the part of my life!"

From my point of vantage, I saw the door of Pietro's shop open slightly, and the Italian boy's luminous black eye appear at the aperture.

"My dear Duke," Ralston said, drawing the ring-bearing hand from his pocket and extending it toward the Duke, "this ring I wear, I assure you, is the imitation I had made."

"What do you take us for?" sneered Mrs. Lansing. "Not fools, I hope; for only fools could be expected to believe you."

"This," and the Duke drew a ring from his wallet, "is the counterfeit that you left in exchange for my jewel. In haste to get away from my home that night, you left top of display case unlock."

"*Tck! Tck! Tck!* Careless indeed of the thief," murmured the boss, unperturbed.

"Marco go to villa you desert. He find evidence we want."

"Determined spies usually do uncover evidence."

"You, my poker-playing American, had not think we would search your villa!" cried the Duke, eyes alight with triumphant vindictiveness.

"Frankly, I didn't."

"The Duke and Marco discovered evidence sufficient to convict you," the Lansing affirmed.

Ralston quietly remarked, "You are sure of yourselves."

"You know we're sure, else we had never come here. We were never surer of anything in our lives!"

"I bow to your omniscience, *madame.*"

Motioning the Duke into a chair, Mrs. Lansing selected one for herself.

"Let us talk business," she proposed, swinging one long leg over the other. "What will you take for the ring on your finger?"

"It is not for sale, *madame.*"

"Mr. Ralston," she said, leaning forward and fixing her keen glance upon him, "you not only robbed the Duke, but you also smuggled that ring into these United States. You could never have declared it; the danger was too great."

"Well?"

"Having made yourself liable under the law of two countries, do you dare refuse restoration of stolen property?"

"I merely refuse, *madame,* to part with the ring upon this finger."

"But it is the Duke's ring!"

"We spare you now!" cried the Duke. "We come without the police, not wishing the much undesirable publicity. We even offer reward for return of the Borgia."

"Then publish your reward," Ralston advised. "Perhaps some kindly disposed soul will find your ring and restore it to you. As for this ring, it remains with me."

"Then we shall call the police!"

It was Mrs. Lansing who spoke, and her words were decisive. Ralston bowed to her again.

"*Madame* has already heard what I have to say about that."

Then, as if suddenly inspired, he drew the ring from his finger. Taking the one the Duke held and laying it beside the other, he cupped the two of them in his hands and shook them about.

"Now," he said, "I have a fair proposition to make. Let the Duke select his ring, and I will abide by the decision." He extended a palm on which the twin rings reposed side by side. "Take your choice, Duke."

The little fire-eater gave the boss a contemptuous look, charged with defiance. He bent over the extended palm, scrutinizing the rings through his monocle. He pawed them about. He tugged at his collar. He held the two rings side by side before him. At length he returned them to Ralston's palm. Drawing a perfumed handkerchief from his pocket, he mopped his perspiring brow.

"You see," Ralston exulted, "he does not know which ring is which! He cannot identify the ring he brought into my house tonight!"

"It is true," the Duke moaned, looking apologetically into the flushed face of his belligerent *aide-de-camp*.

"Now," Ralston continued, "I shall call my artificer, and he will point out the ring he made for me."

The Duke of Vedena yielded Pietro a nasty stare as that young man entered "the tomb" in response to Ralston's summons.

Told to pick out his employer's ring, Pietro considered the rings carefully. Glancing shrewdly into the Duke's eyes, just as a street gamin might, he let a whimsical smile play about his lips. He then selected one of the rings and handed it to the boss, who put it upon his finger. The other ring, Ralston presented to the Duke.

"Are you satisfied?" Ralston asked, addressing the question to Mrs. Lansing.

"I am not!"

With a shrug, Ralston turned to the Duke.

"Are you?"

The Duke regarded Ralston apprehensively. Next he fixed his beady black eyes upon Pietro, who grinned puckishly back at him.

Disturbed by that elfin grin, the Duke swung his glance back upon Howard Ralston.

"*No, signor,* I am not convinced! It is true I cannot distinguish between the rings; but I am positive your artificer has trick me."

"I swear, your Grace, that I gave my employer the counterfeit ring I made for him."

There was a note of sincerity in Pietro's voice. Had his lips not twitched ever so slightly, I myself had been ready to believe him.

That twitching of the lips evidently convinced the Duke that the ring he held was the false **Borgia**.

He hurled the ring to the floor, crying, "Your counterfeit—I give it back to you!"

Although the undersized nobleman actually appeared ridiculous in his anger, Mrs. Lucretia Lansing beamed approvingly upon him.

"Very well," said Ralston. "Since you will not have the truth, we will say that I hold the genuine Borgia—*just* for the jest of the thing."

He went to the Chinese cabinet that stood against the wall to the right of the fireplace and between the fireplace and the double doors leading to the entrance hall.

"Somewhere inside this cabinet," he informed us, opening the doors of the beautiful contraption, "there is a secret compartment, which it is impossible for a person not familiar with the architecture of the cabinet to locate."

As he talked, he managed to open the occult compartment and to conceal the Borgia ring within it.

"Now," he challenged, after securely locking the cabinet doors, "my ring—the genuine Borgia, if you insist—is hidden away in the heart of that black monster. Get it, if you can!"

It was as defiance flung against the teeth of Fate. I went cold all over; and well I might, for the deeds of that stormy night must have been treading hard upon the words of the master of *Windermere*—as subsequent events demonstrated.

"You got that ring dishonestly," Mrs. Lansing declared. "Under such circumstances, you leave us no alternative: we must fight fire with fire. Fire!" She laughed, raucously. "We'll have the ring in that cabinet if we have to burn the house down to get it!"

Close upon her words came a vicious crackling of lightning. The room was plunged into darkness. Flashing lightning gleamed through the windows, illumining the sarcophagus of old Serapion. When the lights came on again, as they did, shortly, the eyes of the Duke were riveted upon the mummy-case.

"Mother of God!" he wailed, shrinking toward the towering Lansing's side.

That lady stared, incredulous.

"The mummy of Serapion!" she muttered. "I recognize the sarcophagus cover."

Like all intelligent antiquarians, the Duke and Mrs. Lansing knew the uncanny superstitions filtering through the world of antiques. Like some antiquarians, they believed in them sincerely.

"The Brothers of Karnak will kill you," Lucretia Lansing breathed. "Even though they are in distant Egypt, they will work their magic and draw the *ka* out of that haunted corpse. The *ka* of Serapion will lay its finger upon your heart, and you will die."

"You are a man accursed!" mumbled the Duke, the muscles of his face jerking with fear.

The storm rumbled like some angered beast straining at its leash.

Mrs. Lansing and the Duke pulled themselves together. There was an exchange of understanding glances; they turned to go. With a last look at the Chinese cabinet, the Lansing said, "We have friends in the city who are familiar with such furniture."

Ralston stood smiling, hand upon the bell strap.

"Will *madame* and the Duke remain for dinner?"

Lucretia Lansing and the Duke sputtered.

"Sorry," murmured the boss. "You deprive me of a very great pleasure. Yourselves, also; for Deborah is an excellent cook."

At the hall door, Mrs. Lansing paused. Opening her bag, she took from it an envelope.

Ungraciously she held it toward Ralston, saying, "As we alighted at your door, a man stepped from the shadows of the shrubbery and requested me to give you this."

Ralston tore open the envelope and extracted from it a card—a card upon which was engraved a scarlet dragon. Startled, he let the card fall to the floor. It landed dragon-side up.

"Ah!" Mrs. Lansing exclaimed. "The shadow of the Scarlet Dragon also has fallen across your path! Mr. Howard Ralston, I pity you infinitely. If ever there was a man about to meet a deserving fate, you are he!"

A reverberating clap of thunder answered her. Before it had echoed into silence, she and the Duke were gone.

"You're an actor, Howard—a great actor!"

M. Cornier grinned his appreciation.

Pietro Martini lifted the discarded ring from the floor, saying, "The real Borgia. I knew that the Duke would fall for my trick."

"Well, at that, you deceived me," chuckled Ralston. And taking the ring from Pietro, he added, "I must exchange the rings at once."

He opened the Chinese cabinet and the secret compartment, saying to Pietro as he did so, "Take the roadster and follow them."

Like a shot, the Italian was gone. A bit later we heard a big car moving down the driveway toward Park Avenue; and, shortly, speeding after it, Pietro's roadster.

"Now examine the work of my artificer," Ralston said, handing M. Cornier the ring that had been locked in the cabinet. "You have already scrutinized the original."

"I cannot credit my eyes," Cornier admitted.

"Keep it and wear it," Ralston suggested. "You cannot have the real Borgia; but you can have the next best thing—a flawless imitation of it."

"But when you return the original to the Duke—"

"Pietro can make me a copy from yours."

M. Cornier and Ralston settled into their customary places on the Spanish divan. They smoked a while in silence.

"How about that wager, Henri?" Ralston finally asked.

M. Cornier laughed.

"Did you think I was convinced—after your colloquy with the Duke of Vedena?"

"If I had, I should have returned his ring on the spot and saved myself Mrs. Lansing's threats."

M. Cornier glanced sideways at his friend, as if deliberating what course he should pursue. In the light of what I learned afterward, I am sure that the only obstacle to his acknowledgement of Ralston's success was in his colossal financial losses.

"Let us wait until tomorrow," he urged. "We'll deliberate the matter in the morning."

And how was Henri Cornier to know, as he uttered those words, that Howard Ralston would not see the morrow's dawn?

3

Hardly had Pietro departed in pursuit of the Duke, than the Ralston limousine drove in and came to pause under the *porte-cochere*. Brookes admitted Miss Mildred Manning and Mrs. Julia Wilmorton. This he was often compelled to do, as members of the household were forgetful about carrying keys. Haunted by fear of being robbed, the boss kept windows and doors bolted.

Mildred announced the presence of herself and chaperon by calling "Oo-hoo!" as they came down the length of the hall.

"In 'the tomb,' Mildred!" Ralston called back.

The two women entered through the double doors.

"Please sit down," Mildred urged Ralston and Cornier. "You big boys look so comfy smoking on your sofa. Don't you think so, Aunt Julia?"

"Why—er, yes, dear—"

I covered Mrs. Wilmorton with a swift glance, really seeing her for the first time since our return home. She appeared pale and haggard. She was not her usual superbly poised self.

Dragging the chic green hat from her bronze head, Mildred said, "Paul and I were afraid the storm would break again before we got in."

"Shall I draw up chairs for you?"

"Thank you, no, Cousin Howard. Your fire is inviting, but we must dress for dinner."

"Was the show good?" M. Cornier asked.

"Gorgeous! One of the best bills I've ever seen at the *Hennepin*. The vaudeville was unusually good, and they had a thrilling movie about a mummy."

"Mummy!" faltered Julia Wilmorton, her eyes seeking the sarcophagus of Serapion.

"Where is Paul?" the boss abruptly asked.

"He went to the garage with Thomas," Mildred explained. "Wants to show him something that needs adjusting on the roadster. Carburetor,

I think, he said. He'll be right in, though; for he knows that M. Cornier is back. Aunt Julia and I told him."

"Yes—yes, we did," absently assented Mrs. Wilmorton.

"Well, Paul won't find the roadster," Ralston said. "Pietro has it out."

No one said anything for a space. It was as if by some psychic agreement they decided the less said about the Italian boy, the better.

"How did you like the show, Julia?" Ralston inquired, a flicker of amusement in his fine eyes—just as if he understood the meaning of that obvious silence.

"Me?—oh—"

"Aunt Julia wasn't there," Mildred hastened to explain.

"Aunt Julia wasn't with you?"

"She felt ill when we reached the theatre, so Thomas drove her out to Dr. Elsing's. She picked Paul and me up at *Dayton's* after the matinee."

"Sorry to learn that you have been under the doctor's care," said M. Cornier.

"It is nothing," Julia Wilmorton murmured.

"Yes it is!" cried Mildred, her tongue running on. "She is nervous. Look how thin she's getting."

Julia Wilmorton showed relief when Paul Ralston entered, and I observed that Mildred's shining eyes sought his face.

"Well, Paul," Ralston remarked, "you come through Pietro's shop, eh?"

"Shortest way in," Paul answered, at the same time shaking hands with Cornier.

"Pietro won't mind."

"So it's he has the roadster out!" Paul wasn't gracious about it. "Just when I wanted Thomas to work on it."

"Pietro will return soon. Besides, Thomas will want to eat now."

"Okay by me if Pietro never comes back," Paul muttered. Cornier's alert ears caught the words, I know; for he shot appreciative glance at Paul.

The boss urged his family to hasten and dress for dinner, relieving the situation of further embarrassment.

Paul and Mildred went willingly enough, but Julia Wilmorton lingered.

"If I have been remiss in my duty, Howard—," she began.

"Not at all," he assured her. "Guess what I have been doing?"

"That would be impossible."

"Showing Henri my three prizes. And he, jealous dog that he is, deplores my possession of any one of them."

"I, too, deplore their presence here," Julia Wilmorton told Cornier. "I am afraid—especially of the mummy of Serapion."

"She knows the superstition," Ralston said.

"Who knows but that there is truth in it?" Mrs. Wilmorton urged.

Ralston strode to the sarcophagus and swung back the lid.

"Where is the *ka* of Serapion?" he demanded. "There is nothing in this embalmed corpse that can touch my heart with an icy finger of death."

Instantly a supernatural hush seemed to descend upon the big room. Then, outside, there sounded an eerie, low-swishing wind—a sound such as the dead might make in brushing wing tips as they take their swift upward flight. The wind swelled in volume, augmenting cyclonically, and climaxed in accompaniment to a soul-rending explosion of thunder that literally tumbled upon the roofs of *Windermere*. Again the lights blinked out. Through the darkness, I heard a hysterical sob. When the lights flashed on a few seconds later, a drawn-faced Henri Cornier had the limp Julia Wilmorton in his arms.

"You shouldn't have done that, Howard," he said, sternly. Without further word, he carried Mrs. Wilmorton out of "the tomb" and up the broad stairs to her apartment on the second floor.

"Feel creepy, West?" Ralston asked me, as he closed the sarcophagus lid.

"Rather," I confessed, dropping into my chair. "It's an unusual procedure."

Cornier rejoined us; or rather, the ghost of him did. I have never seen a man change so in a few minutes. He didn't come back to us the same man that carried Julia Wilmorton up the stairs. He had been gone longer than necessary, I figured; but I was at a loss to account for the sickly pallor of him and the tragic misery in his eyes.

"Leave Julia okay?" the boss asked.

"Shot to pieces," Cornier replied, voice strained. "But she said that she would be down for dinner."

"Funny way women have of fainting!"

"By the way, Howard," Cornier asked, clearing his throat nervously, "isn't that a new maid Julia has?"

"Why, yes. Julia let Frieda go while we were away and took on this French girl—Fifi Burgoyne."

"Fifi is a deep one, and hard as nails. I'd say she'll bear watching."

"Then we'll have her watched. Lord, Henri, what an atmosphere of mystery you are giving *Windermere!*"

"Let's hope it never develops into anything more serious than atmosphere," Cornier replied, knocking the ashes from his pipe. Sticking it in a pocket, he continued, "I observe that the youngsters are still in love."

"Not at all," the boss hastened to protest. "Paul realizes that I intend to marry Mildred."

"You will break two hearts if you marry that girl."

"Are you preaching at me?"

"I'm warning you."

Declining invitation to dinner, Cornier turned to go.

"How's Patterson making it?" Ralston asked.

"Pat's coming fine." Cornier turned. "Best man I ever had; straight as a die. I believe his story that he was framed—"

"Still, he's an ex-convict."

Cornier was standing beside the tabouret on which lay the vengeance dagger. He let his partner's remark pass unheeded, apparently interested in the weapon.

Taking it up, he mused, "The vengeance sword of the Scarlet Dragons—the gentlemen who persist in passing you their picturesque calling cards.

"Interesting relic, isn't it?" Ralston asked, pride of possession shining in his eyes.

"A dangerous one to own, Howard." Cornier grasped the dagger by its dragon-twisted hilt and brought it down in imaginary blow. "How easily it fits one's hand—"

For no apparent reason, he left the sentence unfinished, and returned the dagger to its place on the tabouret as if his hand abhorred the touch of the thing.

Again he declined the invitation to dinner, explaining, "I have a trifling deal on with an old fellow I'm to meet in Faribault tonight.

Expected there at nine o'clock, so I'll grab a bite at home. Patterson will have it ready for me." In the doorway, he paused. "May I ask one more question?"

"Shoot!"

"Why does Paul dislike the Italian so heartily?"

"Paul didn't like Pietro from the first. Since this morning, he has been morosely bitter."

"What happened this morning?"

"I wrote a new will, making Pietro an heir in my estate."

"Do you mean to tell me," Cornier demanded, "that you made this stranger partner with your son in the sharing of your estate?" And when the boss answered that was what he meant, his friend exclaimed further, "Howard, are you losing your mind?"

"You'll learn yet," Ralston insisted, "that Pietro is as true as steel."

Cornier said nothing. Standing there regarding his friend, he took out his tobacco pouch, just as if—having said what he had to say—he couldn't bring himself to take further of Howard Ralston's weed in the jar on the mantel. Later I was to remember the circumstance.

His pipe loaded and lighted, Cornier bade the boss 'good night.'

Ralston couldn't let him go without a parting thrust. "Tomorrow you'll pay up?"

Cornier had no answer for the velvet-like inquiry. He went out of "the tomb," up the broad stairs, and down the long hall to the convenient door over the *porte-cochere*. I heard him unlock the door, open and close it, and relock it.

Left alone in "the tomb" (not counting me, of course), Howard Ralston sat down upon the Spanish divan, lolled back, stretched his feet to the fire—for it had grown chillier. He smoked, meditatively.

I sat and pondered what I had seen and heard, fear gnawing at my heart.

4

When it was evident that Mrs. Wilmorton was not likely to come down to dinner, Mildred ran up to make inquiry. She returned with news that her chaperon had summoned the limousine, thrown a wrap over her dinner gown, and gone out. Fifi, her maid, did not know where.

"I imagine that she has gone to Dr. Elsing's," Mildred said.

"How long has she been ailing?" Ralston asked.

"She has been treating with Dr. Elsing since about the middle of July."

We began our meal.

Howard Ralston had little appetite.

"What seems to trouble Julia?" he finally asked.

"Just seems worried and nervous."

"I don't think Elsing helps her much," Paul remarked. "She's more nervous than before going to him. Has been, ever since you radioed from Venice to make inquiry about the Josephine diamonds."

"H'm. . . . By the way, Mildred, that reminds me!" But Ralston didn't say of what.

The soft glow of light on silver and glass, the soothing music of the radio, the occasional discreet cough of Brookes—these helped us to feel comfortable in the dining room, despite the vicious storm pounding on *Windermere*.

Dinner drawing to a close, Brookes set Ralston's wine before him.

"You youngsters need not linger," the boss suggested. "You've been wanting to get at your ridiculous game, so run along upstairs. *Mah Jong* is *passé;* but you seem to enjoy it."

"If you'll excuse us, Father?" Paul said, rising and moving back Mildred's chair.

"Run along, Boy; capture four red dragons in the good Chinese way."

Mildred went to Ralston. Putting an arm about his shoulders, she bent and kissed his silvering hair.

"You're a darling to let us go," she cooed. "*Mah Jong* is fascinating."

Ralston patted her hand, saying, "You've a right to like what you please."

As Mildred and Paul were about to leave the dining room, the boss called them to wait. Nodding me to follow, he led us into "the tomb." At his command, Paul and I saw that all windows were locked and the drapes drawn.

Ralston took the Borgia from the Chinese cabinet. Holding it up for Mildred's inspection, he informed her that the Duke of Vedena was in Minneapolis and had called for the ring.

"He and Mrs. Lansing left just before you came in."

"How did the Duke come to miss his ring?" Paul asked, his eyes troubled.

Ralston recounted the dramatic interview, concluding, "The Duke departed, leaving both rings with me."

"He'll be back!" Paul cried.

"Mrs. Lansing went so far as to state that if necessary they would burn down the house to get the Borgia."

"Father, we must take every precaution. The Duke might murder you."

"The Duke murder me!" Ralston laughed. "That would be funny."

"He might hire some gangster to do it."

"He'll break in and rob you," Mildred averred.

"As for getting into this room, my dear," the boss answered, "no one can do that. And when it comes to opening the cabinet—only those who know its secrets can do that."

"I wish," Paul muttered, "that Martini didn't know the secret of the cabinet."

"Paul," Ralston said, "I wish you wouldn't mistrust Pietro. If it had not been for him, I should not have secured the Borgia and won my bet with Henri."

"It would have been better to have lost the wager than to have Pietro Martini and the Borgia poison ring in this house. I would to God you had let the wager slide and returned the ring to the Duke. There's no telling what may develop."

"Well, if anything does develop, you may blame it upon Henri's stubbornness. Had he acknowledged that I had secured the genuine Borgia, the jewel would have been returned to the Duke this evening."

"Dad, I'm afraid. The Duke's coming, Mrs. Lansing's threat—"

"Don't be an old woman, Paul. Nothing can happen."

"I'm afraid of your mummy and your dagger, as well as of the ring," Paul persisted. "Take these outlandish warnings— God, it's enough to upset anybody!"

"I'm not afraid of the ring," Mildred broke in, as if to relieve the tension.

Taking the Borgia from Ralston, she slipped it upon her finger—the engagement finger.

Howard Ralston laughed. Taking Mildred's hand, he exclaimed, "Miles too large! But cut it down, and it will make a fine engagement ring, eh?"

Neither Mildred nor Paul answered him. You could hear the little French clock ticking, it was so still in the room.

"Which reminds me," Ralston went on, "that it is time we announced our engagement, according to your father's wishes."

"Yes, Cousin Howard," Mildred murmured.

"Well, my dear," Ralston said, taking the Borgia, "this cannot serve as our engagement ring. Paul, lock it away in that black *cache* of mine."

Paul returned the ring to its hiding place.

The boss then opened a safe in the wall paneling and drew forth the glittering Josephine diamonds. It was a splendid set: slipper buckles, garter ornaments, bracelets, brooch, necklace, tiara, and ring.

"These jewels," Ralston said, "worth a king's ransom, are destined to become the personal property of the Ralston bride. The ring, Mildred, shall be your engagement ring. Slip it on, please. . . . Ah, a perfect fit!"

The gems scintillated brilliantly beneath the electric lights as Ralston held them up for our inspection.

Mildred sighed as she drew the ring from her finger and handed it to Ralston, who took it and kissed it sentimentally.

And I—of course I had to see it—witnessed the agony in Paul's eyes.

"You shall have it to keep," Ralston said to Mildred, "the day our engagement is announced."

Crying out in sharp alarm, Mildred pointed to one of the windows facing upon the curved driveway that swung before the twin mansions.

"What is it, Mildred?" Paul demanded, stepping quickly to her side.

"I thought I heard someone at that window," she whispered.

"You are nervous," Ralston sought to allay her fear. "It is the shaking of the rose trellis."

I observed, however, that the boss lost no time getting the diamonds into the safe.

"We'll have Brookes look about," he promised, "for we cannot afford to take chances tonight."

"I am afraid," Mildred whimpered. "Something dreadful is sure to happen. Dear Cousin Howard, please have the jewels and these three terrible menaces removed tomorrow."

A nasty snarling of the storm sent her panicky into Paul's arms. Ralston smiled. Awkwardly Paul released the girl; and she, confused, turned away.

"Now I shall go back to my wine," the boss said, "and you two go up to your delayed game. I shall dream of the Borgia poison ring,—of dead masters of the black arts,—of Chinese bandits and blood-dripping daggers, while you shuffle flowers and seasons, winds and dragons in your *Mah Jong* game."

Turning to me, he asked, "Join me, West?"

I declined, urging need of catching up my translating; so Ralston, Paul, and Mildred went out, leaving "the tomb" to me.

I switched off all lights, save the one on my desk.

The distant clock boomed the hour of nine; the French clock on the mantel sang saucy echo. The minutes ticked away, but my book lay unopened before me. I had no heart for translating the love life of Napoleon and his Josephine. There was a more profound drama of love and intrigue being enacted before my eyes. Smouldering fires in human hearts and latent evil in rare antiques—all of them gathered in or about "the tomb."

And there was that strange will of Basil Manning's. It hung like a sword of Damocles over the heads of all these actors in the drama being unfolded on the stage that was *Windermere*.

5

The French clock tinkled the quarter hour. Nine-fifteen. I moved the desk lamp to throw a better glow upon my book.

Startlingly, a sound smote my ears. Some one stealthily opened and closed the front door. As I stood there in the shadows of "the tomb", staring at the double doorway, I saw a frightened lady streak across the rectangle of light and scurry up the majestic staircase.

She found difficulty in handling something unwieldy beneath her wet cloak.

For some minutes I stood wondering what it could mean. Where could Julia Wilmorton have been? Why had she walked through the rain from avenue to house? Going into Pietro's shop, I peered through the rain-splashed window toward the garage. Thomas was in his apartment over the garage, reading and smoking. I reasoned that he couldn't have brought Julia Wilmorton home, put the car away, and thus settled himself by the time she got into the house and up those stairs. There was something damned odd about it all.

I returned to "the tomb", perplexed. What with the other happenings of the night—and then I recalled the Manning will.

My heart somersaulted as my meditations were cut short by a harrowing shriek that shattered the silence of "the tomb" and echoed crazily through the house. Leaping to my desk, I snatched my revolver from the drawer. There was another silence-ripping scream, and the door from the servants' hall jolted open. Across the threshold bounded Deborah, Ralston's colored cook. Coming to an abrupt halt just inside the big room, she emitted another shrilling scream. I sprang to the wall switch and flooded the chamber with light.

The blinding illumination elicited a blood-curdling howl from the black woman, who dropped to her knees, wailing, "O, Lawd, Lawd! Ah done seen him!"

I could drag no information from her, nor could I soothe her. She rocked back and forth on her knees, keeping up her infernal yelling.

Howard Ralston, Paul, and Mildred appeared. To the boss Deborah became coherent, if her strange words may be so called.

"Oh, Mr. Howard, Ah done seed de debbil! Ah seed him sho 'nough!"

Julia Wilmorton, followed by her French maid, glided into the room.

"Merciful heavens, what has happened?" she begged to be told.

By this time, Mrs. Delia O'Grady, drawing a gaudily flowered dressing-gown about her ample figure, strode in from the servants' hallway.

"What's the black hussy up to now?" demanded the Irish housekeeper.

"Ah ain' done nuthin'," sulked the cook, her ardour for screaming dampened.

"And it's the loikes of ye to be after tellin' me that! Git up, ye black-hided daughter o' sin and hustle up thim stairs to yer room."

As Deborah, with the aid of a chair, hoisted her bulk, Mrs. O'Grady turned to Ralston, saying, "It's sorry Oi am, Mr. Ralston, that the loikes av her should be disturbin' av the quiet av yer house, and ye home only this blessed day."

Before he let the servants go, the boss learned from his cook that "de debbil" she had seen was like a man's face staring through the kitchen sink window.

Taking an electric torch, Paul went out to learn if there had been anyone at Deborah's window. He reported muddy tracks upon the paving below that window, but these had been rain-washed beyond point of value.

The upshot of the adventure was that Paul insisted that his father remove the three menaces the following morning. Reluctant, because there were so many difficulties and so much money involved, the boss halfway promised to do as his son wished.

"God grant it be not too late!" Paul muttered under his breath.

Then—purely to torment us all, I was compelled to believe—Howard Ralston walked to the mummy case. Pausing there, he suggested that since we were likely soon to part with our antiques, we might as well have a last look at old Serapion.

"Oh, no!" pleaded Julia Wilmorton.

But Ralston, bent upon doing the thing he had suggested, opened the sarcophagus just as the storm, howling like a pack of infuriated demons, lashed its fury again over *Windermere*. A terrific shock of thunder swayed the gigantic house; the lights flickered eerily; the mummy of Serapion pitched forward into Ralston's arms.

The master of *Windermere* laughed with glee; but Julia Wilmorton folded jack-knife-like across my arm, while Fifi jabbered hysterically.

Only Mildred Manning, of the three women, had strength not to lose hold on herself.

To add to the nerve-tearing agony of the situation, the doorbell whirred sharply.

Opening the front door, Brookes found himself confronted by a serious-miened Oriental—not a Mongolian, the butler later explained, but more like an Armenian.

The visitor silently handed Brookes a folded parchment sealed with red wax, and vanished into the storm.

"This," Ralston said, reading the parchment, "supplements the communication that Guissepi Reni delivered me in Venice. It purports to come from the Brothers of Karnak, who by this warn me that at midnight they will summon the *ka* out of that mummy to touch my heart with death unless I radio Al Mirza at Cairo that I will return the sacred corpse."

None of us felt comfortable after hearing that: not with the mummy of Serapion in "the tomb," along with the Borgia poison ring and the Chinese vengeance dagger.

"I hardly think," Ralston said, "that anyone will molest the contents of this room tonight; not with my steel armor in place."

"Your steel armor?"

Mildred was puzzled.

"Let me demonstrate."

Ralston bade Paul and me draw back the draperies at the barred windows of "the tomb."* Then, as we watched him, he stepped toward the fireplace. Fifi Burgoyne, I noted, watched his every movement narrowly.

"When I press a button hereabouts," the boss explained, "a steel plate slides down in the casing of every door and window of this room. Now, keep your eyes on the doors and windows."

While our eyes were off him, Ralston touched the concealed button. At once there was a muffled, whirring sound, as if some mechanism within the walls had started into operation. Before our amazed eyes, solid sheets of steel slid down in every door and window casing.

"Now," Ralston said, "this room is both a prison and a fortress. No one can get in or out without cutting these steel barriers or demolishing these stone walls."

After the barriers were raised again and the window drapes once more drawn, I might have felt relieved when they all went and left me had not fear tightened her hold upon me.

By ten o'clock the storm was wilder than ever. Trying to forget it, I sat at my desk, working on my translation.

At a little after ten, I heard some one fumbling with a lock.

Jittery, I glanced over my shoulder. The noise ceased. Then I heard it again—a faint sound such as one makes when working a key in a lock.

I whirled my swivel chair about and sat staring at the wall from which the sound came. Again I heard the twisting key. But there could

* I should explain here that every window of the first floor of *Windermere* was protected by stout ornamental steel bars.

be no door there—only the solid stone masonry of *Windermere's* wall, veneered on the inside with mahogany.

That key, if key it were, was encountering stubborn resistance in the lock—if lock there were.

My blood flowed like water in my veins. I weakened all over, finding myself powerless to move. I stared at the spot whence the noise came and recalled ghost stories I had heard.

Reason told me that there could be no ghost; I girded up my loins, as it were. Strength returning, I nevertheless determined to be on the safe side. I switched off the desk lamp and gripped my revolver.

None too soon, for I caught the response of the tumblers—or whatever they were—in that hidden lock.

Finger trembling on trigger of my gun, I crept behind a screen standing in the corner beyond my desk. Concealed there, I watched and listened—hearing better than I saw; for in going to the upper floor, Ralston had closed the double doors leading into the entrance hall. There was but faint illumination in "the tomb"—illumination yielded by the low-burning gas-logs in the fireplace.

As I peered through the crack between two leaves of my tall screen, I was dumbfounded to see a panel of that wainscoted wall swing inward.

That door open, I could hear the continuous splash of water from the overrun gutters at the eaves of the *Windermere* roof. Eye to the crack between the leaves of the screen, I watched—for I knew not what.

Quietly, with aroma of damp wool exhaling from him, the intruder stepped through the little door. His coat collar was turned up; his hat pulled over his face. His form seemed vaguely familiar; but in the almost complete darkness I could not divine his identity.

He paused, listening; then cautiously closed the secret door behind him. He stole by my hiding place, his electric torch playing a yellow beam upon the Chinese cabinet and then upon the door of Pietro's shop.

Mildred Manning's laugh rang out above stairs, slicing the stillness of the house with silvery echoes. The searching spot of light vanished. I wondered if my own breathing were as audible as that of the intruder.

Evidently reassured, he moved to the cabinet. The torch beam played over its ornate front, coming to rest upon the lock. I heard a grunt. Followed a hurried struggle with the cabinet fastenings.

He was after the Borgia!

I knew that I should have stepped from behind my screen and covered him with my gun. I can't explain why I didn't. Just one of those psychological things, I guess.

Then, greatly to my alarm, the room was flooded with light. Brookes had opened the double doors and jerked the light switch.

I closed my eyes and waited for the shot, certain that the intruder would shoot the butler down.

Instead, I heard Brookes gasp, "M. Cornier!"

I opened my eyes.

Sure enough, standing with his back to the cabinet, was our neighbor—Henri Cornier.

"Well, Brookes?" he inquired, as if the situation were not unusual.

Brookes, quick to regain his composure, took Cornier's visit as a matter of usual circumstance; for he said, "I came to place the master's slippers and turn up the fire."

"My friend is upstairs?"

"With the young people, sir. Would you wish him down?"

"No, Brookes—no."

Brookes set Ralston's slippers in place and carefully regulated the flame of the gas-logs.

"Has Martini come in?"

"I think not, sir."

Brookes went over and tried the door to Pietro's shop. It was dark and still within the sanctum of the artificer.

At that moment hurried footsteps echoed through the servants' hall and up the service stairway.

"What's that?" Cornier demanded.

Brookes investigated and reported that he recognized the heels of Mademoiselle Fifi scurrying into the darkness above. Cornier took out his tobacco pouch and filled his pipe.

"I ran over after my tobacco pouch," he informed Brookes. "I left it here earlier in the evening."

"Quite so, sir."

"And, Brookes, I came in by the secret door."

Here was jolting honesty on the part of M. Cornier, just as I was endeavoring to figure out why he lied about the tobacco pouch.

"My key doesn't work well," he continued. "I wish that you would file it a bit."

Brookes took the key.

"And," Cornier added, "please let me out the front door. I left my umbrella out yonder. And, my good man, it will be well not to mention my coming over at this hour."

They went out, neither of them—I believe—aware of my presence in the big room. Thinking it best that they shouldn't know that I had witnessed their encounter, I decided to escape to my room *via* the servants' stairs.

As I stepped from behind the screen, I halted, frozen in my tracks; for close without the house I heard a weird calling—just like the screeching of an owl. Three times I heard it. I shivered; for all my life I have hated the call of the screech owl.

And then outside one of the windows I heard a soft scratching—as if some one were sawing through one of the bars.

I escaped through the servants' hall and up the service stairs to the second floor.

There I came upon Mrs. Julia Wilmorton, moving stealthily down the hall toward the windows overlooking the driveway and the *porte-cochere*.

I coughed, discreetly.

"Oh!" she exclaimed, panicky-like, as she spun about to face me.

Seeing that it was only Howard Ralston's private secretary that had surprised her, a look of relief swept over the lady's face. She glided by me and entered her apartment.

I went into my own room. Closing the door, I leaned against it, my heart thumping.

As I paused there, I heard it again—the insistent call of the screech owl.

THE MIDNIGHT OF THE FIRST DAY

1

Hearkening to that call of the owl, I wondered if some one out there in the dark and the storm could be signaling a confederate within the house—a traitor, perhaps, beneath the roofs of *Windermere.*

Then it occurred to me that it might be wise to note the exact time. I felt for my watch, to discover that it wasn't on my wrist. I quickly remembered leaving it on my desk in "the tomb," and I didn't relish the idea of going after it.

I lighted a cigarette, thinking that maybe my nerve would stiffen by the time I had smoked the fag through. I smoked seven of the damned things, my courage diminishing with each. Something—an innate psychic prescience, I now believe it to have been—held me away from that awful chamber: Howard Ralston's "tomb." If not his, then the tomb of Serapion. Like Julia Wilmorton, I dreaded that accursed mummy . . .

It was near to midnight, I judged, when, convinced that I was surrendering to womanly cowardice, I determined to have my watch. I undressed, donned pajamas, thrust feet into my black-leather *Fausts,* slipped into my wine-colored dressing-gown—the gift of my Aunt Martha. Martha West is the most courageous woman I have ever known—absolutely calm and self-possessed under stress of circumstances, brave even though the wildest turmoil swirled about her in maelstromic ferocity. I guess that is why I decided to wear her gift—as a sort of shield for my descent into "the tomb." You know what I mean—with a sort of forlorn hope that some of my Aunt Martha's virtue might be imparted to me through that gift of hers.

I stole through the upper hall, passed the sitting-room where Ralston sat at three-handed bridge with Paul and Mildred, and went down the service stairs. Safely inside "the tomb," I closed the door behind me and snapped the light switch. The current did not respond; the room remained in more than semidarkness, as the gas-logs for some reason were not burning so brightly as Brookes had adjusted them.

I thought I detected the rasp of labored breathing. I strained my ears to locate its source, finally deciding that the effect was produced by freakish action of wind in the chimney.

My inclination toward flight was strong, even though the semblance of human breathing was only wind in the chimney. But my masculine vanity triumphed. I wouldn't be what the boss called "an old woman."

I felt behind me for the lock on the door through which I had come, and turned the key. I stepped to the door leading into Pietro's shop and turned the key there. The double doors I left unlocked, intending to retreat through them when I had secured my watch.

I went swiftly to my desk—my flesh all "goose-bumpy"—and snatched up my watch. No sooner had I done so than the double doors opened and the master of *Windermere* entered. I could see him as he glanced about the room, and I heard him mutter, "Some one must have stepped across my grave!" I thought of the old saying and its basic superstition.

"Better let me come down, Dad," Paul called from above stairs.

"No, Paul," Ralston answered, taking his revolver from his pocket. "I want the thrill of this adventure all to myself."

"But your heart, Father—any undue excitement—"

"That Viennese physician was diagnosing for a fat fee, my boy. The old pump's all right."

He closed the double doors and locked them.

I heard him swear, and understood that he, too, had failed to switch on "the tomb" lights.

I wanted to apprise him of my presence; but I was afraid that he, startled by my voice, might take a shot at me.

The distant clock boomed the hour of midnight; the French clock on the mantel chimed echo—a silvery tinkle suggesting that God was in his heaven and that all was right with the world.

It was the hour at which the Brothers of Karnak threatened to summon the *ka* from out the mummy of Serapion. There in "the tomb" at that midnight hour, the memory of the warning delivered by the unknown Oriental and of all the talk about the *ka* of Serapion that had smitten my ears that night *got* me. . . .

Howard Ralston, revolver in hand, stood back against the double doors and actually chuckled.

"The *ka* of Serapion," he sneered, his eyes fixed upon the mummy case. "Bunk!"

A low rumble of thunder growled over *Windermere*. An awful thing happened.

The lid of the mummy case swung slowly outward, as if propelled by an unseen hand. Howard Ralston gasped. He was no more startled than I, however. I felt as if my eyes would burst their sockets as I stared at the horrid apparition. Stiffly old Serapion stepped forth—slowly, mechanically, as it were. Just outside the mummy case, he paused. Almost, I looked to see the thing turn its head—as one does who endeavors to get his bearings in an unfamiliar place.

He didn't do that, however; just stood there—staring straight before him, what might have been the eyes of him fixed upon Howard Ralston. Then, stiffly, as before, the thing stepped with measured tread toward Ralston.

The boss fired—once.

The bullet went through the apparition, never halting it in its deliberate forward march. The long arm of it lifted a fleshless finger—discharging a ghostly green ray straight at Ralston's heart.

The boss clutched at his heart, his revolver slipping from nerveless fingers. A little sigh of fear, and he pitched forward— face downward— upon the floor of "the tomb."

The storm howled.

My nerves snapped. My head reeled. I swayed uncertainly. I tried to cry out. Then I became conscious of a sharp stinging in my left forearm . . .

"The Brothers of Karnak!"

The words were whispered.

The whispering was followed by muffled, exultant laughter.

I looked about to discover whence voice and laughter came, and I perceived that I was standing amid the ruins of a once mighty temple. About me were towering columns, richly colored and engraved with hieroglyphics. It seemed that I walked invisible; for the white-cowled figures among whom I moved appeared unmindful of my presence. The milling figures halted their movements as one like unto themselves, but larger, stepped from the holy of holies and raised an arm in gesture commanding attention.

"When it is midnight in America," the newcomer said, in tones reminiscent of the moaning of the sea, "we must conjure the *ka*, from the body of our dead Imperator that it may touch that mummy's possessor with death in reward for his sacrilege."

"Can none save him?" I cried unheeded.

The speaker continued: "His heart shall be touched with the icy finger of death if he heed not our warning and return the sacred corpse to the land whence he spirited it away."

I walked among the shrouded forms; and then I saw that I, also, wore the cowled garment. I hugged it to me, glad for effective disguise, and trooped with the horrid company into a dimly lighted cavern beneath the temple. I heard the leader announce that the hour had struck and that no message had come from America. The despoiler of Serapion's tomb had remained silent.

The cowled company formed a far-flung circle about a tripod supporting a brazier into which their leader cast a powder. The powder, igniting, flared up, its flame painting the walls of the cavern with grotesque shadows.

As if moved by common impulse, the figures faced westward, chanting a monotonous incantation. It lies before me now, that chant, printed in an old book from Ben Bailey's collection of rare occult volumes. As I copy the words into this manuscript, I seem to hear them recited—just as vividly as on that terrible night.

> *Come forth, O Ka of Serapion!*
> *Come forth! Come forth!*
> *Touch thou the heart of him*
> *Who hath violated thy house of flesh!*
> *Touch thou his heart with death!*
> *Convey his soul before Osiris!*

The next thing I knew, I was aware that I was lying upon the floor of "the tomb." I combed my harried thoughts for explanation of what had passed. In my browsings in Ben's library and in that of Howard Ralston I had come across accounts of peculiar *adventures in space.* I had heard the boss and Ben discuss the so-called projection of man's astral body. Had I, I wondered, been drawn out of my body by the magic of the Brothers of Karnak and compelled to look upon their mysteries in distant Egypt? I was in a state to believe anything. I who had chuckled up my sleeve at occult philosophy was ready to acknowledge myself a convert. There was no question but that they had summoned forth the *ka* of Serapion and that its icy finger had touched Howard Ralston's weakened heart. With my own eyes I had seen. The threats of the Brothers of Karnak had been fulfilled. . . .

And then I heard their victim groaning. I lifted my head and looked toward him. He was lying where he had fallen, face down upon the floor of "the tomb." From between his shoulder blades protruded the red-tasseled, dragon-twisted handle of the Chinese vengeance dagger.

"Help!" he sobbed, horrible gurgling in his throat.

"I'm coming, sir," I panted, dragging my almost paralyzed body toward him.

It was tedious work—that moving of my heavy body. Only by tremendous exertion was I able to accomplish it. My clothes and my hands were wet with his blood by the time I had reached him. I tried to pull out the dagger, but hadn't strength to do so.

"Mr. Ralston," I wept, "are you hurt?"

"I'm dying—"

He strove to move, but it was feeble effort that he made. "The diamonds!" he gasped.

"I'll see if they're safe," I assured him.

Somehow I got to my knees and crawled to the wall where the diamond safe was located. My vision began to blur. I had to feel every inch of the way. Clutching the side of the Chinese cabinet, I hauled myself into an upright position. I felt along the wall until my fingers touched the lock of the safe. Frantically I tried it. It was locked. The diamonds were safe.

My knees sagged under me. I would have collapsed had I not become aware of a pounding upon the double doors of "the tomb." The thought of succor near at hand gave me strength. Only my determination to reach those doors and unlock them enabled me to retain hold upon consciousness.

Then I heard Paul's voice hysterically demanding that the doors be unlocked.

I reached those doors; my outstretched hands contacted them, coldly.

"West!"

"Yes, Paul! Yes, I'm here!"

"Let me in, West! Open the doors!"

Suddenly I realized why the doors were cold to my touch! I understood, too, why Paul's voice sounded so far away.

"West! Open these doors, I tell you!"

"I can't Paul," I sobbed. "The steel barriers are down."

I heard him pounding and calling as I sank down into soothing oblivion.

2

It is a nasty emotion, being jerked from slumber. Such was my awakening. A jolt; then swiftly following nausea, for I had come-to with one of those heart-dropping sensations that leaves one feeling as if the *Knickerbocker Express* had missed him by a bare six inches.

I lay there, trying to locate myself and endeavoring to recall what had taken place. Gradually I realized that I was in my own room and in my own bed. I tried to puzzle it out; for I remembered last of being down there in "the tomb" with Howard Ralston—and him with the Chinese dagger in his back. . . . Or hadn't I been through that experience? Was it, after all, only hideous nightmare? My brain staggered under Herculean effort to think things through.

Glancing about me, I discovered that at my bedside had been placed a white enameled table with a basin on it, wet towels, and some bottles. Bewildered, I closed my eyes.

Then an idea. I felt at my left wrist. My watch! I couldn't remember snapping it upon my wrist; yet here I was in bed with my watch in place.

I looked at the dial. I had been in bed nearly an hour. I had been asleep. I had been dreaming. . . .

But what was it that jolted me into wakefulness?

I listened with straining ears, hand pressed hard over my jumping heart. I heard nothing. A mantle of quiet rested upon *Windermere*.

Then a vertical line of light struck my vision.

Some one was stealthily opening my door.

I sat bolt upright and cried, "Who's there?"

The door opened wider; I saw Brookes. I batted my eyes to concentrate vision. Shortly Brookes ceased to blur and I saw him distinctly.

He stood there, hand on door knob, quaking from head to foot—a much disturbed old man.

"What's up, Brookes?" I demanded, trying to keep my voice from betraying alarm.

I switched on the lights, hoping thereby to render him encouragement; but he stood there in the doorway, staring at me and looking pathetic in his endeavor to utter sounds.

"Brookes!"

I shouted at him, for terror was shattering the spirit within me.

My effort was rewarded.

"Oh, young sir," Brookes faltered. "It's awful! That's what it is, sir: awful!"

"Calm yourself, Brookes," I admonished, just as if my own blood were not swelling the arteries in my throat and beating hammers at my temples. "Calm yourself. Tell me what has happened."

I was out of bed as I finished the sentence and hunting my wine-colored dressing-gown; but it was not in sight. I opened the closet door. The dressing-gown was not on its accustomed peg. I took another and slipped it on. It was then I noticed that I had on different pajamas.

"What the—?" I began.

"I can't tell you, sir," Brookes mumbled. "But it's the worst that could have happened at *Windermere,* sir."

Windermere!

I had thought it such a beautiful name. Now it sounded uncanny on Brookes' fright-thickened tongue.

"The young master wishes you to come down to the big room, sir. That is, if you feel able, sir—"

"What do you mean: if I feel able?"

Brookes lifted his brows—surprised, as it were.

"Did you—find me—down there?" I asked, glancing from his chalk-white face to the enameled table beside my bed.

I saw then that one of the bottles was labeled "ammonia."

"Quite so, sir. Johns and I brought you round."

"Where is Johns now?"

"In the servants' sitting-room, sir. Keeping the help quiet."

A dozen questions urged expression, but dread of truth held them back.

"You and Johns carried me up here?" I did venture to inquire.

"We did, sir. We put you in a hot bath and did what we could to bring you round. When you seemed well on the road to recovery, we left you to rest."

"Thank you, Brookes . . . Tell Paul I'll be right down."

Brookes departed.

I stared at the door, not thinking of him—but trying to figure out how they got me out of that charnel house. What with the steel barriers and all. Was Howard Ralston dead? If he were, who had killed him? Would they accuse me? Was it the police that wanted me down in "the tomb"?

I brushed the thought aside. It was no time for speculation. Paul had sent for me to come to him. He and I were fraternity brothers. That's how I came to have my job. Job! Where was my job now? . . .

Little dreaming that I would need to be further dressed, I slipped my feet into my *Fausts*. My hands trembled as I knotted the cord of my dressing-gown. Running my fingers through my hair by way of careless arrangement of it, I descended to the lower floor.

Reaching the foot of the stairs, I hesitated—just outside "the tomb": that vast chamber with its incongruous furnishings and its horde of antiques and curios. What awaited my eyes on the floor of that chamber? I hoped they had covered it with something.

Resolutely I pulled myself together. There couldn't be anything worse to face than that which I had been up against.

The "tomb" was candle-lighted, which could only mean that the electric wires had been cut.

Entering "the tomb"—from which I knew not how I had escaped, I saw—not a dead or wounded body, but Paul, Mildred, and Pietro. Just the three of them. Howard Ralston's body was nowhere to be seen.

My heart lightened when I made that discovery.

Then I saw Brookes standing at the far side of the room, his dark eyes wide with horror in his white mask of a face. The worst that could have happened at *Windermere,* he had said. I dragged my eyes from Brookes' miserable countenance, the feeling of lightness flowing out of my heart.

Nor was I happier in looking again upon Paul and Mildred and Pietro. They were fully dressed. Their faces showed effects of some harrowing experience. Paul and Mildred sat on the Spanish divan, which had been turned about so that its back was now to the fireplace. Opposite Paul and Mildred, seated on an old Flemish bench, was Pietro, the exotic Italian, who for two exciting months had been a storm center in the Ralston *ménage.*

After one quick, appealing glance at me, Pietro lumped into a posture of utter dejection, his face hidden in his long, sinewy hands. I couldn't help thinking, even then, that his were beautiful hands— hands that a Donatello would have immortalized in marble. Yet the long, supple fingers suggested evil—strangled throats, perhaps, or gaping wounds made with a skillfully manipulated dagger.

Then Mildred's eyes sought mine; but only for a moment, as they brimmed with tears and dropped their gaze to the floor of "the tomb."

Then I saw it.

Midway between the Spanish sofa and the Flemish bench, in the center of the Chinese rug, was a dark, moist stain. It lay between Paul and Pietro.

"Paul," I faltered, seeking the support of a huge Renaissance table.

His eyes sought the blood-stained, Chinese rug. "My father," he answered brokenly.

So it was no dream, I was compelled to assure myself. Howard Ralston had been murdered, and I had been in "the tomb" when the deed was accomplished.

"Were you—witness to the crime?" Paul asked, as though divining my thoughts.

I became conscious of four pair of eyes burning their regard upon mine.

I groped for a chair, and, sinking weakly upon it, told my story.

"Incredible," muttered Paul, when I had finished. "And yet it all links up. Dear Christ, if any man but you told me such a tale—"

"I know," I said. "You'd brand him a liar. But as God is my judge, Paul—"

"I believe you, West, I can't understand it—that's all."

For a space of time we sat there, with Brookes at the far side of the room. All of us, I think, stared at the blood stain upon the Chinese rug.

My left arm ached and throbbed so painfully that I bit my lip to keep from crying out.

"Would you mind telling me how I got out of here?" I asked, curiosity mastering me. "The steel barriers were down."

"Forgive me for not telling you sooner," Paul said. "Mildred and I heard a shot and hurried down the stairs. The double doors were locked. We tried every door. Then Brookes and Johns came. . . . Brookes—you tell him."

Paul's voice broke; he covered his face with his hands.

"Very good, sir," Brookes replied. Coming forward, he said to me, "I had a key to the secret door—"

"There was no barrier there?" I asked.

"No, sir. Mr. Ralston thought as the door was so well concealed that a barrier wasn't necessary. Besides, sir, he had planned that door for just such an emergency as has occurred. . . . I opened the secret door, and led the young people in. Miss Manning was first to discover the body."

Mildred sobbed.

"We began searching for the spring that would lift the barriers," Paul found voice to continue. "One of us—we don't know which—accidentally touched it. We got the barriers up, and Brookes unlocked the double doors."

"It was then that Johns and I carried you upstairs, sir," Brookes informed me. "When we came down again, Mr. Martini was here with Mr. Paul and Miss Manning. But the body was gone, sir."

"You mean that it had disappeared?" I cried.

"Right, sir."

"It was here when I came in," Pietro interrupted, "and Paul was kneeling beside it."

"Then how could it disappear?"

"Ask him," Pietro answered, yielding Paul an accusing look.

"But if you were here, Pietro—"

"I—why, I stepped out for a moment. When I came back—"

"Quit your lies, Martini!" Paul barked at him.

"What!" Pietro flared, angrily.

Paul ignored him.

"Mildred and I tried to call the police over your desk phone," Paul told me, "but the line was dead. Then we went to the hall phone, only to find that it was out of commission. When we came back to this room, the body was gone."

Vaguely my shocked brain realized that Howard Ralston had not only been done to death, but also that his body had mysteriously vanished.

Paul's hands—they were stained. Not badly—a streak here and there and about the roots of the nails. That he had endeavored to clean them was evident. I noted that Pietro's hands were clean.

"Who could have done it?" I wondered, speaking my thought.

"Him!" Pietro burst forth, pointing shaking finger at Paul.

"You lie!" Paul hurled back at him. "If you accuse me, you know you lie!"

They were on their feet; fists clenched.

"Paul," Mildred urged, restraining hand upon his arm.

To Pietro, she said, "Paul couldn't have done it. He hadn't time to get the body away without your seeing him. And he couldn't have hidden it in this room."

"Oh yes he could!" Pietro retorted.

"Where?" I demanded.

"Here!"

Pietro went to the mummy case and wrenched back the lid. We stared at that sarcophagus with unbelieving eyes. It was empty.

Not only had the body of Howard Ralston vanished, but also the shriveled corpse of old Serapion.

There was a ferocious crackling of lightning; the lights in the hall went out.

Above stairs, Julia Wilmorton shrieked.

3

Then again I was aware of Paul's voice. "Since our telephone is out of order, I am asking Brookes to call the police from Henri's house,

West," Paul was saying to me. "I wish that you would take the roadster and go after Ben Bailey."

"But," I began, shooting a quick glance at Pietro Martini.

"We'll all be here in this room when you return," Paul promised, grimly.

He misunderstood me, for I meant no disparagement of the Italian artificer. I wondered what Pietro would think; but if he took any notice of Paul's words, he showed no sign. Mildred Manning seemed to sense the same thing I did, for she lifted reproachful eyes to Paul's face, and her fingers were laid against his lips to prevent further innuendo.

Even as I looked at them, I felt that Paul and Mildred were made for each other. I had thought that from the beginning. Would they have each other now—after this murder; or would the resulting circumstances forever place barriers between them?

"Will you go, West? Please."

Unmindful of my odd attire, I hastened out through Pietro's shop, through the back porch, and across the drive to the garage. My arm was throbbing and my head swimming as I backed the roadster out and tore down the curved driveway into Park Avenue.

It was a long drive to Ben Bailey's apartment, but I somehow held the wheel and kept going. I seemed to be floating along. Objects I encountered coming toward me were as persons gliding through a slow motion film. My vision blurred, my muscles numbed

Then suddenly the lights at the entrance of Bailey's apartment house shone before me through the mists. I jammed the brakes. I heard their shrilling squeak, but the sound seemed to come from miles away. My head swam; my arm ached. To this day I don't know how I managed to swing the roadster to the curb.

I found Ben still up.

"What the hell?" he demanded, as I burst in upon him.

"Murder!" I groaned. "There's been murder done in 'the tomb'!"

And then, like a damn fool, I fainted.

4

When I opened my eyes, Ben was throwing water into my face and swearing like a Bengal lancer. He got me to my feet, led me to a comfortable chair, and poured real "Scotch" down my throat.

"Now let's have it," he urged.

I didn't answer right off the bat—just sat staring at him, wondering how he'd take what I had to reveal. You see, he was Paul's most intimate friend—member of the same frat.

"It's Howard Ralston," I blurted out. "He's been murdered!"

"Good God! I can't believe it!"

"You'll have to believe it, Ben. Don't you see, it's me telling you? I saw him—dead."

He dropped into a chair and sat staring at me, defiant-like. I realized that it was hard on him; but it was hard on me, too—for you see, my brother and I were *Sig Alphs,* also, and we all sort of hung together. I was the baby of the bunch, and Ben had got me my job with Howard Ralston.

"And the body has managed to disappear," I added. "And damn it, I want to cry like a doggone baby!"

But Ben had neither time nor sympathy for tears. His friend had appealed to him for help. The detective in him was aroused and eager to take the scent.

I related the whole wretched story; and when I had finished, I slumped in my chair. Only the fact that Ben sprang quickly forward and caught me saved me from crashing to the floor. "Snap out of it, kid!"

I did my best, pulling myself together and grinning sheepishly at Ben.

"Let's have a look at that arm."

Kneeling beside me, he rolled up the sleeve of my pajama jacket. He whistled his amazement as he scrutinized the spot where the pain had concentrated.

"Peculiar puncture," he mused. "Looks like an insect sting."

"It couldn't have been that, Ben."

"That puncture was made by a needle," he said.

He went for his kit, took out a powerful lens, and again examined my peculiar wound.

"Just as I thought," he commented. "Symptoms are unmistakable. A powerful Oriental drug has been used—a drug that produces temporary paralysis of the body and induces hallucinations wilder than those attendant upon any opiate commonly known to science. Whoever drove that knife into Howard Ralston's back also shot the devilish drug into you."

At his request, I recalled as best I could the effects I felt from the moment I first felt the stinging in my arm.

My recital finished and particular questions answered, Ben stood me on my feet, stripped me, and stretched me out on my back upon a couch. With patient tenderness, he went over me.

"I can't be wrong," he said, when he finished.

Settling back in his chair, he said, "You've been in terrible shape, kid. Still are, for that matter. Only your damned luck saved you a heavier dose."

"My luck?"

"Luckily for you, the murderer either lost his nerve or was frightened away before he had time to accomplish all he set out to do."

Ben went to his cabinet and brought forth several bottles and a hypodermic needle. Like a practiced physician, he sterilized and mixed.

"I have an excellent counteractant here," he explained. "Another Oriental drug which I have mixed with andrenolin. This will bring you round."

He shot the stuff into me; then helped me into my pajamas.

"Hadn't we better be going to *Windermere?*" I asked.

"We won't be needed there yet. Besides, we'd be in the way of the police."

Drawing up his chair to where he could fully observe me, he settled to enjoyment of his pipe.

"Lie there and don't talk. Rest, and don't think. Shortly I'll give you plenty opportunity to talk, for I shall want to know a number of facts before I go to *Windermere.*"

Don't think, he had said. But my brain was stimulated. Thoughts tumbled over one another. For the most part, they were about Ben Bailey.

Big, handsome, and blond, he had been dubbed "the Viking" by the sorority dames. They ran after him. He didn't run away; just ignored them, his mind intent upon his studies and his hobbies. His studies, insofar as the university program would permit, had been wide and varied. Like myself, he dabbled in anthropology, archeology, psychology, chemistry, physics, languages (including Hebrew, Mesopotamian, and Egyptian dialects, Sanscrit, and what have you?). Took him six years to get his A. B. degree, but he didn't have to hurry—not with his fortune. . . .

His hobby was crime. He read mystery and detective fiction voraciously. He collected an extensive library on crime and crime detection. He made friends with detectives in the city, and was always nosing around police headquarters. The smart dicks kidded him, but many's the time they profited by his hints.

After graduating from the university, Ben went to London, Paris, and Berlin, studying foreign detection methods. Those of the Paris *Surete* made greatest impression on him.

From Berlin he went to India. For years none heard from him. Then he turned up unexpectedly from nowhere. To Paul he imparted information that he had penetrated the recesses of Mongolia and Tibet. With Howard Ralston he spent whole nights discussing occultism and Yogi philosophy. Ralston took these things seriously; but Ben was interested in them only as astounding eruptions within human consciousness. He learned a lot about the tricks of Indian fakirs and about medicines and drugs of Oriental peoples. Howard Ralston was convinced that Ben had become *chela* to some Mahatma and that he could read minds. Ben protested that he did not catch thoughts, but that he had learned how to get at a man's thinking by observing the man's reactions during conversation.

As I lay there looking at him, my mind reverted to the beginning of my immersion into the mysteries of *Windermere*. Howard Ralston had wanted a "bright young chap with a flair for archeology and ability in Romance languages." Ben recommended me, and I was hired on the spot—without so much as an interview. And I, just receiving the little old A. B. degree and wanting a job—wasn't I tickled pink! But as Ben drove me to *Windermere* that night of June 15, had I known what I was to experience the two months that followed, it is likely I should never have gotten out of Ben's *coupe* when he slid under the *porte-cochere* serving both *Fontainebleau* and *Windermere*.

Lying there recalling it all, I wished I had accepted Ben's earlier invitation and gone with him to Hawaii, from which spot he had just returned.

And having arrived at that point in my forbidden thinking, I recalled that Ben had gone to Hawaii to investigate a new drug a certain school of criminals was using. . . . Ben had said that an Oriental drug had been shot into my arm.

"You think," I finally mustered up courage to ask him, "that the drug administered to me stimulated in my consciousness a vision of the Brothers of Karnak and of the *ka* of Serapion?"

"Yes, to the first part of your question, Win. When the drug got you, the thought of the Brothers of Karnak was uppermost in your mind. That was natural, you having seen the *ka* walking out of its mummy case. Your mind received further suggestion when you heard the name of the Egyptian organization whispered to you. Inevitably, when your brain responded to the hallucination-creating stimulus of the injected drug—"

"I had visions of the Brothers of Karnak. But what about that invocation I heard them chanting?"

"That's in an old book of Egyptian rituals I have on my shelves. At least, one similar to it is there. You've done a heap of browsing among my books, you know."

"What about the *ka?* Did I dream that, too?"

"There is no such thing as a *ka,* Win. Pure superstition. Don't ever fall for any of this pseudo occult stuff. It has ruined more people than Wall Street. See what it's done for Howard Ralston."

"Ben, I couldn't have been drugged when I saw that mummy case open and the *ka* float out into the room—"

"It floated?"

"As sure as I'm lying here."

"Okay, kid. If you saw it, you saw it."

"Well, we found the mummy case empty."

"I'm not surprised."

"How do you account for that?"

"By facts filed under *L* in this cabinet."

He went to an olive-green steel cabinet, opened a drawer, and extracted a number of folders. Returning to his chair, he ran through them—sorting out a few for future reference.

"*L?*" I murmured. "Mind telling me what you're getting at, Ben?"

"My lad, a good detective thinks—and keeps his mouth shut."

"You won't tell?"

"Not now. But I'm wanting you to tell me things—about what's happened at *Windermere* between the dates of June 15 and August 15."

"I can't tell you much, for we've been away. Returned home only yesterday morning."

"Then tell me about the few days you spent there before you accompanied Ralston abroad."

"Where shall I begin?"

"With the night I took you to *Windermere*."

I related how warmly Howard Ralston received me; how he himself showed me to my room.

"Located where?" Ben interrupted.

"Second floor, front, adjoining the upstairs sitting-room and right across the hall from Julia Wilmorton's apartment."

"What is Mrs. Wilmorton like?"

"Beautiful then. Kind of woman you imagine the second Mrs. Tanqueray to have been, or Mrs. Erlynne, if you know what I mean—but in looks and manner only. Don't get me wrong, Henri Cornier's crazy about her."

"Indeed?"

"I'm telling you."

"After Ralston showed you to your room, what?"

"He stayed while I dressed for dinner. Talked about the university and about the work he wanted me to do. Then we went down to 'the tomb,' where he showed me an old French book that he wanted translated. He had just purchased the Josephine diamonds, and he wanted to run down facts that would throw light on their history."

"What about the Josephine diamonds?"

"Wonderful set that Napoleon gave Josephine. For years the boss had been after them. They cost him a million and a half—at least that's their estimated valuation."

"And he keeps them at *Windermere?*"

"In a secret safe in the wall. Over by the huge fireplace."

"H'm. I'd call that risky."

"I worked on the book until dinner time. At dinner I met Mildred Manning, the girl Ralston expected to marry."

"And what's she like?"

"Oh, Boy, you're asking me something! I could rhapsodize about her. Slender and graceful. A complexion of rare ivory, with faintest glow of rose blushing through. Lovely hazel eyes. Hair with the sheen of bronze—"

"Hold it! You'll be having another fainting spell."

"Just let me carry her over the dance floor—just let me hold her once in my arms, and I'll willingly die," I replied. "She's as sweet as she is beautiful, too. Paul's wild about her. They fell in love at first sight the night Paul met her at the station."

"So Arthur sent Launcelot to fetch the Guinevere home, eh?"

"Is funny, isn't it, Ben, that the son should fall for the girl his father was to marry. Pietro's crazy about her, too." I had to tell Ben about Pietro then.

"How does Mildred Manning behave under those conditions?"

"I told you that she's as sweet as she is beautiful. She loves Paul, but she meant to go through with that marriage. She never did a thing out of the way."

"Naturally you'd speak in her defense."

"Wait until you see her."

"I'm all anticipation," he laughed. "Suppose you tell me about that wager now."

"The wager was made that first night—right after dinner. Cornier had come over and was talking with the boss about antiques down there in 'the tomb.' I was working at my desk, so I heard it all. Ralston said that he meant to have the mummy of old Serapion, the vengeance dagger of the Scarlet Dragons, and the Borgia poison ring. He had a deal on with an Italian agent named Guissepi Reni, who knew that he could get the mummy and the dagger—the latter through a Chinese agent in Shanghai. But the Borgia, he said, Reni was uncertain about. 'But I'm going after it!' he declared. Cornier laughed. He said, 'You'll stand about as much chance of getting that Borgia poison ring from the Duke of Vedena as I stand of getting England's crown from little King George.'

"That nettled the boss, and the upshot of the ensuing argument was that a bet was laid—fifty thousand to fifty thousand. Julia Wilmorton was given the stakes to hold—a personal check drawn by each of the partners."

"A hundred thousand dollars! That was a lot of money for Mrs. Wilmorton to be responsible for. No wonder she's looking not so good these days. Does she make a satisfactory chaperon?"

"Does she? She even warned Paul to give up all thought of marrying Mildred."

"Now that's interesting, in the light of Basil Manning's will!"

"You know about the will?"

"I've heard enough about it to know what it means to the folks at *Windermere*. What does Henri Cornier think of the proposed marriage between Ralston and Miss Manning?"

"That Cornier's a shrewd one. He saw through the situation the first night. He warned Ralston then, but the boss only laughed at him."

Ben sat and smoked. I watched him, wondering what his thoughts might be.

Presently he knocked the ashes from his pipe.

"How feel?" he asked.

"Better," I replied, sitting up and reaching for my dressing gown.

"Let's get going," he said, rising.

He assembled his paraphernalia and we went down to the roadster. I still felt too unnerved to take the wheel, so Ben drove the road to *Windermere*.

5

"Will there be any objection to your working on the case?" I asked, as we rode along.

"Never can tell. If the dick in charge doesn't prove obstreperous and the district attorney doesn't forbid a non-professional operating on the scene of action, I ought to get along. It's Paul's request, anyway; not my officiousness this time." He laughed. "How'd you like to play along with me, kid?"

"Me? Help you?"

"I need a guy like you. A little chemistry, a little physics, perhaps, and an adept at shorthand."

"Gosh, I'd like to, Ben."

"Job's yours," he said, pinching my leg.

"Hey!" I yelled.

"Good!" he chuckled, when I winced. "Old Doc Bailey brings 'em round."

"Ben," I asked, hesitatingly, after some reflection, "am I apt to be listed as a suspect?"

"Right! The police have every person who has been inside *Winder-mere* the past twenty-four hours down as a suspect. But I'll get you off with light sentence." He grinned at me. "Why, you couldn't swat a fly without shedding apologetic tear over the insect. You've a complex that way. Now, of course, according to certain schools of psychology, such a complex is indicative of—"

"Surely they wouldn't suspect Brookes," I cut in. "He's been with Howard Ralston for years."

"Ah, but family butlers have sometimes proved to be wolves in sheep clothing."

"Not Brookes. He's what sentimental ladies call 'a dear old lamb'."

"I call him that myself," Ben said.

"I don't believe that you much suspect the Brothers of Karnak or the Scarlet Dragons," I hinted.

"I wouldn't go so far as to say that! To you, as my assistant, I will say—confidentially—that the type of showmanship displayed in this affair doesn't savor of their style."

"What do you mean by 'showmanship'?"

"Didn't you notice that I consulted *L*-file in my records?"

"Okay," I assented, perceiving that my inquisitive mind was not yet to be eased, "only I'd like to know."

"So would I. And we're going to find out!" He turned into the *Wind-ermere-Fontainebleau* driveway, adding, "Provided, of course, that the professional detectives aren't too resentful."

"I'd forgotten," I said. "Of course there will be regular detectives—and as dumb as Mississippi oxen."

"Not always," Ben assured me. "There are some smart boys among them."

"Not one of them can hold a candle to you, Ben," I gushed prideful-ly, as he assisted me from the roadster.

As Ben had surmised, the police had come during my absence. They had gone over the place, more or less thoroughly, and, departing, had left behind them a detective named Harrison Denny—"Hal Denny" to his familiars, and an assistant that we heard called only "Sleepy Wall-ingford." No one, apparently, took him seriously.

I at once set Mr. Harrison Denny down as a rather intelligent and likeable chap, with more than a bit of the Irish in him.

Several policemen, I also discovered, had been stationed about the premises—both inside the house and out; quite in accordance with traditional methods of the blue-coated fraternity. One of these, after a grilling cross-examination of Ben and myself, went into consultation with Hal Denny. He returned from that consultation and admitted us to the house.

Paul and Mildred and Pietro were still in "the tomb", sitting much as I had left them. Hal Denny had been questioning them. They looked fagged out.

Paul glanced up with a sigh of relief as we entered.

"Mr. Bailey is my nearest friend," he explained to Denny. "I want him here with me. I thought, too, that he might help—"

"Sure," Denny said. "Be glad to have him around. I can fix it with the D. A. Bailey don't need introducing to me, though."

"You know each other?" Paul asked.

"Oh, yeah—in a way. Me and him—"

Paul waited, but Mr. Denny had no further offering to make.

"This is Mr. Winston West, my father's private secretary," Paul then said, presenting me.

Removing the cigar butt from his mouth, Hal Denny looked me over.

"So you're the lad what saw the murder done, are you?" he asked.

"I was in the room when it was done," I stammered, "but—"

"I've been wanting to talk to you."

Thinking his tone menacing, I shivered; but felt better when Ben laid his hand upon my arm.

"I'm sorry to have kept you waiting," I said, by way of apology.

"It's all right, young feller. Only next time don't skin out when yuh know the police is coming."

"I told you the circumstances," Paul cut in.

"Let's all set down," Denny suggested, ignoring Paul's defense of myself.

THE DAWN OF THE SECOND DAY

1

Detective Denny began on me. But for the assistance I received from Ben and Paul—with occasional confirmation from Brookes, I would have been set for the "hot squat." Only they hang in Minnesota, thank the Lord! Denny dragged from me every detail of the night's happenings; then cross-examined until I was ready to admit anything and assume full responsibility for the murder of Howard Ralston.

If Paul, Pietro, and Mildred—along with Brookes—were suspects, I wondered why Denny let them sit in on his interrogation. I remembered Ben once said that while the examination of witnesses should be conducted as soon as possible after the crime, each person should be taken separately. I was soon to learn, however, that Detective Denny did things in his own sweet way and that there was no turning his feet from the path in which he elected to set them.

"Well, Bailey," he remarked, when through with me, "I guess he's been doped all right."

"Might have taken my word for it at the beginning," was Ben's dry rejoinder.

Hal Denny glared at Ben Bailey; Ben Bailey glared at Hal Denny. Sleepy Wallingford chortled his delight and bit a mouthful from an apple he apparently kept about his person.

Denny looked away first, I was comforted in observing. Setting that fact down as "score one" for Ben, in what I considered was to be relentless warfare between the two detectives throughout the case, I relaxed as the big Irishman gave his attention to Paul.

"Mr. Ralston," Denny requested, "please go on from where you was when Bailey came in."

"Well," Paul began, "after Father put the diamonds back it the safe and locked the Borgia in the cabinet, Miss Manning and went to the upstairs sitting-room for a game of *Mah Jong*."

"What time was that?"

"I don't know, Mr. Denny."

"Go ahead."

"Father came up afterward and took a hand. Then Aunt Julia came in."

"She join the game?"

"Looked on a few minutes; then went across the hall to her rooms. It must have been about ten o'clock when Father called Brookes and asked him to set his slippers before the fire down here."

"Slippers still there," Hal Denny indicated to Ben. "Mr. Ralston never put 'em on."

"Are they as you left them, Brookes?" Ben asked.

"No, sir. They had been kicked aside like. I set them where they are now—after we found the body."

"Can you remember the position into which they had been kicked?"

"Quite, sir. I observed at the time that the position was unusual. I thought then that had they been in my way, I should have kicked them toward the grate. But they were kicked out and away from the fireplace, sir. Quite unusual, I thought—as none of us who first came into 'the tomb' went anywhere near them."

Ben got out his yellow notebook and made a memorandum.

"Now what?" Denny demanded, seemingly irritated at having the questioning taken out of his own hands. "What you writing down there amatoorish-like?"

"Just a little reminder, Denny—an item that apparently fits in with a theory I'm concocting. By the way, have you interviewed Mrs. Wilmorton?"

"We seen her in her rooms, but she was too bad shaken up to talk. She won't get away if that what yuh driving at."

"I'm sure that she won't get away, Denny. Pray pardon my interruption."

Hal Denny nodded self-conscious graciousness, and, after thoughtful consideration of his stogy, asked if Mr. Ralston had continued at the game of *Mah Jong*.

"For a while," Paul answered. "Then we switched to *bridge*. Father had Brookes knock at Aunt Julia's door and ask if she felt like taking a fourth hand; but Fifi said that her mistress was indisposed."

"Uh-huh. Then what?"

"We played three-handed until nearly midnight. Then Father remarked that he had an appointment in 'the tomb' with the *ka* of Serapion."

"What's that? West said something about a *ka,* too."

"The ancient Egyptians," Paul patiently explained, "believed that the ego of a dead man could be magically vitalized and compelled to remain with that man's mummified body as guardian spirit. The *ka* was also believed to follow and punish persons who molested the mummy or despoiled the tomb wherein that mummy reposed."

Denny didn't seem to grasp the idea.

Paul continued, "I begged Father to let me accompany him, but he wouldn't. He came down alone. That—that was the last time I saw him alive."

He bit his lips to keep back the tears.

"What did you and the young lady do when you was left alone?"

Paul shot a questioning glance at Mildred, but she kept her eyes lowered and tugged at the bit of linen and lace in her fidgety hands.

"We decided to come down to Father and make a clean breast of it."

"Didn't he approve of your being in love?"

I coughed, yielding Ben warning glance; but Ben repaid my effort with negative shake of the head.

Paul dragged out the bitter words, telling how Mildred had come from Long Beach, California, to marry his father, and that she did it in accordance with her father's will.

Under Hal Denny's heartless insistence, Paul and Mildred both admitted to love at first sight.

"But Mildred intended to go through with the marriage," Paul declared. "I was a fool to endeavor dissuading her—"

"Oh Paul," Mildred broke in, "I was at fault in listening to you!"

Pietro fixed appealing eyes upon Mildred as she made that avowal; but she took no notice of him.

"Well," Denny carried on, "you started down to have a serious talk with Mr. Ralston—but yuh never reached him, eh?"

"We had just started when we heard a shot."

To me, Denny said, "You saw Mr. Ralston killed with a dagger!"

"I didn't see him killed," I replied. "I saw him fall when the *ka* pointed its finger at him. Then I must have fainted. When I regained consciousness, I found him with that dagger in his back."

"H'm," Denny pondered. "That means we don't know whether he was shot or stabbed. That's something we got to find out."

"I'll say it is," Bailey agreed.

"And we'll find out, huh? And now, young man, when yuh finally got into this here room, you found your father dead?"

"Face down, Mr. Denny—in a pool of blood. . . ."

"Where is the dagger?" Ben asked of Hal Denny.

"The boys took it with 'em. Liable to be lots of good fingerprints on that there knife."

"You've taken fingerprints of everyone in the house?"

"You bet!"

Thrusting the anemic stogy between his teeth, Denny gave his attention again to Paul.

"Mr. Ralston, have you no idea who could have did it?"

Paul accused Pietro then and there.

"I—," Pietro began.

Hal Denny silenced him with, "That's all right, Boy. Hold everything until it's your turn to talk. Go ahead, Mr. Ralston."

"I was going to add," Paul said, "that as soon as the barriers were up, Martini and a strange boy came in from the shop."

"Stranger, you say?"

Hal Denny snatched the stogy from between his yellow teeth.

"Yes, Mr. Denny. Handsome chap. Smaller than Pietro. Miss Manning and I both noticed how young he was, with chin too smooth to have known a razor."

"Can yuh describe this here stranger?"

"He was slender and wore a rather untidy blue serge suit and a greasy cap," Paul contributed.

Mildred Manning added, "We couldn't see his eyes, because they were shadowed by the cap which he kept pulled down over his forehead."

"Would yuh know 'im if yuh saw 'im again?"

Paul and Mildred thought that they would.

"Then what?"

"Then Martini accused me of killing Father."

"But you didn't do that, did yuh, Mr. Ralston?"

Looking up at Hal Denny with surprised eyes, Paul answered, simply, "Why, no."

"What did yuh do when yuh discovered the body?"

"I started to turn it over, but Mildred warned me that I shouldn't touch it."

"But you did touch the body?"

"I reached under to see if the heart beat. . . . But it was still."

"Sure of that?"

"Absolutely sure."

"Did you touch the dagger?"

"Yes."

"Recognize it?"

"It was the vengeance dagger Father sent from China."

"Yuh couldn't be mistaken?"

"It is said to be the only one of its kind in the world."

Detective Denny strode up and down the length of the room, coming to pause before Paul and asking, "Yuh didn't see no sign of a bullet wound, did yuh?"

"No. I didn't, Mr. Denny."

Ben spoke, saying, "If Mr. Ralston was standing as West described him, the bullet would have had to come from the direction of the sarcophagus. West heard no shot other than that discharged from Mr. Ralston's gun. Paul saw no bullet wound in the body. . . . But—if there had been a shot and it had missed or passed through Mr. Ralston's body, it would be lodged in the wood of or near those double doors."

"Well, there ain't nothing there," snapped Hal Denny. "Leastwise, nothing what's visible. But we'll be looking later on." He then asked of Paul, "What did yuh do next?"

"It was then that Martini and the strange boy came into the room."

Denny cast a sharp glance at Pietro, but the Italian averted his face.

"When did yuh try calling the police?" Denny next wanted to know of Paul.

"Right away. The telephone on West's desk and the one in the hall were dead. The wires must have been cut."

"So you was out of the room, huh? And when yuh come back, the body of your father was gone, eh?"

"It was. Martini and the stranger, too."

"But I came back," Pietro threw in.

"Alone?"

"Yes—alone."

"Humph!"

To Paul, Denny said, "Could Martini have carried the body out?"

"I don't know, Mr. Denny. He and the stranger might have done so. Anyway, I looked in his shop and around—"

"But yuh found no trace of the body?"

"None."

"Any sign of the strange boy?"

"No. But I thought I heard a car getting away down the drive."

"Didn't yuh look to make sure?"

"I did, but it was dark and there were no lights—car lights, I mean."

"H'm!"

The stogy underwent merciless chewing.

"When yuh got back in here, what?"

"Martini accused me of hiding the body. He said I could have put it in the mummy case. He jerked the lid of the sarcophagus back to see. You may not believe it, Mr. Denny, but that coffin was empty."

"But there had been a mummy in it, huh?"

"The corpse of Serapion."

"Can yuh beat that?" Denny demanded of Ben. "Two corpses disappear in a jiffy—just like that!"

"Baffling," was Ben's non-committal comment.

"Damned funny, if yuh ask me!" Denny grunted. "Mr. Ralston says his father had these here French windows locked every night. They was all tight when I got here, same's all the windows on this floor. It wouldn't have made no difference, though, if they hadn't been locked, because not even a child could crawl between the steel bars set in every window frame."

Detective Denny's glance swept the room and he grunted again—a grunt that might have been an expression of no considerable appreciation of Howard Ralston's carefully protected antiques.

Paul must have caught the same idea I did, for he said to Hal Denny, "You may not regard what you can see as worth much, Mr. Denny; but the stuff is valued at hundreds of thousands. Locked in the wall safe are diamonds worth a million and a half."

He went to the safe, lifted his hand to spin the dial, and started back with a cry of alarm.

"Ben, there are bloody fingerprints all about the safe!"

Both detectives leaped to Paul's side.

"Open up, Paul! Quick!" Ben commanded.

Paul worked feverishly, anxiety and haste hampering control of the tumblers. Then he had the safe open—just when it seemed my own anxiety would smother me, and yanked out the purple plush case with its imperial monogram done in gold. He thrust the box into Ben's hands, and Ben snapped up the cover.

There they reposed, the glittering horde—every piece, Paul certified.

"But some one was after them," Ben affirmed. "Whoever he was, he was frightened away."

He returned the diamonds to Paul, who locked them away.

"Frightened away," Denny repeated. "After committing murder and all. Say you," and he turned upon Pietro, "it could have been that stranger you drug in here!"

"No, no!" protested the Italian. "You are mistaken."

"Yeah! That's what you say. But we've got his fingerprints on that safe—yours, too, maybe. Come on, Bailey, let's find out."

"There's no need to do that, Ben," I faltered. "The prints are mine."

2

Ben didn't seem particularly interested in my confession. He and Denny took my fingerprints. That done, Ben got out his magnifying glass and examined the bloody prints on the wall safe.

"Visible prints such as these are not clear enough to yield satisfactory results," he told us. "But if you will notice closely, Denny, there are elements discernible, in spite of smears, to certify identity. Clearly,

West left his prints on the safe when he examined it at the dying man's request."

"Well now, young feller, ain't that interesting? I know yuh told us that your hands was wet with Mr. Ralston's blood, but—"

"Go easy, Denny," urged Ben.

"Sure I'll go easy! We've got a damned good clue. The sooner we get this thing settled, the better it suits me."

"Me, too," sighed Sleepy Wallingford, regaining consciousness sufficiently to stifle a heavy yawn. "Me, I want to get home to the old woman and the kids."

"Say," Denny demanded of me, "what was you doing to that there safe if yuh didn't mean to open it and lift them *rocks?* Just finding out if the safe was locked didn't make it necessary for yuh to get your fingers all over the place."

"Don't be an ass, Denny," Ben admonished the big Irishman. "Remember the condition West was in. A man doped as he was would be more than likely to get his hands 'all over the place'!"

"An' don't you be no ass, Bailey. This young feller's smart, see."

"If he were guilty, would he come for me and return to *Windermere* with me? Wouldn't he have taken it on the *lam* as soon as Paul Ralston let him out of the house?"

"Wise dick you are!" Denny's look and tone were withering. "This young feller would naturally know it was better to return to the scene of his crime and take a chance, hoping us guys is dumb."

"Do you happen to have a duplicate set of the dactylographs made in this house tonight?" Ben inquired, smiling down Denny's belligerent glare. "I ask because I recall that you always wisely make it a point to secure two sets: one for headquarters and one for your own reference."

"Sure I got a extry set," Denny replied, thawing under the implied compliment Ben was paying his sagacity. "Hey, Sleepy, wake up!"

"Yeah!" protested Sleepy, rousing under Denny's rough handling. "What the—where's the fire at?"

"Never mind no fire. Give me them fingerprints."

Sleepy produced them, and dozed off once more.

Ben and Denny laid the charts out on the Renaissance table and checked them, I keeping tab for them.

"Anybody's print missing?" Ben asked me.

"All here, Ben."

Ben opened his kit, extracting from it a small blowpipe and a fine whitish powder. The powder he gently blew over the safe door and the wall surface adjoining. With magnifying glass he hunted for indistinct fingerprints that would naturally escape the naked eye. Here and there he focused the light of his powerful torch.

"Ah!" he exclaimed, at length. "There have been numerous fingers busy here. Fingerprints not much good, however; for West smooched them. And, by George, here's what I'd call smears left by a gloved hand!"

"Huh?"

"Now, who could have wanted to guard against leaving fingerprints at a place like this?" Ben wanted to know.

"Well," opined Denny, his eye in turn covering Paul, Mildred, and Pietro—and myself, "diamonds worth a million and a half bucks would tempt lots of folks."

"Quite true, Denny," Ben murmured. "But I'm thinking—"

"You're thinking what?"

Ignoring Hal Denny's query, Ben continued his scrutiny of safe and wall.

"The powder brings out other prints on the glossy surface of the wall. Of course you'll have them photographed, Denny."

"You bet I will!"

"We'll want a thorough check-up on every one," Ben went on. "In the meantime, we'll see what we can determine for ourselves."

And "we" determined plenty. Comparing Denny's dactylographs with the safe and wall prints, we found that Julia Wilmorton and Paul had also left their signatures there. That was to be expected, Ben explained, as Paul had opened the safe that night, and that he and Mrs. Wilmorton had opened the safe when—according to Paul's story—Howard Ralston had radioed them from Venice to ascertain if the jewels were safe. The dimness of the Wilmorton prints would indicate that they had been made some time back. Hal Denny wanted to argue that point, but Ben ignored him.

Because one of the prints showed a peculiar marking right in the center of the underloop of the twin loop of a left thumbprint, Ben and Paul identified it as that of Howard Ralston. Mr. Ralston had a wart on his left thumb that would have made just such a mark.

"Look at this one, will you?" Ben advised Denny. "Another freakish print. See, there's a mark across it such as might have been made by a welt. Sometime or other the owner of that finger had the tip of it ripped open by a sharp instrument—"

"That would be Henri Cornier's fingerprint!" Paul exclaimed.

"Indeed?" murmured Ben, lifting a brow. "Then it seems that M. Cornier has an interest in the safe containing the Josephine diamonds. . . . There's one more fingerprint," he concluded. "Look at it, Denny."

"Smooth, ain't it?" commented the Irishman. "Hardly enough to make it look like a finger had left it."

"I should say that it was left by a finger that had been sandpapered," advised Ben.

"You mean some professional cracksman has been after them sparklers?"

"Such is my deduction."

"Whose?"

"Your guess is as good as mine."

"Huh?"

"Criminals sometimes seek to avoid leaving fingerprints by wearing gloves, you know. There is evidence here that one hand laid upon this wall was gloved. Perhaps our cracksman found it difficult to work in gloves and had to remove the glove from his right hand—"

"How d'yuh figger that?"

"Examine the spot where the hand rested. Could the right hand be placed in such a position?"

"I get yuh!"

"Mr. Cracksman evidently anticipated difficulty with gloves and so came prepared. Knowing that he might have to bare his hands, he sandpapered—"

"I got a hunch you know who was that smart, Bailey—smart enough to sandpaper his fingertips. Come on, be a sport."

"We'll say more when you have the fingerprints photographed and—," Ben returned, packing up his kit and smiling tolerantly into the eyes of the official investigator.

"You mean we may have his dactylographs down at the bureau?"

"I wouldn't go so far as to say that."

"Then what the hell will yuh say?"

"I'm saying nothing yet, Denny. But if that fingerprint was left there by the party I suspect, we're up against a tough proposition. Unless we are alert, there will be a second murder at *Windermere* within twenty-four hours."

3

I was glad when Denny asked our artificer to account for his movements during the night.

Lifting darkly circled eyes, Pietro looked about at all of us. His was such a woebegone expression that I pitied him, despite the fact that he had laid heinous accusation against Paul.

"When the Duke and Mrs. Lansing left here," he began, "the Master told me to follow them. Taking the roadster, I trailed them to the Nicolett Hotel. I located them in their suite; and, under a Spanish name, I engaged the rooms adjoining. . . . Sitting on the floor, I put my ear to the keyhole in the door communicating with Mrs. Lansing's suite."

"Hear anything?"

Detective Denny leaned expectantly forward, the frazzled stogy shifting nervously in his fingers. Ben lounged comfortably in his chair, smoking his English cigarette with delightful insouciance.

"Come on! Spill it!"

Momentarily the old radiant smile lighted Pietro's haggard features, only to fade quickly as he glowered at Paul.

"What does it matter what I heard?" he demanded. "The murderer is here!"

"If it's just the same to you," Denny said, coldly, "we'd like a report on that conversation you overheard."

Pietro shrugged.

"Well, first of all, the Duke stormed and threatened. He must have been walking up and down the room, for his voice drew near one minute and receded the next—in regular rhythm. I could hear Mrs. Lansing's voice all the time, so that I concluded she must be sitting near the door at which I was listening."

Detective Denny spat a portion of his shredded stogy into my wastebasket. Then, rolling the remaining shreds pleasantly on his tongue, he wanted to know if Pietro could repeat the words that passed between the Duke and his ally.

"Pardon my interruption," said Ben, "but West here is a stenographer and can take all this down, if you will permit."

"Not a bad idea."

So began my function as official reporter on the case. I am glad now; for, with book after book of detailed recordings made during the investigation, I am able to give this story—not only completely, but also accurately.

Pietro told how the Duke bewailed the theft of his Borgia-jewel in his family four hundred years.* He expressed resentment over the fact that his daughter Francesca had been made innocent accomplice in the theft.

"What did the Lansing woman say to that?"

"She said, 'Duke, it is perfectly evident that Ralston got your ring; a blind man could see that. But Ralston failed to take Marco into consideration. There's where he gave himself away.'"

"Marco!" In his surprise over the introduction of a new character into the already lengthy cast of the *Windermere* drama, Detective Denny swallowed the last of his stogy. "Who is Marco?" he demanded.

Pietro explained that Marco, member of the Venetian secret police, had been acting as *major-domo* to the Duke of Vedena.

"I guess so," acquiesced Denny, his brow wrinkling. "Did this here Lansing have anything else to say about that there Marco?"

"She said, 'Marco, thank heaven, had sense enough to go to their villa when he learned they had fled Venice so abruptly, and so found the drawings Ralston's artificer make in connection with his work in counterfeiting the Borgia. Just the evidence we needed.' She laughed over that, Mr. Denny, and said further, 'They might have known that it was reckless to leave that junk lying about.'"

---

* This ring, one of two such known to be in existence, bore the date 1503 and the motto of Cesare Borgia in Old French. It is owned by the present descendant of that Cardinal who was a victim of the notorious son of Pope Alexander VI. I refer to the present Duke of Vedena. The family of the murdered Cardinal never let the instrument of his death leave their coffers, although at different time they were offered fabulous sums for it. Numerous attempts were made to steal it—each attended with either misfortune or death for the would-be thief. The Borgia had come to be regarded with dread by the superstitious.

"Why did yuh leave things that-a-way?" Denny asked.

"We hadn't meant to leave a single clue," Pietro told him. "We sold our stuff to a dealer, who promised to remove it immediately. That was the Master's particular stipulation. Fate seems to have played us a nasty trick there."

"Fate's a nasty old trollop," Denny made dry comment, thrusting a fresh stogy into his mouth. "But we can't blame her for everything—not by a damn sight, we can't. Most of the jams we get into is due to our own cussed carelessness."

Having thus philosophically delivered himself, he lighted his stogy— much to our dismay—and was promptly saturating the atmosphere of "the tomb" with a filthy odor.

"Trot along the rest of your story," he directed Pietro.

Pietro revealed how Mrs. Lansing reproved the Duke for not keeping the ring that had been placed in his hand, for, said she, "It would be like that imp of Satan to trick you."

"Meaning me, when I gave him the genuine Borgia right here in this room," Pietro enlightened Denny.

Grinning impishly, he related the full circumstance of that devilment of his.

"You did sure enough trick the Duke, then?" Denny chuckled.

"That was because he is such an ass," Pietro sneered.

His eyes dropped their glance to the blood-soaked Chinese rug.

"The Master, he got the ring, and I think there must be a curse on it. Francesca told me that she believed that there was a curse upon the Borgia poison ring, because every one who had sought to steal it met with misfortune—or death. I thought she was trying to shoot a scare into me; but the Master—now he is dead—"

Urged to continue, Pietro related how Mrs. Lansing expressed opinion that the genuine Borgia was locked in Ralston's Chinese cabinet. That meant, she advised, that the Duke must get a Chinese to open the cabinet.

"And she named our venerable friend, Dr. Lao Wong," Ben murmured.

At which Denny exclaimed, "Ah, ha! Now we have got something definite to go on." He alternately puffed at and chewed on his stogy. "A genuine clue, I say."

Pietro was unable to hear more after Mrs. Lansing brought the name of Lao Wong into the conversation, which led him to conclude that she and the Duke had gone down to the hotel lobby or to one of the lounges.

He went down, but saw nothing of them. He did, however, encounter a young Egyptian gentleman.

"Egyptian!" Ben cut in.

"Now what?"

Hal Denny bristled.

"Unusual, don't you think, Mr. Denny, for a young Egyptian gentleman to be in Minneapolis?" Ben quietly asked.

"Well, now—maybe."

Pietro told us how he made acquaintance with the Egyptian and learned that he was a wholesale rug merchant who had been some weeks in the city. Pietro also expressed to Ben the opinion that the Egyptian, whose name was Youssuf, could have had nothing to do with the *Windermere* murder.

"Interesting, nevertheless," Ben said.

Denny disdained Ben's interest in the Egyptian rug merchant, and wanted to know what Pietro's next move had been.

"I came back here, Mr. Denny."

For some reason my eyes were held by the glow at the tip of Ben's cigarette. Held lightly between long fingers, it burned like a fiery stud against his white shirt-front, where he stood motionless as a statue.

"You say yuh came back here?" I became aware that Denny was asking Pietro.

"Yes, sir."

"Straight back?"

It was Ben that asked the question, and again I was conscious of that cigarette glow against his shirt-front.

"Right back, Martini?"

"Yes," whispered the Italian, eyes questioning Ben's right to press for an answer.

"Yet you were gone something like six hours," Ben reminded him. "Further, if you came straight back here, you were in the house when Howard Ralston was murdered."

"No, no!"

"Ha!" cried Paul. "He's telling on himself. Let him talk, Ben. . . . He killed my father! Blast the confession out of him!"

"Well?" Ben sternly demanded of Pietro.

"Now looky here, me lad," snarled Detective Denny, "you can't get away with this! You'll tell the truth and tell it straight, or—"

He paused, fingering his fireless stogy menacingly.

I thought of the glow at the tip of Ben's cigarette and the lifeless scorch at the end of Hal Denny's stogy. I wondered if there could be anything symbolical in that matter of fire and lack of fire.

"Come clean," Denny counseled Pietro. "Where'd yuh *go* after yuh left the Nicolett?"

"I drove to my cousin's," Pietro answered.

"Who's you're cousin, huh?"

"Victor Martini. He is chief chemist for *Maris and Maris.*"

"Them boys what makes perfumes?"

"Yes, sir."

"Why did you drive out to see your cousin Victor?"

Pietro hesitated.

"Well!"

"Because I resolved that no one should steal the Borgia poison ring from the Master and live."

He uttered the words quietly, each with nice distinctness. None of us in "the tomb" seemed to breathe. Every eye was fixed in surprise upon the face of the Italian artificer.

Ben broke the silence.

"Are we to infer, Martini, that you sought your cousin, who is a chemist, to secure poison to put into the bezel of the Borgia?"

Pietro's eyes lighted, evilly.

"*Si, si!*" he cried. "You must understand that the thief would put the ring upon his own finger and fortune would be kind and cause him to press the claw of the lion into his own flesh."

The horror of Pietro Martini's vicious purpose shocked me. If he had succeeded, who might not have been innocent victim to his scheme?

"You secured the poison?" Ben asked.

Pietro nodded.

"Did you put it in the ring?" Denny demanded.

"I came too late."

"Too late?"

"The roadster broke down."

Once again the Italian did not seem inclined to talk, but Denny drove him on.

On his way home from his cousin's laboratory, he had trouble with the Ralston roadster. It unexpectedly stopped on him, and would not respond to any effort he knew to make. The trouble appeared to be in the carburetor.

That might have been so, I knew; for Paul had spoken to Wayland Thomas, the Ralston chauffeur, about that very thing.

"But I didn't find the trouble at first," Pietro told Denny.

"But you was looking for it all the time, wasn't yuh?"

"I was."

"Didn't mind the weather none, did yuh?"

"It wasn't a question of the weather, Mr. Denny."

"Sure not. I understand that."

Pursing his lips, Denny endeavored to appear unconcerned; but only long enough to permit Pietro to acquire sense of security.

Then he suddenly came out with, "Your clothes is damp, but they ain't soaked, when I first seen yuh tonight, and yuh hadn't time to change them neither. And I think there's a button off your right cuff, and your collar is torn, and your face is scratched—but there ain't no dirt or grease on your clothes or hands. Huh! Car trouble, sez you!"

Pietro seemed to shrink, withdrawing into himself, as it were.

"Huh?" demanded Denny, removing the stogy and applying a match to its dead end—a match he scratched into flame across the top of Howard Ralston's Renaissance table. Puffing violently, he glared upon Pietro.

"Who was this strange boy with yuh, huh?"

Pietro looked up, appealingly; but meeting only sternness in the eyes of the detective, he answered, "He helped me with the car, so I gave him a lift."

"The young feller just happened along, I suppose?"

"First thing I knew, he was there."

"Yeah!" Denny's tone was acrid. "An' you was that grateful yuh gave him a lift! Nice story you're telling, Martini!"

Pietro remained silent.

"Had to *lift* him clear here to Mr. Ralston's house, huh?"

"He didn't seem to want to get out anywhere."

"Oh, he didn't? Well, well!" And to Bailey, "What d'yuh know 'bout that?"

Ben Bailey smiled—first at Pietro, then at Denny.

"Looks as if he enjoyed the ride, Denny."

"Huh!"

If a look could have blasted Pietro, he'd have shriveled like an autumn leaf under the scorching heat of the burning regard in Hal Denny's eyes.

"You didn't invite him into the house after yuh drove the car into the garage, I suppose?"

"He just followed me in. . . . I didn't know—"

"Sure, you didn't know! And all the time you was thinking of putting poison into that there Borgia ring to kill the thief that yuh knowed was coming after it! Sure, that there strange boy just followed you in, all unbeknowns to yourself."

"Well, no—"

"I don't suppose he was a-hiding with yuh in your shop back there when Mr. Paul Ralston and Miss Manning tried the lock on its door, huh?"

"Well, what if he was?" flared Pietro, momentarily defiant.

Detective Denny caught his breath in surprise. He stared in astonishment at the artificer.

But quick to regain his composure, he next demanded, "Where'd the strange boy go after that?"

Pietro shook his head.

"Mean to say yuh don't know?"

"I didn't see him leave. He just slipped away—"

"Sez you!"

Shooting accusing finger before Pietro's face, Denny charged him with lying.

"Before God, I am not!" cried the frightened Italian, recoiling.

After that dramatic moment there was a lull—tense like it is before a heavy storm breaks. I stole a glance at Paul and saw that his eyes where shining with vindictive gloating over Pietro's discomfiture.

As for Ben Bailey, he appeared indifferent—slightly disapproving, perhaps.

Denny chewed ferociously on his stogy, several times belching his disgust.

"Did yuh learn the stranger's name?" he suddenly demanded.

"He told me that his name was 'Romeo'!"

"*Romeo!*" Detective Denny laughed. "What else did you find out about him?"

"Nothing."

"You wouldn't!"

Denny looked at Ben.

Ben looked at Denny.

"Well?"

Denny was over-belligerent.

Ben shrugged his shoulders, indolently lighting another cigarette.

"Tell me why you was so ready to suspect Mr. Ralston here of killing his father."

"Well—," and Pietro hesitated. "Must I answer that question, sir? I would rather not—under the circumstances."

"It will be wise for you to answer that question—under the circumstances."

Pietro looked down at his tightly interlocked fingers.

"Well, Paul and his father had a violent quarrel yesterday afternoon."

Out came the stogy. Detective Denny whistled softly. "What did they quarrel about?"

"About—Miss Manning."

"Tell me about this quarrel," Denny commanded, biting the chewed end off his stogy and spitting it into my wastebasket.

"Let me tell about the quarrel, Mr. Denny," Paul begged.

"Okay, Mr. Ralston."

Detective Denny waited, expectantly.

Ben stirred, uneasily.

Paul gulped, and I saw his fists clench until the knuckles seemed fair to burst through the skin.

"My father," he said, "thought that I was paying too much attention to Miss Manning. He cautioned me to be careful and to bear in mind the fact that he was to marry her. I lost my temper, I guess. We had words."

"Just what, if you please?"

"My God!" ejaculated Paul. "Must our souls be bared in this ordeal?"

"We are trying to collect every shred of evidence that will help run down the murderer, my dear young man. It won't pay nobody to be squeamish."

We waited while Paul pulled himself together.

"It was this way," he started. "Father saw me with Mildred in my arms. She and I were in the conservatory at the time. When I came in here afterwards, Father was waiting for me. He sent West on an errand, and then spoke pretty plainly to me. I told him that I loved Mildred— that he didn't, couldn't love her. Then I accused him of trying to wreck my happiness—of caring more for Martini than he did for me—"

"What made you think that of your father?"

"Because he showered Martini with gifts and let it in every way appear that he preferred his companionship to mine. Only yesterday he put Martini into his will."

"I see. . . . What else passed between him and you?"

"Well—," and Paul's voice faltered.

His eyes shifted and his gaze lowered; but he lifted his eyes again, quickly, defiantly, I thought.

"Nothing more," he declared. "I flung myself out of the room, slamming the door behind me."

"He lies!" cried Pietro. "I came in from my shop as he was about to strike his father."

Detective Denny eyed Paul, coldly, the unspoken question in his eyes.

"It's true," Paul confessed, miserably. "But I didn't do it. I wouldn't have struck Dad for the world. I'm sorry I didn't tell you the whole truth."

My soul, but it was quiet in "the tomb" when Paul said that! So blamed quiet that I could hear the heart in me pounding against my ribs. My forearm ached.

The little clock on the mantel chimed.

"Denny," Ben suggested, "what about letting these harassed folks get a little *shut-eye?* It's three o'clock."

"I could use a little myself," mumbled Sleepy Wallingford, stretching upward from the depths of his chair.

"Surest thing," Denny agreed, in answer to Ben's suggestion. "Tod-dle along, you folks. We'll carry on in the morning."

They rose wearily and went out—Pietro through the shop; Paul and Mildred through the double doors.

"If you please, gentlemen," Brookes volunteered, "I'll show you to your rooms."

"Okay," yawned Denny. "I can't sleep, but I sure can do a heap o' thinking."

"Don't bother about me, Brookes," Ben said. "I'll bunk with West."

"And I suppose I'll have to be cooped up with this lummox," Denny complained, regarding Sleepy with disfavoring eye.

"I'm afraid so, sir," murmured Brookes.

"Don't think it'll be no pleasure for me," Sleepy put in.

Brookes waited for us to file out, locked the doors leading from "the tomb" to Pietro's shop and to the servants' hall, extinguished the candles—save one, which was to light us up the stairs. Last to leave "the tomb," he locked the double doors, depositing the keys in his pocket.

We were a solemn procession as we ascended the wide stairs, four silent men, following the candle-bearing butler and wondering what dawn would bring.

We paused at my door.

"At seven, what say?" asked Denny.

"Seven it is," Ben agreed. "Good night."

"Night."

"Just a moment, Brookes," Ben called softly. And as the butler turned back, "Might I have the key to the double doors of the big room? I may want to go down there."

Brookes gave Ben the key.

So we parted for four hours of needed rest—at least, so we thought.

4

Neither Ben nor I got to bed that night. By candlelight, Ben sat and read the red-leather diary I had been keeping since the day I found employ-ment with Howard Ralston. Sitting on the arm of Ben's chair, I watched him mark passages. He thrilled me by saying that he thought the red-bound volume was enabling him to get somewhere. He apparently had decided upon the guilty parties before his arrival that night at *Windermere,* and the diary seemingly was clinching his theory.

What he figured out, he declined to tell me. Cautioned me against banking heavily on him, declaring that he might be wrong.

Shortly after five o'clock, Hal Denny sauntered in.

"Up?" he said, feigning surprise.

"Did you expect to find us snoring?" Ben grinned.

"Well, not you," Denny replied, lighting a fresh stogy. "But I do think the kid needs sleep."

"I'll never be able to sleep until the murderer is apprehended!" I vowed.

"What you got there?" Denny asked Ben.

"West's diary. Sit down, Denny, and let me read you excerpts from its pages."

"No diaries for me. But I'll set down and let you give me some information."

"Okay by me," Ben agreed. "But you ought to read this journal. West's a keen observer; his comments, it seems to me, are illuminating."

"Later," Denny promised, dismissing my record with a wave of his stogy.

"Lock your red book away, West," Ben said to me. "We don't want it lost."

"I'll put it here," I said, going to my secretary over by the door to the hall.

As I turned the key and opened the secretary, my ear caught the sound of a rustling movement on the other side of the door. Noisily closing the desk and turning the key with as much clatter as possible, I paused, listening. No further sound came to me.

"Well, it's safe in that secretary," I said, lifting my voice sufficiently to enable anybody loitering in the hall to hear me.

"What the—," began Detective Denny.

Ben silenced him with warning gesture.

I wanted to see who could be eavesdropping, but decided against doing so. Instead, I went to the opposite side of the room and touched a spring that caused a wall-panel to slide back. Into the exposed cavity I thrust the diary.

"Regular mystery house," Denny commented.

"Howard Ralston delighted in Gothic romances with castles and manor houses crammed with trap-doors, secret passages, and hidden chambers," Ben said. "It would have been like him to build this house in conformity to Gothic pattern."

The diary secreted, I glided to the hall door and jerked it open. The hall was empty, but in the air lingered odor of perfume. I thought I saw the door to Mrs. Wilmorton's apartment—right across the hall—close abruptly; but I couldn't be sure. My senses had played me so many tricks that night, that I doubted their reliability. I reported the circumstance to my companions, however.

"Just as I thought," swore Denny. "The murderer's still loose in this house."

Ben yawned.

"Anyway," he suggested, "we might give our eavesdropper a chance at this room."

"Pretty soon," Denny acquiesced. "Right now I want the lowdown on this man, Howard Ralston. You've known him personally a long time, what?"

Stretching out his heavy legs, ankle crossing ankle, Detective Denny lolled in his chair.

"And of his friend, M. Henri Cornier?" queried Ben. "Might as well include him."

Ben snapped open his cigarette case and very deliberately selected a fag. As the lighter's flame moulded his features into relief, I noted that they were set in thoughtful reflection.

"Yes, I've known the Ralstons a long time," he began, flicking his cigarette. "Ever since Paul and I started County Day School together. So I understand pretty much what you want to know."

"I leave selection of details to your judgment."

Ben leaned lazily on the radio, smoking dreamily.

"Huh?"

"Well," Ben smiled, pulling himself out of some reverie in which he seemed about to lose himself, "Howard Ralston and Henri Cornier were antiquarians—both vocationally and avocationally, if you'll permit my use of the terms."

"Sure. Talk as you please."

I laughed, mentally—as it were, knowing darned well that Mr. Harrison Denny wasn't certain of Ben's meaning.

"They gradually established a reputation for themselves, eventually coming to be recognized as ultimate authorities in their field. They knew the history, authenticity, and value of every antique possessed by man. A remarkable friendship held the two men together. It began all of thirty years ago, I guess—when as youngsters they met at a convention in Baltimore, where each had gone to lecture on aspects of archeological research then being done in Mesopotamia."

"Is this here Cornier an American?"

"Naturalized. Frenchman by birth."

"That why he wears the waxed mustache and funny little whiskers?"

"The *imperial,* I believe, is an affectation of his family in loyal gesture to the memory of Napoleon III."

"Uh-huh."

"M. Cornier sold his estates in Brittany and emigrated to the States and to Minneapolis."

"Wanted to be near his friend, eh?"

"They formed a partnership."

"Married, did they?"

"Cornier never did."

"They made money, I suppose, in this antiquarian racket?"

"Plenty of it. But they were already millionaires."

"So?"

"I suppose I really should say that they made antiques their avocation."

"What?"

It was evident that Hal Denny meant to know the meaning of the terms Bailey was tossing about so glibly. Ben explained. "I get yuh!" the Irishman grinned. "Nice playthings, antiques."

"Rather. If you've got the money to indulge in such expensive toys. Ralston and Cornier had it. . . . Cornier joined Ralston here in Minneapolis, as I was saying. They bought this property—an entire city block. Each man built for himself a stone house. Like French chateaux, the two houses are—identical in exterior design."

"Does Cornier's house have one of these here curiosity shops?"

"Sure. But neither as large nor as interesting as that at *Windermere.*"

"Damned queer idea, if yuh ask me."

"Suppose," suggested Ben, "we go out front and have a look at the twin mansions. Our absence will give West's eavesdropper opportunity to do a bit of snooping."

"And maybe drop a clue, eh?"

We went out into the gray, rainy morning, and walked across the lawn to a point near the avenue, whence we could obtain excellent view of both *Fontainebleau* and *Windermere.*

"As like as two peas in a pod, only more so," remarked Denny.

Being an integral part of the Ralston *ménage,* I looked upon the two great houses with pardonable pride. They did resemble the chateaux one sees in the valley of the *Loire.* Romantically veiled in the mist-like rain, they appeared imposing.

"What's that there thing?" Denny asked, indicating the connection between the two houses.

"That's the *porte-cochere,*" Ben explained.

"Funny looking *porty-coachery,* if yuh ask me," Denny said. "Looks kind-a like one of them double-decker trolley cars they used to run when I was a kid."

"Looks that way because the friends built a glassed-in hallway over their double *porte-cochere,*" Ben explained. "At each end of the hallway is a doorway admitting to its respective establishment. Each owner carried two keys, one to each door."

"Queer guys! . . . Well, that *porty-coachery* must have been convenient."

"Rather, permitting, as it did, easy method of communication."

We walked back across the lawn and through the Ralston side of the *porte-cochere* to the terrace back of the houses. At the ends of the terrace, which was a balustraded promenade, were located the coach houses. Howard Ralston had converted his into a garage; M. Cornier had made similar transformation only in part, still maintaining stables for his blooded horses. Beyond this terrace was a sunken garden, copied from the D'Orsini estates near Florence. Beyond the gardens, the park again—in the midst of which stood the gardener's lodge.

"Hadn't we better go back to my room?" I urged, when I thought that Denny had seen enough. "I don't want it wrecked."

"I want to give our prowler plenty of time," Ben advised.

"And if there be a prowler?" I asked.

"It will prove that Mr. Denny is correct in his surmise that the murderer or an accomplice is still at large in the house."

Eventually returning to the house, we went into "the tomb."

"Aha," exclaimed Denny, "cigar smoke!"

"A man has visited this room since we left the house," said Ben. "Secure in the conviction that we would not return so soon, he's been here for some definite purpose."

"I saw women smoking cigars in Denmark," I offered.

"Our smoker could have been a woman," admitted Ben. "Might have used the cigar to throw us off the scent."

"But who could-a had a key to this room?" asked Denny. "That butler had 'em all—except the one you asked for."

"You've got me there," Ben acknowledged. "Better look about to see if anything's disturbed."

Lighting every candle, we searched the big room, but could find no further evidence of an intruder.

Our examination of "the tomb" completed, we adjourned to the second floor, where, after the city dick explored the *porte-cochere,* we went into my room.

"Sure enough!" I cried. "He's been here!"

I pointed to my secretary, which had been pried open and the lock left broken. The contents of the desk were in a jumble, despite attempt to rearrange them.

"This," crowed Denny, "proves I'm right."

"That the murderer is still in the house?" I faltered.

"Not quite," Ben quickly answered. "It proves that his accomplice is here."

"What yuh mean, 'accomplice'?"

"Just that, Mr. Denny. A murderer as clever and as skillful as the man who executed the bizarre crime last night would never have bungled a desk-breaking job. Clearly the work of an amateur."

"Huh!"

THE FORENOON OF THE SECOND DAY

1

After breakfasting with Paul in the upstairs sitting-room, we descended to "the tomb," where Hal Denny was to interview the servants of the household.

On our way, we were joined by lugubrious Sleepy Wallingford. He had expected to breakfast with us, but had found the comfort of his bed too enticing.

"Just wake up?" Denny greeted him.

"Gosh, that was a swell couch," yawned Sleepy. "How's tricks, Chief?"

"Not much doing. But there will be, now that Sherlock Holmes is out of bed."

"Sherlock Holmes, that's me," mumbled Sleepy, good-naturedly, dragging an apple from his pocket.

The questioning began with Brookes. Evidently determined to make the best of a distasteful predicament, the butler squared his shoulders, smoothed down his thinning, "brownatoned" hair, and moistened his lips.

"You see, sir, it's very unusual," he began. "I hardly know where to begin—things happened so unexpected-like. . . . It's very difficult, sir, for me to talk at all, having been so many years in Mr. Ralston's service."

"Knew your master well, I take it."

"I knew most all about him, sir."

"Did you ever hear him mention anyone—an enemy, maybe, who might have reason to wish him dead?"

Smoothing trousers down over sharp knees, the butler replied, "Mr. Ralston had only friends, sir."

Denny paced back and forth in front of the fireplace, muttering, and rolling the stogy between his heavy lips.

"Say!" he exclaimed, whirling suddenly about.

Whatever it was he meant to say, we never knew; for the stogy fell to the floor, much to Denny's consternation. Before he could retrieve it, Ben offered him a two-bit cigar. He smelled the gift; accepted flame from Ben's lighter; let his raddled face register pleasure at the first draw.

"Brookes," he asked, "can you tell me if Mr. Ralston ever got mixed up in any shady deals before?"

"Not to my knowledge, sir. You see, he was a theosophist."

"What kind of a animal's that?"

Brookes lifted thin brows in pained surprise.

"A theosophist, sir, is one who believes in *karma*."

"What's *kur-mur?*"

"One who adheres to the doctrine of *karma,* sir, wittingly does no wrong; for he believes in the law of cause and effect—that each deed brings its own reward in kind. And if he does evil, knowing about *karma,* the reaction is many times more severe."

"Jeez! What a idea."

"You see, sir, believing as he did, Mr. Ralston wouldn't knowingly do anything wrong."

Denny puffed extravagantly at his two-bit cigar. Evidently Brookes embarrassed him and left his ignorance standing naked, as it were, within the circle of the intelligent.

Brookes narrated the events of the night pretty much as I have already set them down, with Denny quizzing him closely upon one or two points.

The quiz brought out the fact that Mrs. Lucretia Lansing had said, as she and the Duke left the house, "We'll show them a trick or two before the night is over!"

Brookes' account also elaborated upon the incident of the tobacco pouch and the key to the secret door.

"It was unusual about M. Cornier, sir," Brookes had remarked.

"So! Why?"

"Well, you see, Mr. Denny, M. Cornier came back when we all thought he was at Faribault."

Brookes told of his surprise encounter with the slouch-hatted, collar-muffled French partner of Howard Ralston the night before.

When he had finished, he let his eyes fall to the crimson-stained Chinese rug. His body quivered with a shudder he strove hard to control.

"What was unusual about that?" Denny demanded. "Mr. Cornier came and went as he pleased, didn't he?"

"Quite so, sir," Brookes responded, moistening his lips and then all as nervously brushing them with the back of his claw-like hand. "Quite so, sir. M. Cornier informed me that he had run over after his tobacco pouch. I noticed then that he had it in his hand and was filling his pipe from it. He said that he left the pouch here earlier in the evening, sir."

"Do you think that West here can have been correct in saying that he was sure Mr. Cornier was lying when he told you that?"

"I wouldn't say that of a gentleman, sir; but I do know that M. Cornier is not a forgetful man—and he never lets his tobacco pouch off his person."

Denny took to pacing again, smoking more extravagantly than before.

"Yes, sir," Brookes continued, when Denny paused and stood regarding him, "it was unusual, sir, for M. Cornier to come in by the secret door."

Hal Denny's brows contracted as he regarded the panel that was the secret door.

"One wouldn't hardly look for a door there, Bailey," he observed.

"Hardly," Ben agreed.

Denny turned again to Brookes, who almost stammered in haste to resume his narrative.

"M. Cornier told me that his key didn't work well, and asked me to file it for him."

"Yeah, we know all that—"

"But, sir," and Brookes was reprovingly dignified, "the key worked easily when we opened the secret door later on."

"H'm, yeah. Point well taken, my man."

"Quite so, sir," murmured Brookes, moistening his fingertips and gently smoothing his sleek hair again.

"Where's the key now?"

Brookes handed it to Denny.

"I've been carrying it in my pocket, sir. For reasons which I am sure you will understand."

Chewing on his cigar, Denny examined that key to the secret door.

"Odd looking key. Must be foreign make, eh?"

"English, sir."

"Had it made over yonder, did yuh?"

"In Salisbury, at the master's request."

"Of course you have another like it."

"Oh, no, sir. I ordered just the two: one for the master and one for his friend. You see, sir, it was a sort of secret between them—that little door hidden in the wall."

"But you knew."

"I did, sir."

Holding the key out before him, gripping it with tips of thumb and forefinger, so that the shaft pointed directly at Paul, Denny said, "So you had a duplicate, eh?"

"I?" Paul stammered.

"You did, didn't yuh?"

"He couldn't have, sir," Brookes interposed.

"Let the young man speak for himself," snapped Denny. And to Paul, "You did, didn't yuh?"

To my dismay, Paul answered that he did.

"Where is it now?"

"I don't know. It disappeared."

"When?"

"I missed it last night. I had kept it in the box of brushes on my bureau."

"When did yuh have the duplicate made?"

"While Father was away this summer. He left his with me."

"Why'd yuh duplicate it?"

"Because I feared that there might sometime happen just what did happen last night. I was afraid it would happen when the barriers were down, and I would want to get in—"

"Foresighted, wasn't yuh? . . . When you found them there double doors locked last night, I suppose yuh ran right up the stairs after your duplicate key, huh?"

"That's when I first missed it."

"And you knew that Brookes had one, didn't yuh?"

"I didn't believe that he did, since Father requested but two of them made."

"There wasn't nothing to prevent your butler having three made, was there?"

"Brookes isn't given to underhanded things like that."

"No, I suppose not," Denny retorted, sourly. "Wonderful sight of confidence you have in your butler. . . . And I want to know, young man, if you was down in this here big room this morning."

"No."

"You smoke cigars?"

"Sometimes."

"Got any on yuh?"

"Several."

Paul offered Denny a cigar.

"I want you to smoke it," Denny told him.

Paul hesitated, puzzled.

"Go ahead, Paul," Ben advised. "Our friend is following a powerful clue."

"Cut the sarcasm, Bailey," Denny said, his temper ugly.

Paul lighted one of his cigars and impudently blew the smoke into Hal Denny's face.

"Hey! What yuh think you're doing?"

"Giving you what you asked for."

I noted a dangerous glint in Paul's eyes.

"Yuh don't need to keep it up," Denny growled. "It ain't the same smell."

Paul's eyes narrowed as he looked straight into those of the detective.

"Have you been implying—," he began, angrily.

"Hold it, Paul," Ben warned.

"Yeah!" Paul snapped back at him, rather ungraciously, I thought. "Well, I don't relish being subjected to insinuating questions before servants—that's what!"

"Denny meant no offense."

"I apologize," Denny offered, "if I overstepped myself. But in the interests of the case—"

"There's a sitting-room upstairs," Paul reminded him. "Or my own room is available."

Denny relighted what was left of his cigar.

"It seems, Brookes, that M. Cornier also had a duplicate key, eh?" Denny asked of the butler. "Likely had it made from the one Mr. Ralston give him."

"I wouldn't know, sir."

"H'm. Of course not. He wouldn't be confiding in yuh, would he? Did he go home after leaving his key with you?"

"Yes, sir."

"Then what was unusual about his visit?"

"Just this, sir. Why, on such a stormy night, should he find it advisable to use the secret door?"

Detective Denny was startled—quite as though the butler's question had shunted him onto a new train of thought.

I observed that Ben's eyes swung interested upon Brookes.

"What yuh mean, my man?" Denny demanded.

"Don't you see, sir? M. Cornier came over by the driveway in the rain with an umbrella."

"Well, I'm damned! Bailey, what yuh think?"

"I'm just listening," Ben shrugged.

"Well?" Denny blurted, again addressing Brookes.

"It would have been more convenient and certainly much pleasanter, sir, for him to have come the usual way—through the hallway over the *porte-cochere*."

"Well?"

"And when he returned to *Fontainebleau,* sir, it would have been equally convenient for him to have returned by the same route."

"He didn't go that way?"

"No, sir. He left by way of the front door. Of course, sir, he wanted to pick up his umbrella he had left outside the house."

"Yeah. Sure."

"On the other hand—," Ben began.

"On the other hand?" queried Denny, wheeling to face Ben.

"M. Cornier probably didn't want to be seen. Not when he was supposed to be at Faribault."

"Well now," pondered Denny, removing the stub of his cigar, "that's a idea. . . Mr. Bailey's probably right, Brookes. It don't look like Mr. Cornier wanted nobody to see him."

"That's what I was thinking, sir."

Again Brookes moistened his lips and brushed them with the back of his hand.

"I don't wish to appear officious, sir; for I hope I know my place—," Brookes resumed, his long fingers slipping up and down over his shiny knees.

"Go ahead, my man. By all means."

"When I went upstairs to rest a bit, sir—after letting M. Cornier out the front door, I saw Mr. Howard Ralston coming down the hall from the windows overlooking the driveway under the *porte-cochere.* Of course, he might have gone to see if the windows were safely locked; but instead of going from there back to the company of the young people, he went into Mrs. Wilmorton's apartment."

"Er, what?" grunted Sleepy Wallingford, suddenly alert.

"And what if Mr. Ralston did go into his sister-in-law's apartment?" asked Denny.

"Why—," and Brookes was embarrassed by Sleepy Wallingford's leer, "the master wasn't in the habit of visiting the rooms of the ladies, sir."

Sleepy snickered, but sobered under the reproving eye of his superior officer.

"Really, Mr. Denny," Paul interposed, "that couldn't have happened. Father wasn't out of the upstairs sitting-room after he joined Miss Manning and me—except to step to the door once, until he came down here."

"And that one time he stepped to the door, he didn't get out of your sight and go down the hall or across to Mrs. Wilmorton's apartment?" Denny queried.

"He did not," Paul affirmed, looking at Brookes in an odd kind of way.

"How was your father dressed when with you and Mildred after dinner?" Ben asked.

"In dinner clothes," Paul replied. "Why?"

"I merely wondered," Ben said.

"But, sir," Brookes spoke up, "when I saw Mr. Ralston coming down the hall, he had changed to a business suit."

"Brookes must be mistaken," Paul said, sharply.

"I may have been mistaken," the butler murmured, flushing under Paul's regard.

Ben offered Hal Denny another two-bit cigar, which was accepted with alacrity.

"I told you, Denny," Ben said, as he flinted his lighter for the city dick, "That you should have read West's diary."

2

Such was the testimony of the Ralston butler. It had me guessing why Brookes was so anxious to tell more than was demanded of him. But my speculations were cut short by Detective Denny'ₛ next words.

"Since it might embarrass you to hear what the rest of the servants has to say," he was advising Paul, "it might be just as well for you to get some rest."

"I think Denny is right, Paul," Ben supplemented. "There is no need in your sitting through the questioning. It'll only harrow your sensibilities. You'll be needing rest before we get through with the investigation."

Paul retired to his room.

Denny remarked to Ben, "Young Ralston's a keen chap. I hate seeing him messed up in this murder."

"If there's been a murder," muttered Sleepy Wallingford.

"Say, what yuh mean by that crack?" Denny irritably demanded.

"Well, the body was disappeared when we got here, wasn't it? How do we know it's been killed?"

Hal Denny bit the end off another of Ben's cigars. Regarding Sleepy contemptuously, he sneered, "Of all the dumb dicks, your're the dumbest I ever seen."

"Dumb. That's me," grinned Sleepy.

With out-flung gesture of his hand, Detective Denny dismissed the subject and turned to Johns, Paul's valet.

Johns apparently knew little more of what had taken place the previous day, except that Paul had stormed up the stairs and into his room sometime during the afternoon.

"He doesn't own a gun, does he?" Denny asked.

"Yes, sir."

"What kind?"

"I'm not sure. Derringer, I think."

"Where does he keep it?"

"In the top right drawer of his bureau, sir."

"Does he ever use it? For target practice, or anything like that?"

"No, sir."

"Does he ever handle it; ever take it outen the drawer?"

"Seldom."

"When was the last time you knowed him to have it out of that bureau drawer?"

"Yesterday afternoon, sir," Johns replied, after a moment's hesitation.

"What became of that revolver, huh?"

"It's still on the bureau, Mr. Denny."

"Yuh sure?"

"I saw it there an hour ago."

Denny paced and smoked.

Then, "What yuh know about this here Italian guy?"

"Seems a decent sort of chap," Johns testified.

"On pretty smooth terms with the boss, wasn't he?"

"Regular pals, Mr. Denny."

"You couldn't see no motive for this here Martini having a hand in murdering his boss, could yuh?"

"None whatever."

Mildred Manning's maid, a prim little piece, who seemed to entertain a liking for Johns, was next.

"My name is Mary Rose Blodgett," she replied to Denny's query.

"How long yuh been Miss Manning's maid?"

"About a year."

"An' yuh entered Miss Manning's service before yuh knew Johns?"

"I never knew there was such a person as Johns until I came to *Windermere* with Miss Manning," Mary Rose answered, with defiant toss of the head.

Sleepy Wallingford blinked approvingly at her.

"Very good, Miss Blodgett. And now will your haughtiness condescend to tell where you come to enter Miss Manning's service?"

"At Long Beach, California. I came to Miss Manning highly recommended."

"How come Miss Manning didn't keep her former maid?"

"Her former maid was drowned."

"Drowned, huh? Was she alone when that happened?" And as Mary Rose yielded him a covertly suspicious glance, "Well, was she?"

"Edith was swimming out to a float with a message for Miss Manning."

"Yeah? An' Miss Manning was by herself out there on that float in the ocean?"

"Why, yes."

"Just sat there and watched her maid drown, I suppose?"

"As soon as Miss Manning saw Edith Bellew throw up her hands and sink, she plunged into the water and swam to her assistance."

"Didn't reach the maid in time, huh?"

"She did reach her. People on the beach saw them struggling in the water."

"A struggle, eh?"

"Drowning people usually are difficult to handle, aren't they?"

Sleepy Wallingford snickered, as Mary Rose gave Mr. Hal Denny a despiteful look.

Ignoring the maid's look and Sleepy's snicker, Denny continued. "And this here struggle was in vain?"

"The timely arrival of the life guard alone saved Miss Manning from being dragged under by Edith."

"Now, that's a interesting bit of information," opined Detective Denny. "Did you ever go swimming with Miss Manning?"

"I have never learned to swim. Besides, Mr. Denny, maids don't swim with their mistresses."

I decided that if Hal Denny was trying to bring forth evidence that Mildred Manning already had one murder to her credit, he wasn't going to receive assistance from Mary Rose. That maid was nobody's fool.

"Miss Manning's quite rich, ain't she?" Denny proceeded.

"I should say that she will be, if she isn't now," Mary Rose replied. "Her father speculated in oil, successfully, I'm told. He owned a good slice of Signal Hill."

"She'd be losing a lot of money by refusing to carry out her father's wishes about marrying Mr. Howard Ralston, wouldn't she?"

"I'm not supposed to know anything about any marriage, if you please," Mary Rose evaded.

Detective Denny showed his mettle then.

"You'll answer my questions, Miss Blodgett. And don't tell me yuh don't know nothing about your mistress' affairs."

Mary Rose pouted; but to no advantage, for Denny came at her again.

"She would lose a lot of money by refusing to carry out her father's wishes, wouldn't she?"

"I believe so," the maid admitted reluctantly—and then only after an encouraging nod from Johns.

Denny apparently didn't like that nod, for he whirled upon the valet with the startling question; "Ever been in trouble with the police?"

Ben cut in, saying, "Johns is straight. I've known him for years."

"Okay, if you say so, Mr. Bailey. And what about this here butler? Can you put the stamp of approval onto him?"

Brookes sputtered with indignation.

"He's been with the Ralstons since Paul was a baby. Sound as a dollar."

"Thank you, sir," Brookes whispered, almost tearfully.

But Hal Denny was not through with Johns—or with Mary Rose, either, much to our immediate sorrow.

Of Johns he asked, "What you know about this surreptitious romance what has been going on between Miss Manning and young Ralston?" And as he saw Johns glance at Mary Rose with troubled eyes, he demanded, hotly, "What now?"

Mary Rose threw herself into the situation, declaring, "It's none of anybody's business; but since you'll get it out of us anyway, here it is. Several times I saw Mr. Paul making love to Miss Manning. Once I saw him kiss her."

"You told Johns about that, of course?"

"Why not?" flashed Johns. "Mary Rose and I are engaged."

"So that's how the land lies! Well now, Miss Blodgett, what else did yuh tell Johns?"

"Well," and Mary Rose dropped her eyes, reluctant to reveal 'what else.'

"Come on!"

"I peeped sometimes at the mash notes Miss Manning hid in her glove box. . . . Mr. Denny, I'll hate you the rest of my life if you insist on my telling."

"Come on. Slip it off your mind."

Evidently convinced that Denny meant business, Mary Rose said, "In one of the notes, Mr. Paul wrote that he would kill his father rather than let him have Miss Manning."

"Hey, Bailey. This beats West's diary, don't it?"

"You're getting along famously, Denny," Ben replied, at the same time smiling reassuringly at the frightened Mary Rose.

"Sure. I'm getting somewheres. These mash notes'll tell the story."

"I wouldn't bank too heavily on those notes, Denny," Ben cautioned. "Mash notes contain a lot of foolish stuff written on impulse and without a thought behind it."

"So, yuh don't like seeing me build up a case against your friend, eh? Well, it's dangerous business writing without thinking. An' how d'yuh know young Ralston didn't put a heap o' thinking behind what he wrote? . . . Getting this down, West?"

"Everything," I replied, my pencil flying.

"See," exclaimed Pietro, who had come in, "did I not tell you? You would not believe me when I said that Paul killed his father. And there will more evidence come. You wait."

"My, my," and Denny regarded Pietro suspiciously, "but you and Paul Ralston sure do love each other, don't yuh? Both of you under suspicion, and for good reasons—if yuh ask me."

"How come?" insisted Ben.

Detective Denny was quick with his enumeration. "First," he said, "because of indiscreet admissions; second, because of what the servants has said; third, because both guys profit by Mr. Ralston's death—Paul Ralston getting the girl, and Martini a nice inheritance."

"That's slander!" cried Pietro.

"Well, you are in Howard Ralston's will, ain't yuh?"

"What if I am? Is that proof that I would kill him—the Master I loved?"

"Humph!" grunted Denny.

With nothing more to say to our artificer, he demanded of Mary Rose what else she had to contribute.

"Nothing else, Mr. Denny."

"I can tell by the look of you there is. Out with it!"

"I'd rather not."

"Yuh gotta tell—now or later."

"Very well," and one could see that the maid was more than reluctant to talk further. "I saw M. Cornier carry Mrs. Wilmorton up the stairs last night. I went to proffer my assistance, but Fib sent me about my business. Later I saw M. Cornier come out of Mrs. Wilmorton's suite, and I heard him say, 'Don't worry, Julia. I'll keep my mouth shut. And I'll stand by you.'"

That statement so excited me that I almost forgot to set it down in my stenographic notes.

"That all?"

"Yes, sir."

"You wasn't in the house at the time of the murder, was yuh?"

"Not until afterwards, Mr. Denny," a chastened Mary Rose replied. "Johns and I went to a movie and then had dinner and danced at the *Golden Pheasant*."

"Got a alibi?" Denny demanded of Johns.

"We can get one."

"I'm anxious," Ben suggested, "for you to read West's diary, Denny. Especially after the testimony you've just heard."

Striking a match on the polished surface of the Renaissance table, Denny snapped back at Ben with, "To hell with West's diary!"

3

Detective Denny chewed on his cigar, reflecting; then applied his match. He regarded the scratches he had made on the Renaissance table, wetted his finger and rubbed them over with saliva. That gracious act accomplished, he addressed the Ralston chauffeur.

"Been with Mr. Ralston long, Thomas?" he asked.

"Ten years."

"H'm," grunted Denny, "this seems to be a regular family, if yuh ask me. You must have been a youngster when Mr. Ralston hired yuh?"

"Seventeen."

"Live on the premises?"

"With my mother in an apartment over the garage. My mother is in Omaha this week, and I eat in the house with the other help."

Further questioning elicited nothing of value. Wayland Thomas, it appeared, spent his time, while not in service, studying architecture.

"With your permission, Denny," Ben said, "I'd like to ask Thomas a couple of questions. . . . Will you tell us, Thomas, whether or not there has been late trouble with the roadster?"

"Mr. Paul spoke to me about the carburetor yesterday. I was working on it this morning when Mr. Denny sent for me."

"Tell us about any drives you made about dinner hour last night."

"I drove Mrs. Wilmorton to Dr. Elsing's."

"At what time did you bring her back?"

"I didn't bring her back. Mrs. Wilmorton told me that she would take a taxi home."

Detective Denny appeared so interested in what Wayland Thomas had said that I thought he was going to continue the interrogation Ben had begun; but instead he turned to Mrs. Wilmorton's French maid, Fifi Burgoyne.

"What's your name?" he demanded.

Fifi appeared unaware of the fact that she was being addressed.

"Them *Frogs!*" grumbled the burly Irishman, disgusted.

"Perhaps she doesn't understand English," Ben advised, mildly. "That being the case, she would not suspect that you were addressing her."

The corners of the Irishman's mouth crinkled, skeptically.

"Permit me," Ben further suggested. Turning to Fifi, he said, in French, "Detective Denny is addressing you, *mademoiselle.*"

"*Ooh, pardonez-moi, M'sieu. Je ne parle pas Anglais.*"

"Looks like I'm going to have trouble with this dame," opined Denny, his brow wrinkling. And to Fifi, he said, "Maybe yuh don't speak English, but yuh understand it, huh?"

"*Le comprenez-vous maintenant?*" Ben asked her.

"*Je n'en comprends pas un mot,*" replied Fifi, the French slipping easily from her glib tongue.

"I asked her," Ben interpreted to Denny, "if she got your meaning, and she replied that she didn't understand a word."

"Now ain't that too bad," Denny murmured. "Her and me might make a real interesting conversation."

Through all this, Mademoiselle Fifi sat in apparently blissful ignorance of what was being said about her.

Then Denny, taking *mademoiselle* off guard, pointed a finger at her and sharply asked, "Ain't that a spider on her collar?"

Like a flash the French maid whisked the imaginary insect from her person. Realizing herself trapped, she flamed anger into her eyes.

"Tell the beast," she hissed in French, "that I indeed have some ability to understand, but none to speak the English."

"Sez she!" muttered Denny, sententiously, when Ben translated. "Tell her she was overheard talking English last night."

"*Non, non,*" protested Fifi.

"Oh yes you was, *madamzelly,*" Denny shot at her. "You said that the police would be here fast enough—said it to your mistress in her rooms upstairs. Mrs. O'Grady told me at the time."

Our Irish housekeeper beamed expansively, evidently proud to have contributed materially to the success of the investigation her fellow-countryman was conducting. As for Fifi, she shrank back in her chair, regarding Hal Denny with fascinated eyes.

"Know anything about this affair last night, Miss—er, *Madamzelly* Burgoyne?"

"*Non, M'sieu.*"

"Does your mistress know anything about it?"

"Only since eet happened, *M'sieu.* She ees prostrate."

"Suffers from nerves, eh?"

"*Oui, M'sieu.*"

"Been in her rooms all night?"

"*Oui, M'sieu.* All the night."

"Thomas says she went to Dr. Elsing's last night."

"Oh, *oui, oui, M'sieu!* I forget. The English, eet ess so difficult for me."

"What time did she return?"

"About nine o'clock, *M'sieu.*"

"Where does this Dr. Elsing live?"

Fifi gave an address on Pillsbury Avenue.

Detective Denny consulted the new telephone directory on my desk. With a grunt, he turned from it, apparently satisfied, and resumed his questioning of Fifi.

"Did Mrs. Wilmorton carry a gun with her?"

"Oh, *non, non, M'sieu!* Her leetle revolvair, eet ees een her desk."

"That's all from me," Denny said to Ben. "Want to ask her anything?"

"Believe I do," Ben answered.

Fifi looked up at him with easy eyes—eyes of hazel color. "Did Mrs. Wilmorton take anything out of the house with her when she went to Dr. Elsing's?" Ben asked.

Fifi's jaw sagged. Had Ben been the devil, the maid could not have regarded him with greater alarm. But she shook her head in negative reply.

"Well, did she bring anything back with her?"

"*Non, M'sieu,*" Fifi Burgoyne replied in faltering tone.

"Anyone been with her in her rooms?"

Ben's shrewd eyes regarded Fifi narrowly as the color receded from her face, leaving the rouge like two ugly daubs to heighten the terror in her eyes. That Fifi was afraid of Ben was evident to me. She bit her lip, struggling to a semblance of composure I was certain she did not feel.

"Myself only, *M'sieu,*" she finally whispered in reply to Ben's question.

"You have been up all night with your mistress, I imagine?"

"Nearly all zee night, *M'sieu.* I doze on zee *chaise-longue* een her bedroom."

"Have your clothes off at all?"

"*Non, M'sieu.* I was too fearful to retire. Not yet have I made zee change of garment."

"Were you down on this floor at any time?"

Fifi shook her head.

Ben stood close beside her, looking grimly down into her upturned face and compelling her gaze to his.

"Tell me then," he said, "who it was that Brookes saw going through the servants' hall at a little after ten last night."

Fifi seemed literally to shrink, but she protested that she did not know whom the butler could have seen.

Denny's eyes, followed by Sleepy Wallingford's interested stare, traveled down Mademoiselle Fifi's slim leg to a splotching of dried mud on the ankle of her sheer chiffon stocking. Fifi glanced down and saw the mud. She made swift gesture to brush it away, but Sleepy was too quick for her. He seized and held her wrist in iron grip.

Ben, stooping and examining the splotch on the stocking, said to Denny, "It's some of the red earth that borders the front drive. She's been out toward the avenue."

Badly scared, Fifi began talking. She told that she had been but a short time with Mrs. Wilmorton, and that Dr. Elsing had secured the place for her. She had been in America three years, coming from Rambouillet, France. Previous to her employment at *Windermere,* she had been personal maid to Mrs. Stanley Brown-Coppersmith III in Chicago. Being ill, she had followed Mrs. Brown-Coppersmith's advice and sought Dr. Elsing, who had once been the Chicago woman's physician.

To Ben, Denny said, "We'll have to check on her there."

Fifi started to say something, but for some reason decided against doing so.

Detective Denny paced the hearthstone, chewing on the remnant of his cigar and meditating. Then, coming to an abrupt halt before Fifi, who, cat-like, had been watching his every move, he demanded that she tell why she went to Dr. Elsing's the night before.

"But, *M'sieu,* I did not admit that I go to see *le docteur Elsing.*"

"No? But yuh went just the same, didn't yuh?"

"*Oui, M'sieu.*"

I was surprised at the docility with which she admitted the fact.

"What'd yuh go for?"

"For zee medicine. Madame need eet so badly."

"Did yuh walk there?"

"I hire zee taxi."

"What kind of medicine did yuh get for your mistress?"

"How should I know zat, *M'sieu?*" Fifi replied.

Detective Denny renewed his pacing, his brows contracted in further rumination. Once he paused and regarded Mademoiselle Fifi with puzzled eyes. She smiled back at him with eyes that to me seemed yellowish where they should have been white.

With impatient gesture, Hal Denny discarded his shredded cigar, and, before Ben could offer him a third two-bit weed, lighted one of his stogies.

After which Ben, I noted, made a memorandum in his yellow-covered book.

4

"Now," and Detective Denny expanded pompously, "it seems to me we're getting somewheres. Eh what, Bailey?"

"I shouldn't be surprised," replied Ben. "But if you'd—"

"Don't say *diary!*" yelled Denny.

"I won't," grinned Ben. "But really, I think we'd save time at that."

"Save time? What the hell!" He jerked the stogy from his mouth. "Say, you amatoor dick, who's conducting this here investigation?"

"You are," Ben affably conceded. "I merely ventured—"

"Huh!" Denny jammed the stogy into his mouth and eyed Ralston's black cook with belligerent eye. "What's your cognomen, eh?"

"Lan' sakes, Mr. Law, Ah didn't know Ah had one."

"Had one what?"

"Coggy-man. Ah's one 'spectable woman, Ah is. Sho nuf!"

"What's your name?"

"Mah full an' complete name what mah pastah done baptise me to am Deborah Stella Dolly Madison Oh Grave Whar Am Thy Victory Jones, an' I is from Alabam'.'"

"Well strike me pink!"

"Yes'm. Mah mammy she done tole me dat when Ah was born on Eastah Day dat de angel ob de Lawd come an' sit on de foot ob de baid an' say, 'Sis Jones, des you call dat sweet gal baby Deborah—'"

"Yeah? Well, that's enough."

"Yes'm is, sho nuf!"

We welcomed laughter as brief respite from the nervous tension that had gripped us.

"You had a scare last evening, I'm told," Denny said to Deborah.

"Ah sho did!" Deborah declared. "Ah jes finish ma dishes an' Ah look up an' seen de debbil peerin' at me fru de windah ovah mah sink."

"You saw him right plain, huh?"

"Yes'm." Deborah shuddered, jellily. "Des as plain's Ah sees you right now, Mr. Law."

"Horns, tail, and cloven hoof, I suppose?" Ben prompted.

"No'm, Ah ain seen none ob dem things, but Ah sho knows dey war dar."

Led on by Hal Denny's more or less pertinent questioning, Deborah related her frightful experience and its smothery aftermath beneath the pillows of her big bed.

"De debbil look lak a yallah niggah wid a low-down white trash look on he face," Deborah concluded.

The searchlight of Detective Denny's interrogation focused next upon the Ralston housekeeper, Mrs. Delia O'Grady.

"Shure and Oi've somewhat to be telling yuh!" she answered Denny. "An' haven't Oi the patience av Job himself to be setting here waiting to be telling it?"

"Very well, Mrs. O'Grady, we'll be after listening to the story yuh have to tell," said Detective Denny, grinning as he fell easily into the rhythm of Delia's own brogue.

Removing an amber sidecomb, Delia ran it vigorously through the sorrel strands of her tightly drawn hair. Then, shaking the comb coquettishly at Denny, she said, "Ye'll not be after belavin' the story Oi'm telling yuh. . . . Oi was reading in me bed, if ye please, Mr. Denny, whin Oi came to the place in me story that told av the lovely rid geraniums the loidy hero had in her windy. Now, Oi've some geraniums av me own, an' Oi'm that proud av thim! So Oi took it into me head to git up an' see if the storm had broke any av me plants in the windy box."

"Were they hurt, Mrs. O'Grady?"

"Just damp with the moisture, Mr. Denny. They was sheltered from the rain, the Saints be praised!"

"And then ye went back to bed, I'm after thinking, Mrs. O'Grady?"

"Oi did not, Mr. Denny!" Delia O'Grady drew in her lips and bent upon Detective Denny a profoundly oracular look. "No indade, an' Oi did not! . . . Because Oi thought Oi heard some one on the roof av the house!"

Detective Denny's smoking stogy nearly escaped the grip of his yellow teeth, as he exclaimed, "Mrs. O'Grady!"

"Blessed Mither, it's the truth Oi'm after telling yuh, Mr. Denny! A man on the roof av the house!"

"Holy St. Patrick, Mrs. O'Grady!"

"Yuh see, Mr. Denny, me room is on the third floor, directly over the *porty-cochairy*. And as Oi stood there at me windy, straining the ears av me to catch the sounds over me head, Oi saw a man climb down the trellis. Oi did that! And he came across the roof av the *porty-co-chairy* an' swung in at a windy some one had opened for him. A woman's hand it was at that sash, Oi'm telling yuh, Mr. Denny."

You could have heard a pin drop, it was that still in the big room— each of us waiting, with what must have been varying emotions, for Mrs. O'Grady to continue her account of the man on the roof.

"Mrs. O'Grady," asked Denny, breaking the tense silence, "who was that man?"

"Oi thought at first it must be some one as had gone up to examine a leak about the roof. But now Oi'm thinking—"

She paused, glancing apprehensively about the room.

"What are yuh thinking, Mrs. O'Grady?"

Her face sobered as she answered, "It's the loikes av me to be afraid av opening me mouth in this bewitched house."

"There'll no harm be befalling yuh, Mrs. O'Grady. Not with me about," Detective Denny assured her.

"Shure thin," she faltered, "and Oi think the man on the roof was the boss himself."

"What's that you say?" demanded Ben, suppressed excitement in his voice.

"Shure, young man, Oi'm after thinking it was Mr. Howard Ralston that Oi saw on the roof av the *porty-cochairy*."

"But that's impossible, Denny!" Ben exclaimed, staring at the official investigator.

A creepy silence ensued—a silence broken at length by the Ralston butler.

"Begging pardon, sir," Brookes said, moistening his fingers and sleeking his hair. "That's in harmony with what I said, sir—begging the young master's pardon. It was Mr. Ralston that I saw come down the upper hall from the *porte-cochere* and go into Mrs. Wilmorton's suite."

"*Non, non!*" protested Fifi Burgoyne.

"It is true, sir," Brookes held. "And then, more strange than ever, when I had gone to test the windows and returned, I saw the master standing in the door of the upstairs sitting-room—"

"In his tuxedo?" Ben interrupted to ask.

"Quite so, sir. And he asked me to inquire if Mrs. Wilmorton would join him and the young people at bridge."

"Say!" cried Detective Denny, perplexed and therefore irritated, "Is everybody 'round here going coo-coo?"

"Do you remember what clothes Mr. Ralston had on when Miss Manning discovered the body, West?" Ben inquired of me.

"Tuxedo," I replied.

"Looky here, Brookes," Hal Denny wanted to know, "you hadn't taken a drink, had yuh?"

"I am against repeal, sir."

Mrs. O'Grady beckoned Detective Denny to her side, and, as he bent over, I heard her distinctly whisper, "The hand that opened the windy for the man on the roof was wearing an emerald ring, Mr. Denny."

"It couldn't have been Mrs. Wilmorton!" I involuntarily exclaimed.

I glanced at Brookes, but his eyes were fixed upon the floor.

"Madamzelly Fifi," Denny addressed the pale maid, "please tell Mrs. Wilmorton that I shall want to speak with her in about an hour."

"*Oui, M'sieu.*"

Fifi started for the double doors.

"Wait a minute!" Denny called after her. And as she turned, brows raised, he continued—addressing all the servants, "You boys and girls may go about your work; but don't none of yuh try to leave the place or communicate with no outsiders. The grounds is in charge of the police."

As the servants rose to go, he added, "You, Joe Hofer—you and your wife wait a few minutes."

The gardener and his wife settled nervously back into their chairs, enviously watching the other *Windermere* help quietly leaving "the tomb."

When the servants had gone, Denny instructed Sleepy Wallingford to close the double doors.

"Now, Hofer," Denny said to the gardener, "I want you to repeat to Mr. Bailey and me what you've been after telling Mr. Thomas."

"He told you already?" asked Hofer.

"Some of it, but I want the story from you and your wife." Joe Hofer did most of the talking, his wife nodding or shaking her head as he proceeded.

"Me unt Annie vas coomin' home from de movies unt a cup of coffee mit our frents, yen ye seen a taxi standing out by der sidevalk curb yet. Der motor vas racin' unt der vas a voman in der back seat already."

"You sure about that, Hofer?"

"*Ach, ja!*" exclaimed Joe, while his wife nodded vigorous confirmation.

"So then what?"

"Ye coom along der drive unt took der valk through betveen der two houses. Ve vas only coom to der back yet, ven we heard a shot—"

"Was that shot inside the house?"

"*Nein.* Outside it vas, I tink."

"*Ja, draussen,*" asserted Annie Hofer.

"Me unt Annie, ye run back qvick already yet unt see *zwei* men running like dey vas crazy for dot taxi by der sidevalk curb. Unt yen dey got in dot taxi it got avay like a hurry yet."

"Then what?"

"*Das ist alles.* Me unt Annie, ve say maybe der police vas after some no good hoodlums, so ve go home unt got in der bed."

"It was I who fired that shot," said Paul, appearing at the double doors. "When we went outside, I saw a man sneaking around the corner of the house. I called to him to halt, but he kept going. I let fire at him."

"Hit him?"

"I don't know. I started to run after him, but fell. When I got to my feet, he had disappeared."

"Joe here says he saw two men."

"I saw only one, and he ran toward the back of the house. I did hear a car start away from the curb, though."

Paul sauntered into the room and dropped into a chair. Somehow or other, his manner didn't seem convincing to me. The thought made me uneasy.

Detective Denny's eyes swung upon Pietro.

"How about that strange boy?" he demanded.

"It—it couldn't have been he," murmured Pietro.

"Why didn't yuh tell me this before?" Denny demanded of Paul.

Paul hesitated—the barest fraction of a minute.

"Because," and he spoke as with sudden determination, "I picked up a monogrammed handkerchief out there. It was Henri Cornier's."

And me—I wished that Paul had remained upstairs. Denny dismissed Joe and Annie.

To Pietro he said, "Open that cabinet. I want to see that ring and make certain you didn't put no poison in it."

Pietro, with Paul at his elbow, opened the black monster and drew forth the secret drawer.

"Here it is," Pietro said, taking out the ring.

Then, staring at the ring, while the color drained from his face, he cried, "No, no, it is not the Borgia!"

"What yuh mean, it ain't the Borgia?" exclaimed Denny, snatching the ring from Pietro's trembling fingers.

Paul Ralston and Ben Bailey stared at each other. And me, I told them that Howard Ralston had given the duplicate to M. Cornier and locked the genuine Borgia in that Chinese cabinet.

"That leaves but one conclusion," muttered Ben.

"It sure looks bad for that Frenchman," remarked Denny, stooping to roll up the Chinese rug.

"But," Paul argued, "I don't believe that Henri Cornier took the poison ring."

"But it's gone," Denny pointed out. "And the mummy's gone, too."

Returning the counterfeit Borgia to Pietro, he said, "Lock it up."

"The three terrible menaces," sighed Paul. "Two of them vanished, and the other in the hands of the police!"

"And which of them is primarily responsible for the death of Mr. Ralston?" I wondered, speaking my thought aloud.

"Find the person who wanted all three of them and we have our murderer," commented Denny, tying a cord around the rolled Chinese rug.

"If—"

But no one paid Sleepy any attention, except myself—and I wished that he had finished his sentence.

5

The two detectives—Mr. Harrison Denny, representing the city of Minneapolis, and Mr. Benjamin Bailey, private investigator for Paul Ralston—retired to the upstairs sitting-room to talk over the situation. I was rather surprised at this, in view of the fact that Hal Denny had, to my way of thinking, resented Bailey's introduction into the action of the *Windermere* drama—and that despite Denny's pretensions toward affability.

Black Deborah, under the benevolent eye of Mrs. Delia O'Grady, served us Danish pastry and black coffee. Paul sent Brookes up with a box of choice "weeds." These Denny and Sleepy scooped up, leaving Ben and me to the enjoyment of our plebeian cigarettes.

"Well, what yuh think, Bailey?" asked Denny.

"You know, Denny," Ben replied, "Scotland Yard prides itself on its superior team work. It credits that team work with its outstanding successes. Get me? I'd like to play ball with you, but, being human, I naturally want a little credit for myself."

"I appreciate all that, Bailey; but don't be—"

"Selfish?" Ben laughed. "I'm not selfish, Denny. All I ask—"

"You'll get your share of the glory."

"Who got the glory in the Footlight Murder Case?"

"Well, of course O'Rourke—"

"Never mentioned me in any of his reports, let alone to the press."

"But I'm different, Bailey. I don't think you're selfish, and I'm not a hog. You're good. You got ideas. This here case is baffling—about the worst I ever tackled. Murder done, and the body disappeared."

"And you can't proceed according to cut and dried formula, eh?"

"That's right. Now you—"

"Find such a case to be a *honey,* what?"

"Well, you got peculiar methods of your own."

"Such as my theory of psychic contact?"

"Well, *yes.* That—and other things."

"Things I get laughed at for by you city dicks. Humph, I ought to play ball with you boys!"

"Looky, Bailey, I ain't made you sore, have I?"

"What, you?" Ben laughed. "That's good, Denny. As if you could."

I knew that Ben was not the lad to surrender the advantage to be gained by such deductions as he might have made—not when they were to be yielded at a loss to his subsequent prestige. It was clear, that, having been *stung* so badly in the matter of the Footlight Murder Case,* Ben wasn't going to put himself in the way of any more hornets such as Barney O'Rourke.

*Citizens of Minneapolis will recall the strange case of Charlotte Chambray, who died mysteriously while singing before the footlights of the Blank Street Theatre, back in 1929. Had it not been for Ben Bailey, O'Rourke would never have found the minute poison dart that had been blown at her from the darkened house.

"You ask me what I think," Ben continued. "Suppose I ask you what you think?"

Hal Denny eyed the younger man appreciatively, with just the suggestion of a smile. Then, with a shrug of his broad shoulders, he discarded the dead stogy, laying it primly upon an ash tray. And while Ben and I made leisurely completion of the repast Mrs. O'Grady had provided, Denny drew one of Paul's cigars from his bulging pocket and set himself for a contented smoke. Leaning back in his chair, he flung his left leg over the right, locked his hands behind his head, and sat gazing meditatively upward at nothing in particular.

"Well," he answered, at length, "I gotta confess I'm at a loss for a sure lead that points right square at positive identification of the bird that killed Howard Ralston. And I ain't got the faintest idea where the body could of been took."

"But you said that it looks bad for M. Cornier," I reminded him.

"Yeah, I said that. But it looks bad for several folks around this swell joint, if yuh ask me. But then maybe more particular for him than anybody else. Still—"

He swung his left leg down. He took the cigar from his mouth, and, leaning forward, legs spread, forearms on knees, said, "Suppose we begin with an analysis of possible motives."

"This is your party," Ben reminded him.

"Uh-huh. . . . Well, we'll begin with the son of the house, then."

Ben and I smoked, waiting.

"Young Ralston," said Denny, "quarreled with his father yesterday over this here pretty Miss Manning. We have Martini's testimony to that; young Ralston himself admits it. And the valet and Miss Manning's maid had damned interesting bits to add."

He puffed lazily on his cigar. Ben and I still waited.

"Young Ralston is a determined lad. You can see that, easy. Once desperately in love, he ain't one to give up. Now, if his father was like him, there was dog-gone sure to be a head-on smash of wills. Huh?"

"Paul's a chip from the old block," Ben conceded.

"Okay! There you have it. Two wills smash head-on, father and son, both wanting the same girl. One of them will have to shift into reverse—back up, surrender. Get me?"

"I get you."

"All right. Then tell me, would either of the Ralstons back up?" Ben looked at me.

"They were both strong willed," I admitted, cautiously, realizing that Ben didn't want to express an opinion. "But I am inclined to believe that if it came to a show-down, Paul would yield to his father."

"But if he was passionately in love?" Denny persisted. "And there's that statement he wrote to Miss Manning."

"I'm not putting much stock in that mash note," Ben said.

"It's mighty damning, Bailey, if you ask me."

"I'm not asking you. I'm telling you. Paul wouldn't—couldn't carry out such a foolish threat."

"You're prejudiced! Young Ralston's your friend."

"He is my friend; but if he killed his father, I'd say he ought to swing for it. Look, Denny. Paul didn't do it. West was in 'the tomb'—"

"Proving what?"

"You have his testimony."

"Sure, I have his testimony, but what's it worth. Paul Ralston's his friend, too. Besides, West was doped—he's not accountable for what he saw and heard. So what?"

"Just this!" Ben snapped back. "You keep talking about a revolver. You seem to forget that the vengeance dagger of the Scarlet Dragons served as the murder weapon."

"Not by a damned sight I ain't forgetting that there fact. But there was a shot fired, wasn't there? Young Ralston admits using his gun, don't he? How do we know whether Ralston was killed with a dagger or a bullet from a gun? West didn't see the murder, he declares. And just because the body was found with a dagger in its back ain't no sign. Damn it, where's that body anyway? We can't do nothing without no *corpus delicti!*"

"Rot! And don't overlook the fact, Denny, that you make wrong use of the term *corpus delicti!*"

"Me? Say, me lad, I was prodding them there things while you was still in the nursery."

"What about a motive? You haven't determined that, Mr. Denny."

"Oh, haven't I? What about Paul Ralston's being crazy in love with the Manning girl?"

"That motive is not strong enough for murder in this case. Paul could have eloped with Mildred."

"Yeah? And been cut off in the old man's will. Heck no, Bailey! Paul Ralston was after the money as well as the girl."

"Have your own way," Ben retorted, grimly. "I think you're all wet."

"Time'll tell."

"You're right—time will tell. And that before long. This case isn't twenty-four hours old yet. . . . What about Paul's alibi? Miss Manning's testimony ought to be worth something."

"She's in love with Paul Ralston ain't she? So what's that make her testimony worth? Who knows but what she had a hand in killing the old man?"

"Mildred Manning? Don't make me laugh!"

"I'll make you laugh before we're through with this mess, smart boy. Looky. That drowning of her maid out to California looks funny to me. How do we know Edith Bellew wasn't murdered, huh? How do we know Mildred Manning ain't a natural killer? How—"

"How do we or how don't we know a lot of things? In defense of Mildred Manning, there's Paul's testimony. Hold it, Denny! I know what you're wanting to say—"

"But—"

"And don't forget that you yourself said that in looking for the murderer we should seek the individual who coveted all three of the menaces. Where does that get you? What about the tampering with the Borgia poison ring? What about the disappearance of the mummy of Serapion?"

"Hooey!" grunted Hal Denny. "Bluff—to throw us guys off the trail."

"But West saw the *ka* walk."

"Yeah, an' you *say* West was doped, and I agree. So where does that get yuh, huh?"

"Have you considered the *ka* angle?"

"No. And I ain't going to consider it!"

"Okay. I am."

"That's your privilege. Chase around after mummy clues if yuh want to; but don't forget that old pal Denny is telling you it's all hooey and bluff."

Followed a lull in the storm—and the lighting of another of Paul's cigars.

"Mr. Denny," I made bold to remind him, "you said that it looks bad for M. Cornier."

"I know I did, youngster; and I ain't forgot. That Frenchman has got as good a motive for killing his friend as anybody mixed up in this mess. We'll give him plenty of attention."

"And yet," I made bold to continue, "you said that the murderer is in this house."

"I said it, and I believe it. Anyhow, what's to prevent Mr. Cornier from coming and going as he likes in this here house, huh?"

"Nothing," I admitted.

"If it ain't anybody living right here, it's him," Denny declared.

"In your last statement, you may be nearer the truth than you surmise, Denny," Ben offered.

"So—you're beginning to see eye to eye with me, huh?"

"Not quite. I'm not fixing the guilt. I admit only that the murderer's accomplice may still be—in all likelihood still beneath the roofs of *Windermere*."

"I heard you say that before. Mr. Cornier could have a accomplice over here, couldn't he?"

"Who?" I asked. "Not Pietro. M. Cornier hates Pietro."

"Mr. Cornier might be a damned good actor," Hal Denny offered.

"He might at that," smiled Ben. "And what about Julia Wilmorton?"

"That swell looking dame?" Denny asked the question as if his admiration for the beautiful sister-in-law of Howard Ralston had eased his inclination to suspicion of her. Then, as though embarrassed in the revelation of that admiration, he hastened to say, "I'm not forgetting her, neither, Bailey. She could be Mr. Cornier's accomplice."

"She owns an emerald dinner ring," I contributed.

"Huh! What's that? She does? By heck, now that's interesting."

"And I hear she's in the Ralston will," I added, as further contribution. "In Basil Manning's will, too."

"We gotta see that Manning will," Denny declared.

"We're going to see it," Ben stated. "In fact, I—if not we—intend seeing a number of things and people."

"What about the Italian?" Denny suddenly thought to ask.

"There's plenty of motive there," Ben had to admit.

"He'll bear further investigating," Denny affirmed. "In short, all the Ralston employees will. Including yourself," Denny shot at me.

"Leaving out West, that might be a good idea," Ben said. "There's the French maid, for example. She's dynamite, if you ask me."

"Let's get back to Paul Ralston," Denny urged. "He's put himself in a bad light."

"Paul seemed to give up his struggle for Mildred Manning the night we left for Europe," I told Denny.

"Let's have that story," urged Denny.

It was Ben's opportunity: the psychological moment he had been awaiting.

"You asked me to play ball, Denny. Well, I'm pitching."

"Yeah! What you tossing me?"

"West's diary."

Detective Denny grinned at Ben, as much as to say, *Well, you've cornered me.*

"Trot it out," he said to me.

I rose and went out into the hall on my way to my room to get the red diary. As I approached my door, I noticed that it stood slightly ajar. Stopping dead in my tracks, I began wondering who could have invaded my private domain. None of the rooms had been done as yet, I knew, Mrs. O'Grady not having made her customary rounds with Annie Hofer. Cautiously I stole to the door and listened at the aperture. Distinctly I heard movement within the room. I observed, too, that the room was in darkness. That discovery startled me, for I had left the window drapes pulled back when I went out that morning. Who could have drawn them, and why?

At that moment I noticed the play of a spot of light upon the wall exposed to my view. I realized that some one was after the red diary—some one who must have heard our conversation in the sitting-room next door.

Brookes came up then and went down the hall to Paul's room. He didn't notice me as he passed, the tired eyes of him almost closed. I was thankful that he didn't, for it wasn't my desire to have the occupant of my room apprised of my presence outside the door.

But that intruder must have heard Brookes, for the spot of light vanished from the wall.

I waited a moment; then decided to enter my room and confront the burglar, if such he proved to be. Taut in nerve, I cautiously pushed the door inward. As I did so, I was certain of quick, soft tread away from the other side of the door. I am not a coward, but the muffled beat of those retreating feet gave me an uncomfortable feeling. . . . Tiptoe, I entered the room. Pushing the door shut behind me, I stood inhaling that same strange cigar odor we had encountered that morning in "the tomb." I concluded that my intruder was a man, and I was thankful that I enjoyed reputation for some athletic prowess. But the room appeared empty.

I glanced toward my secretary and saw that it was open.

Mr. Intruder was after my diary all right.

From the corner of my right eye I caught the slight movement of the curtains that hung before my closet door. . . . He was in there. Armed, perhaps.

I had no weapon. In whatever emergency developed, I would have to depend upon my two strong arms. Legs, too, maybe. I was glad that Pietro had taught me the art of *la savate* those days we spent in Venice. . . . I wished that I had thought to summon Ben and Denny. It was too late now. Once I began backing toward the hall door to give the alarm, Mr. Intruder would become suspicious. He might take a shot at me. . . .

Resolved to end the suspense, I edged toward the closet door, going sidewise like a crab and endeavoring to keep out of bullet line. I neared the curtains. I reached out my right hand to touch them. Mr. Intruder's breathing was audible—the cigar odor stronger.

Quickly I jerked the curtains aside.

At the same instant something seemingly bashed in the side of my head. I saw stars a plenty. I did not collapse, however. Blind with pain and anger, I lunged, only to receive a hard thrust in the stomach. One thought raced through my mind: Mr. Intruder was a master of *la savate*. Backward I went, striking my head upon a chair. I was conscious of fingers at my throat. Vainly I struggled. Black fog swirled about me. Midnight encompassed my consciousness.

When I came around, Ben and Denny had me on my bed, and a jittery Brookes was moving a bottle of ammonia at my nostrils.

Brushing his hand aside, I pulled myself to sitting posture. My head nigh to bursting with pain, I was close to nausea of the stomach. For the moment I believed that I was going under again, but I jerked myself free from the octopus-tentacles of unconsciousness.

"Did he get it?" I demanded, hoarsely.

"The diary is safe, if that's what you mean," Ben assured me.

With a groan I sank back upon my pillow. Again for me the light went out.

THE AFTERNOON OF THE SECOND DAY

1

The luncheon hour had passed when I regained consciousness.

Ben and Hal Denny were eating at a small table Brookes had brought in for them. Sleepy Wallingford, half-eaten apple in hand, snored in a chair pulled into a remote corner. As soon as I was able to sit up, hot beef broth was brought me. I swallowed three bowls of it, confessing that I felt better for its stimulating warmth.

Ben wanted to know what had happened, so I recited my adventure as well as I could—my throat hurting me in my effort to talk.

"Only a man could have gripped my throat like that," I said.

"That might be," Ben opined. "But some women are handy at strangling."

"But the cigar odor," I argued.

"Didn't you tell us this morning that you had seen women smoking cigars in Denmark?" Ben smilingly reminded me.

I could think of no woman at *Windermere* who smoked cigarettes, let alone cigars.

"What's going to happen next?" pondered Denny.

"Murder, if we aren't alert," answered Ben. "Twice they've tried to get West—"

"Which supports my contention that the murderer is at large in this here house," added Hal Denny.

"His accomplice," Ben corrected.

"Looky, why yuh keep saying that?"

"Hunch, I guess."

"One of your psychic hunches, huh?"

"Maybe," murmured Ben, ignoring Denny's sarcasm.

"Well, let's get out West's diary," Denny urged. "We got no time to waste."

Ben retrieved the red-leather diary from its hiding place behind the wall-paneling. He thumbed through the pages and found the passages he sought.

"This is the entry giving you the account you asked for just before West was attacked," he said. "Read under date of June 17."

Hal Denny took the book and read aloud, his voice low-pitched.

Paul saw us off tonight, but I could note the feeling of constraint *with which he took his father's hand in farewell. Mr. R. sensed it, I could see, and must have guessed the cause; for he said: "My boy, there is but one on this earth who can occupy your place in my heart; that's yourself. . . . You are unfortunate in having your mother's inclination to suspicion and jealousy. . . . The sea will soon be between us, and much can happen while we are separated. I wish, therefore, to impress two things upon you. First, although I like Pietro exceedingly—and find him deserving, I shall never let him come between you and me. Second, I leave Mildred here; but when I return, I shall fulfill her father's wish. I consider myself bound by the desires of the dead. . . ." Paul wrung his father's hand. "Father," he said, tears in his eyes, "you have nothing to worry about so far as I am concerned. . . ."*

"That," I said, as Denny paused, "answers your question. Doesn't that sound as if Paul had given way to the priority of his father's claim?"

"Sure, it sounds that way; but look at his attitude since. I still think he could have done murder because of his infatuation for the girl."

He bent over the diary, pondering that which he had read aloud.

"Young Ralston sure is jealous of that Italian feller. He'd like to pin the crime on him. That shows he's got a vindictive spirit, and I don't like that none. Makes me want to believe that he plunged that dagger into his father's back."

Ben said nothing. Hal Denny skimmed through the pages of the diary, pausing now and again to read aloud such items as interested him.

"Mighty valuable information," was his comment, closing the book.

"West is a keen observer," Ben said. "The comments he makes are pertinent."

Reaching for the diary, he asked, "May I read a few passages which I regard as significant, and which might yield us a better basis for our speculations?"

"Shoot!" was Denny's laconic reply.

Denny listened intently. I lay there tickled pink to think that maybe I was making definite contribution to the council of the sleuths.

June 16. . . . Martini moved in this evening. Ralston had a contractor in for consultation on construction of a 'shop' for his artificer to use upon our return from this momentous journey we are about to undertake. This shop will be directly off the "tomb" and communicate via the servants' hall with the kitchen and back porch. It will be rigged up while we are away. . . . Martini has clamped his eyes on Mildred Manning. No wonder, for she's some woman! Tawny hair, such as Titian thrilled to paint, with provocative glints of gold in it. S. A. and to spare. No wonder the men in this house find her easy to look at! Disturbing, I say. Martini won't stand a chance; she has fallen for Paul.

June 17. Ralston via radiogram today engaged a villa in Venice. Sent instructions for fitting up there of a workroom for Pietro. R. means to win that wager made with M. Cornier. . . . Pietro has joined family circle with surprising ease. Sang for Mildred in music room last night. Family all present. Paul left shortly, looking moody as Pluto, and drove away in the roadster.

June 18. Up early to exercise in gym. About to step out of my room, I heard voices in passage over the porte-cochere. What I heard arrested my steps. . . . "You've got to marry me, Mildred!" Paul was saying, passionately earnest. I stepped back inside my door, listening. Wonder of it is that the whole second floor didn't hear them, for they were so concerned with themselves that they weren't cautious. I heard Mildred say, "You know I can't Paul." But Paul wouldn't hear to her saying that, for he came right back at her with, "You've got to, I say!" She seemed to hesitate; then said, firmly, "No, Paul, I don't have to; and I won't. You mustn't talk so to me; not when I'm promised to another." "Promised!" he retorted, bitterly. "Who made that promise? You didn't. Good God, Mildred, can't you see this thing as I do?" "My father made it impossible for me to do anything but marry your father," came her answer. "I consider myself bound—" Paul broke in with, "Do you think I am going to submit passively to the wrecking of both our lives? . . . You love me, don't you?" "Paul, it came like a revelation from God when you met me in the Pullman the other day. All that night—" At that moment the door of Mrs. Wilmorton's suite opened and Freda came out. . . .

"Freda?" Hal Denny interrupted Ben's reading to ask.

"Freda was Julia Wilmorton's maid at the time," I informed him.

"What became of her?"

"None of us know. Fifi had taken her place when we returned from abroad," I replied.

"Uh-huh. Well, rattle on, Bailey—keep piling up evidence against young Ralston."

Ben continued to read.

This evening I went onto the terrace overlooking the sunken garden . . . Mildred and Pietro were strolling the graveled paths. . . . They came to a central grass plot, where Mildred put the sundial between herself and Pietro. Their hands met across it. Ten minutes passed, with Mildred doing most of the talking. Paul came out about then. His hands clenched; I heard him mutter something uncomplimentary about Pietro. Presently Mildred turned toward the house, walking slowly, with drooping head. Pietro stood by dial, watching her go. When she passed into the house, he dropped to his knees, covering his face with his hands. Paul angrily followed Mildred. . . . Later, the contractor came with plans for Pietro's Windermere shop. When the contractor left, Mr. R., Paul, and Pietro had a session on the big Spanish sofa in "the tomb", talking over definite plans—what we should do in Italy and China, and what Paul would do while we were away. As the three of them talked, I noticed how Ralston always had ready ear for Pietro—turning from Paul to hear what the Italian had to say and leaving Paul to address the air, as it were. The look that came over Paul's face at such moments wasn't pleasant to see. After a while he slouched back into his corner of the sofa, glowering darkly. . . .

June 19. This afternoon Julia Wilmorton and Paul held forth on the Spanish sofa, indifferent to my presence in the room. "Paul," she said, "why did you have to fall in love with Mildred Manning? You knew about that ridiculous will." "Sure I knew." "You must give up this idea of marrying Mildred," Mrs. Wilmorton urged. "Can't you see what the consequences will be? Mildred will lose her fortune, and you will be cut off by your father—" Paul insisted that if Mildred loved him, she'd let the fortune slide. "It will go to you then, Aunt Julia. . . ."

Ben paused, ostensibly to enjoy another cigarette.

"As pretty a yarn as I ever listened to," said Detective Denny. "Makes it darker and darker for Paul Ralston. Throws a shadow of suspicion over Mrs. Wilmorton, too—don't it? She sure had a motive for murdering Ralston. Jeez! What a mess it all is. There's the Italian's infatuation for Miss Manning. . . . But—Mrs. Wilmorton. Huh!"

"You don't think that Julia Wilmorton would kill Howard Ralston to keep him from marrying Miss Manning, do you?" I asked.

"Why not?" demanded Denny. "The money left by Basil Manning goes to her if this here Miss Mildred don't marry Ralston, don't it?"

"I know about the will only as I have picked up remarks here and there," I answered. "I don't know that Mildred's inheritance goes to Mrs. Wilmorton in case of Ralston's death before the marriage—that is, providing Miss Manning were agreeable to going through with the wedding."

"Well, that's a item we gotta find out about. In the meantime, Bailey, you might as well tell me what idea's bitten you. Who killed Howard Ralston?"

"I have my suspect spotted," Ben answered. "But you wouldn't believe me if I told you."

"I might laugh, at that—if you got your suspect outen this here diary."

"I sensed my suspect before ever I saw this diary. The very nature of the crime told me what the suspect would be like. The diary merely confirmed my suspicion."

"Why don't you nab the murderer?"

"We require something more than suspicion behind an arrest, Denny. There's checking to be done—certain facts to uncover."

"Here's wishing you luck!" Denny mocked. "Hal Denny has his suspects listed, and he's going to get the murderer through a nice little process of elimination."

"And your present suspects are?"

"Sure, I'll tell. Paul Ralston, Pietro Martini, Mrs. Wilmorton, Mr. Cornier, Miss Manning, and Winston West."

"Nice list, Denny. And here's wishing you luck!"

Ben could mock, too—only his mocking of Hal Denny made that gentleman red in the face.

"Since you have included my name among your suspects," I wanted to know of Denny, "why not include the Duke of Vedena and Mrs. Lansing, the guys that have been passing dragon cards to Howard Ralston, and the Brothers of Karnak—"

"Huh?"

"What about Fifi Burgoyne?" Ben asked.

"What about the whole damned outfit?" bellowed Hal Denny. "What about you, Benjamin Bailey? How do I know you wasn't in on this murder?"

"How indeed?" murmured Ben. "I could have been. I'm a frequent visitor at *Windermere,* you know."

"Say," yawned Sleepy Wallingford, roused by the shouting of his chief, "I dreamed we found the body."

"Aw, shut up!"

Sleepy obliged, settling back for another nap.

"How much consideration have you given the missing mummy, Denny?" Ben asked. "That disappearance is rather singular, you know."

"Just a bluff," Denny insisted, reverting to his original idea on the subject. "That mummy'll turn up, and you'll see that it don't have no connection with this here murder."

2

The conversation was interrupted by a knock upon my door. Denny admitted a smiling Mrs. O'Grady, who came bearing a tray in her hand.

"For me?" I asked, pleased at her thoughtfulness.

"Oi'm that sorry, Mr. West," Delia replied. "It's a malted milk for the Eyetalian. He ain't feeling so good."

"We could all do with one," Denny broadly hinted.

"Ain't that loike the Irish in yuh?" Delia retorted. And of me she inquired, "How is our patient now?"

"Feeling punk," I told her.

"Just a minute," she said, moving toward the door. "Let me set this tray on the table out in the hall. Oi'll be right back, sure now."

Delia went out into the hall, placing—as we afterwards learned—the tray with Pietro's malted milk on a console table that stood between Paul's room and mine. Returning to my room, she closed the door and ordered Ben and Denny to keep their distance while she communed with me.

Into my ear she whispered that maybe I could do with a "nip" from her private stock. I assured her that I jolly well could, and whispered back that it would be generous of her to treat the other boys, too.

"Sure now, and that's what Oi'm planning to do, only Oi thought Oi would be after asking you first. Oi'll be back in a jiffy. Soon's Oi've served the Eyetalian."

As she opened the door to pass out, she was confronted by Paul. She stood aside to let him enter, then went her way.

"How's West?" Paul inquired of Ben.

"He'll be feeling jake when he gets what Delia's bringing him," I answered ahead of Ben.

"Sounds as if I'd better stick around," Paul grinned.

"We'd rather you didn't," Denny bluntly told him. "We're discussing aspects of the case."

"What I want is action!" Paul snapped back at him. "If you'd quit discussing and let Bailey tell you what to do and how to do it—"

"Yeah! An' is my face red? Me letting an amatoor dick tell me what to do!"

In truth, his face was red. What might have been said further, I could only guess; for Delia poked her sorrel head in at my door to say that Pietro wanted a sandwich and that she would be delayed in bringing my refreshment. I assured her that it was quite all right to wait upon Pietro first.

"Why do you hate the Italian?" Denny asked Paul.

"Why shouldn't I hate him? He's tried to rob me of everything I hold dear in life—the girl I love, the affection of my father—"

"Hold everything, Paul," Ben warned. "Be careful what you say."

"I'm convinced that Martini killed Dad," Paul stubbornly persisted.

As the words fell from his lips, the picture of him and Pietro sitting down there in "the tomb" with Howard Ralston's blood staining the floor between them flashed before my mind. "You'd like to kill him, wouldn't yuh?" Denny purred.

"It would be doing him as he deserves!" Paul retorted.

"Please, Paul," Ben begged.

"Oh, all right!" Paul grumbled, and left us.

"Young Ralston's got hatred in his heart and blood in his eye," Denny said.

"Paul says things impulsively," Ben argued. "Things he doesn't mean, just as he did in that mash note to Miss Manning."

"Yeah? Well, I don't want that second murder you been talking about."

Down the hall, Delia O'Grady's voice shrilled in high quavering scream, and there was a crash of china.

I leaped from the bed and plunged after Denny and Ben as they dashed from my room and tore down the corridor. Bursting into Pietro's room, we saw him on the bed. His right arm hung limp over the bed's edge, and below his relaxed hand lay a glass from which the malted milk had not been entirely drunk. What was left of the beverage spread pool-like upon the polished floor.

"He was loike that whin Oi came in with the sandwich," wailed Delia.

Denny bent over Pietro, laying ear to his heart. He felt for the pulse.

"Dead?" whispered Ben.

"I don't know."

To Sleepy Wallingford, who finally mosied in, Denny said, "Go down and call Dr. Kelsey."

"What if the line ain't repaired?" queried Sleepy.

"Go where there *is* a phone."

Denny regarded the fallen tumbler.

"Poisoned, I calculate," he said. "Mrs. O'Grady, who mixed that drink for Martini?"

"With me own hands, Oi mixed it, Mr. Denny."

"Anybody see yuh doing it?"

"Deborah."

"Did she get near it?"

"She did not!"

"Anybody else—"

He broke off, whistling softly as a thought struck him. "Mrs. O'Grady, you left the malted milk on the table in the hall while you visited with West. . . . Where is Paul Ralston?"

"Oi saw his door closing as Oi came up with the sandwich," Mrs. O'Grady informed Denny.

"Why ain't he here?" Denny demanded. "He could of heard Mrs. O'Grady screaming."

"So could any of the others," Ben reminded him. "They aren't here."

But some of them were—Fifi, Deborah, Brookes, Johns, Mary Rose. They came crowding to the door; and shortly after them, the policemen who had been in the house.

Denny brushed them all aside. With Ben at his heels, he crossed the hall and burst unannounced into Paul's chambers. The rooms were empty. As we stood there, wondering where Paul could be, the whisper of trickling water came to us from beyond the closed door of Paul's bathroom. Ben rapped upon that ominously closed door.

"Paul!"

There was no response.

"It's I, Ben!"

Only the whisper of trickling water answered him. Ben tried the door, but it was locked—bolted on the inside.

"My God!" groaned Ben. "He's in there—maybe dead!"

"Probably killed hisself," mumbled Denny, "after knocking off the *wop*."

Ben turned fiercely upon Denny.

"You great big blundering ass!" he shouted. "If Paul's dead by his own hand, you've driven him to the deed!"

"Hey, you!" Denny yelled back. "What you accusing me of?"

Ben's face sobered.

"Forget it, Denny," he begged. "Remember, Paul's my best friend."

Hal Denny clasped Ben's hand.

"Forget what I said, will yuh?" he begged, in turn. "I guess I'm nerts over this here case. As sure as we're here to talk about it, there's a maniac loose on these premises. There's no telling what's going to happen next."

By this time Brookes had fetched a chisel and was busy at the bolted door. Feverishly he worked, chipping and prying, all the time praying under his breath that the young master wasn't dead. We who stood watching him wondered what that door, when opened, would reveal. Brookes' efforts were fruitless. The bolt, like all bolts of *Windermere*, was long and firmly set.

"There's nothing but to bust it in," Denny advised.

Two beefy policemen threw their combined weight against it, time after time, until finally the hinges gave and the heavy door crashed inward, falling upon Paul's body, where it lay—half-clothed—upon the bathroom floor. Both spigots were turned on and the water was trickling over the side of the tub in whispering splash upon the tiled floor of the bathroom.

We lifted the door and picked Paul up.

"Well?" Ben fiercely demanded, as we lay the unconscious boy upon his bed.

"I don't know," was Denny's dull answer.

"Look," I pointed out, "he must have been washing his teeth!"

Clenched in Paul's right hand was his toothbrush. His mouth was still foamy from the scrubbing he had given his teeth.

From Paul's contorted features, Ben's glance swung to Denny's startled blue eyes.

"Howard Ralston!" Ben whispered, awesomely. "Pietro! Paul! . . . Denny, there's but one heir left! Quick, we must get to Miss Manning's room!"

3

Like madmen we raced down the hall to Mildred Manning's room.

"She isn't here!" cried Mary Rose.

"Where is she?"

"I don't know," the frightened maid replied. "She was here fifteen minutes ago when I went down to the basement."

"Didn't you come from this room when yuh run down there to where we was with the Italian?"

"I had just come from the basement, where I had gone to burn some trash for Miss Manning—"

"Trash!" ejaculated Denny.

He was about to investigate Miss Manning's room, when a shriek from the adjoining suite spun him about.

Following Ben's lead, he dashed into Julia Wilmorton's apartment. There we found Mildred Manning slumped in a chair, unconscious, breathing faintly. Her pallid hands were pressed against her stomach, as though she had suffered intense pain before passing out. On the bed, in the room beyond, lay Julia Wilmorton, apparently dead.

There was nothing to do but to have Fifi and Mary Rose and Johns get their respective patients into bed and await the arrival of Dr. Kelsey from headquarters. Brookes was assigned to care for Pietro. Those tasks set, Denny and Ben retired to my room.

"I had a teacher oncet who read me a story about somebody killing seven at one stroke," Denny rumbled, as he strode to and fro, "but I ain't never seen nothing like this before. Four at one stroke! What you make of it, Bailey?"

"One of two things," Ben calmly replied. "Deliberate attempt at murder, or a successful attempt to hinder four parties from contributing anything toward the solution of this crime."

"They can't get away with it," Denny boasted. "They tried it on West here, and he's still talking."

"True. But whoever did this can accomplish a great deal while we're working on these people he's laid out. The four won't be able to talk for some time, and he can elude us in the meantime."

"Let him try it!" thundered Denny, his cigar flaming like a Pittsburgh furnace. "I've got this place surrounded."

"Criminals as clever as those with whom we are dealing can walk invisible, Mr. Denny."

"Seems to me you did mention secret rooms," Denny said, derisively. "Heck, they don't build houses like that these days."

Ben merely lifted his brows and carelessly flicked ash from his cigarette.

"Of course," Denny conceded, "this here Howard Ralston must have been the queer one. There's no telling what kind of a house he'd build."

Denny strode to the window and jerked back the drapes. "Why the hell don't Kelsey get here?" he demanded.

"We're out some distance," Ben said. "Remember, you've only just called him. It will take time for him to make the drive out here."

"Let's do something," Denny urged, facing us. "We got to pass time."

"We might go on with West's diary."

"Anything goes! I'm too blamed flabbergasted to care what. Shoot the works!"

As Ben was selecting passages to read, Sleepy Wallingford barged in with information that Dr. Kelsey was on his way. That message delivered, he sprawled in my favorite chair and was soon whistling in slumber.

"Crew all settled?" Ben asked with a chuckle.

Casting a disdainful glance at his assistant, Denny grunted, "Let's go!"

"Righto!" said Ben. "This next section gives items concerning the voyage from New York to Cherbourg and introduces an intriguing lady, whose honest-to-God name didn't appear on the passenger list."

"Now what?" Denny wanted to know.

"Keep your ears open, Denny. I'm playing ball with you." Ben began reading.

June 22. Second day out. . . . This afternoon I eluded Pietro, weary of his playing mollusk to me. . . . Tonight as I was entering the promenade deck for a stroll and a quiet smoke before calling it a day, I came unexpectedly upon him, leaning on the rail and gazing out over the waters. In the palm of his left hand lay a miniature. . . . Pietro did not stir when I joined him, except to close his hand over the miniature. . . . "You ought to be in a chair beside one of the nice girls we have aboard," I said. "They do not interest me." "Off the women?" "Forever!" "I've said that myself; but we always go back to them." "Not so with me," he averred. "My heart is too strongly held." And then, impulsively, he confided in me, saying, "I am hopelessly in love. The very despair of it is poignantly beautiful!" "Miss Manning?" The name slipped unbidden from my lips. . . . Pietro opened his clenched hand, frankly displaying a miniature carrying her lovely countenance. "She has told me that she is going to marry the Master. But she was angel-kind—she gave me this!" He carried the portrait to his lips. "She will marry him; but I shall hold her enshrined in my soul forever. He cannot deny me that privilege. . . . No other woman shall ever reign there! And as a symbol of the goddess enshrined within, I shall always wear this blessed miniature over my heart."

"So that way the wind blows!" muttered Hal Denny. "And the odor it carries ain't so pleasant in my nostrils neither. That wop could have did it, Bailey."

"Reserve your judgment," Ben advised him, and read on.

June 23. Third Day. . . . Pietro didn't appear at dinner. I started out to search for 'him' and found 'them' . . . in the verandah cafe. . . .

"A skirt chaser, is he?" Denny interrupted.

"Evidently the miniature over his heart was no protection against love darts," Ben murmured, drily. "But listen."

June 24. Lonely day for me. Ralston played cribbage with first mate; Pietro danced attendance upon his blonde British-er. She's wistful, making me think of Tennyson's Elaine. Last night he woke me up when he came in. He raved about 'Gwendolyn Seabury.' "Isn't it a beautiful name! . . . Tomorrow we land. The next day she has in Paris; and I plan to be with her and her Aunt Amy. . . ."

June 25. Paris. . . . Busy day. . . . No glimpse of Pietro since we left Cherbourg. . . .

June 26. Aboard Rome Express. . . . Pietro arrived just before our departure. He was a sight. He mumbled something about being 'beaten up' by an infuriated chauffeur who had run him down on the boulevard. I noted that the diamond no longer sparkled on his finger. . . . Finally we got the truth out of him— the story of his Parisian misadventure and the fact that he no longer had an account at our Minneapolis bank. "You!" Mr. Ralston derided. "To let the blonde Gwendolyn Seabury lead you like a lamb to the slaughter!" "Well," Pietro complained, "how was I to know that 'Aunt Amy' was her husband?"

Hal Denny shook with laughter—boisterous laughter that was echoed by Sleepy Wallingford.

"Damned interesting account of the smart boy being out-smarted," opined Detective Denny, wiping tears from his eyes.

"Damned vital account, I'd say," was Ben's comment.

"Vital, huh! What you mean?"

Smiling cryptically at Denny, Ben said, "I want to be helpful, but not too helpful. I've led you to what I regard as the spring of knowledge in this case. Drink if you want to."

"Okay!" The big Irishman was good-natured about it. "So where do we go from here?"

"We might go to Italy and to China."

"Let's get on our way, so long's it don't cost nothing to travel."

But the journey wasn't made just then, for Brookes ushered Dr. Kelsey into the room.

4

"Well," demanded Denny, when Dr. Kelsey returned thirty minutes later to report on his examination of the four victims.

"Poisoned," was the police surgeon's laconic reply.

"Poisoned!" we echoed.

"And lucky to be alive," said Kelsey. "Young Mr. Ralston's in the worst shape of any. He may not pull through."

"He's got to live," Ben muttered, hoarsely. "He's got to live to see this thing cleared up."

"Better call in the family physician," Kelsey advised. "I'd like to consult with him."

I ran down to put the call through. Fortunately the telephone company's men had come and gone, leaving the telephone as fit as ever after repairing the wires where they had been cut up under the eaves.

Dr. Kelsey was summarizing his findings when I returned to my room.

"The Italian," he was saying, "must have been poisoned by the Malted milk. I'm sending the glass and such of the spilled contents as I could scrape up to the laboratories. Mrs. Wilmorton and Miss Manning seem to have drunk from the carafe in Mrs. Wilmorton's bedroom. That carafe, with its crazy water, has also gone to the laboratory."

"Crazy water?" queried Denny.

"Made by dissolving crazy water crystals in ordinary drinking water," Dr. Kelsey explained. "Lots of people drink it. Regard it as a sort of cure-all. Mrs. O'Grady informed me that Mrs. Wilmorton lately had begun using it. They prepare it for her in the kitchen, and a fresh supply had just been poured into the carafe."

"That'll bear looking into," opined Denny.

"What about Paul Ralston?" Ben anxiously inquired. "What had been given him?"

"You mean what did he take, huh?"

Ben disregarded Detective Denny's insinuation, keeping his eyes upon Dr. Kelsey.

"I don't know, Mr. Bailey," Kelsey replied. "But that toothbrush and the foam on his lips look suspicious to me. The brush has gone to the laboratory."

"How long will our patients be out?" Denny wanted to know.

"That depends, Denny. Maybe twenty-four hours. Not knowing the poisons, I can't venture a safe guess."

It was decided that there was nothing to do but to mark time. We would go on with the diary, Denny agreed, until the Ralston physician arrived.

Taking the diary, Ben cleared his throat, preparatory to further reading.

"Hold it!" Denny suddenly commanded. And as Ben looked inquiringly at him, he asked, "Is that all there is about that there English dame?"

"No," Ben softly replied, "that isn't all. We'll hear of her again in these next episodes, which also introduce the 'signorina' and throw further light upon the secret love-life of our passionate pilgrim—heart-ensnaring Pietro Martini."

"Well, I'm glad he ain't dead, at that," swore Denny.

Ben read on.

June 27. Rome. Antona Reni, swarthy and suave, met us upon our arrival and accompanied us to our hotel. . . "How about my three prizes?" Ralston at once demanded of his Italian agent. With much sighing, much rolling of bulging eyes, and considerable gesticulation with pudgy hands, Antona Reni answered, "The mummy of Serapion—si, si, signor, I have that! and the vengeance dagger of the Scarlet Dragons, yes; but not the Borgia poison ring! Son of the Virgin—that it was impossible to obtain." . . . Ralston dismissed the apologies with wave of hand. "Venetian villa and shop ready?" he asked. They were . . . . And the Syrian representative of Ralston's Italian agent was waiting, Reni informed us. H. R. gave the word; the Syrian was shown up. . . . "Meester Ralston, yes, the mummy is ready for shipment; but the risk and the cost has been much greater—" . . . It was arranged that the money be deposited with Signor Reni, to be paid to the Syrian after Ralston returned home and found the mummy genuine and in satisfactory condition. With benedictions upon the head of his benefactor and with handsome gratuity in hand, the Syrian smirked out of our lives.

"Who knew that there mummy was being bought and shipped?" asked Denny.

"Nobody was supposed to know, other than the parties involved in the transaction," I answered.

"What yuh mean?"

"Well, Mr. Ralston was tricky about that," I replied. "He had the mummy encased in what was apparently a solid slab from a Babylonian palace. It was shipped from Port Said, frankly addressed to *Howard Ralston, Esq., Minneapolis, Minnesota, U. S. A.* The continental journals carried stories telling how the noted American archeologist anticipated that inscriptions on the slab would make specific contribution to a problem long puzzling Mesopotamian scholars."

"But some one must of knowed," declared Denny.

"Some one did know," Ben offered.

"Yeah?"

"Later, Denny."

Hal Denny regarded Bailey suspiciously, but finally urged him to continue his reading.

With the mummy business dispatched, Signor Reni informed Ralston that the vengeance dagger of the Scarlet Dragons would be delivered to us in Shanghai. Reni laid in R's hand a disc of pale green jade, engraved with characters that would identify R to Reni's Chinese agent. . . . "But the poison ring! Ah, signor, I am unutterably chagrined. There I have failed you. The Duke will not sell." "Does he know for whom you sought the ring?" "I have been too discreet for that, signor." "Good. You need not worry, Signor Reni. I anticipated just such a situation, and have come prepared to meet it. . . ."

June 28. Venice. Today sees us established in our villa here. I contacted the Duke of Vedena, who was delighted to learn that so distinguished an antiquarian as Howard Ralston was in Venice. He invited us to call and view his collections. We were prompt in the appointment. 'Marco,' pompous major-domo of the ducal palace, received and conducted us into the presence of the Duke, who proudly displayed his collections, and graciously permitted us to examine the Borgia poison ring. . . . At four we were back at the villa. Ralston and I watched Pietro execute drawings of the ring of death. Following a satisfactory completion of the general sketch, Pietro enlarged upon

*details, making calculations and notes. He made memoranda
of contours and measurements that the next examination of
the 'Borgia' must yield him.*

*June 29. Tonight we were the Duke's guests at the opera. 'Tro-
vatore' was the offering. Pietro sat bored through three acts.
The first seen, of the last act had ended, when Pietro's attention riveted upon the box opposite. A beautiful woman had
entered it, arriving late—after the Italian fashion, I concluded—solely to hear a single favorite number. Pietro alarmed
me with the boldness of his stare, but the fair unknown took no
notice. . . . At the ducal palace, to which we were invited after
the opera, we found a cosmopolitan crowd assembled in the
brilliantly lighted rooms. I remained close to Ralston, in the
card room; but now and again I glimpsed an exuberant Pietro
in the company of the lady of the opera. She was Francesca,
nineteen-year-old daughter of our host. Francesca was slim
and athletic, with boyish features through which lovely fem-
ininity managed to reveal itself. Her short hair was golden
brown, in color like the autumn leaf, and clusteringly curly.
As I watched them together, I wondered if Pietro would again
be swept off his feet. . . . When we returned to our villa about
six this morning, Pietro came into my room to rave. "What of
Miss Manning?" I asked. He paled and his hand covered the
spot where the miniature reposed, hidden against his flesh.
"Mildred is my true passion!" he breathed. "But she is for me
beyond obtaining. She is the Master's, and I am loyal to him.
But, Francesca—"*

*July 1. Letter from Paul. He writes: "You saw and heard
enough to realize the situation. I love Mildred; she loves me.
The only way in which we can have each other is to break and
run away; neither of us will do that. However, this state of
affairs cannot endure endlessly. I shall stay here to look after
things while you are away; but as soon as you return, I'm off
for Chile or the Argentine. . . . West, I want to ask a favor of
you. Keep an eye on Martini. I don't like his psychology, and I*

don't want his hold on Dad strengthened. He might not stop at blackmail. . . Have you ever thought that Martini might possess sadistic tendencies? . . . And he would take Mildred, if he could get her. . . ."

July 2. Pietro spends much time in his shop, perfecting plans for creating duplicate 'Borgia.' Last night he was with Francesca. That she loves him, he is positive. That he loves her? Ah, in a man's way! He will keep her guessing. . . . What the Duke thinks of this romance, I cannot surmise. Anyway, Francesca is as much of a pagan as Pietro. . . .

July 5. Situation resolves in our favor; for while Ralston is with Duke, Pietro is with Francesca—she madly in love with him. On many strolls through the collection rooms, Francesca humors Pietro's desire to examine the 'Borgia.' As a result, our artificer has been able to make necessary corrections in his drawings and measurements. He has mastered the vicious mechanism of the ring. . . .

"Phooey!" exclaimed Detective Denny. "This here diary's interesting enough, but it ain't getting us nowheres."

"Think not?" Ben quietly asked.

"You heard me!"

"It's telling us everything we need to know in securing a working basis for the solution of this case," Ben stubbornly insisted. "If you'll only listen while I finish it, we can go into discussion of its revelations."

"All right, big private investigator; but make it snappy."

Before Ben could resume his reading, Dr. Kelsey came in with Dr. Howard, the Ralston family physician. Both men looked grave.

"None of the patients will die," Kelsey assured Denny. "They've had close calls, but indications are that they should pull through. A special nurse, I believe, had better be called in. I'll attend to that for you Denny, sending out Miss Lutie, who is a regular member of our department."

"That," said Denny, "ain't a bad idea."

"That's about all we can accomplish until the analyses come from the laboratory."

"Poison, you both agree?"

"No doubt of it, Denny."

"Then there's a sure 'nough devil loose in this house, and we gotta get him—"

"Or her," Ben finished.

5

Now where do we go from here?" Detective Denny, looking and acting like a perplexed man in a London fog, inquired of nobody in particular.

"You requested me to play ball with you," Ben murmured—somewhat wearily, I thought. "In view of that fact it might be wise to continue reading West's diary."

"That damned diary ain't telling us nothing!"

"It has told me a great deal," Ben insisted. "But then you and I would look at this case from different angles."

"I figger," Denny said, crustily, "that we better run down this here poisoner. Don't you realize, young feller, that there's a criminal at large in this here house?"

"I know," Ben returned, "that he isn't going to get away if you boys are alert. Our criminal doesn't dare make a move toward escape. I know, too, that until you get that laboratory report on the suspected poison, we aren't in possession of sufficient facts to act on. Now West's diary—"

"Go ahead," Denny groaned, resigned to his fate. "It'll help pass time, if nothing else."

"I advise," Ben admonished him, "that you give discriminating thought to what I read; for, unless I be mistaken, the key to our mystery lies right here."

"You may be all wet," complained Denny, lighting one of his stogies.

"My treat if I am."

"Mine, if you ain't."

Denny smoked glumly, Sleepy dozed, I listened intently.

July 8. This morning Howard Ralston looked up from the Paris edition of 'The Chicago Post' to stare at Pietro. "What—?" the Italian began. Howard Ralston read the following, which I afterwards clipped:—

The notorious international swindler, Chic Quayle, known as 'king of world crooks,' is believed to have entered the United States *via* Canada, New York police announced today. It is thought that he is accompanied by his clever partner in many crimes, who is known to the police of three continents as Marietta Gale, *alias* Riviera Fannie, *alias* Gwendolyn Seabury. . . .

"Oh, my 'Aunt Amy'!" I exclaimed, in my turn staring at our artificer. "I imagine," H. R. said, "that during tender exchange of confidences with the dreamy-eyed lady of our crossing, you let her pump considerable information from, you?" "Please forgive, Mr. Ralston," Pietro implored, miserably, "but I did tell her about the Josephine diamonds. . . ." "Tell her anything else?" the boss drily queried. "Yes, about the mummy—" "And the dagger and the ring," I finished for him. . . . There ensued a flock of radiograms, bringing reply from Paul that he and 'Aunt Julia' had found everything intact. . . .

July 9. Last night Pietro regained his place in Ralston's good graces by displaying the finished duplicate of the 'Borgia.' R. immediately planned exchange of duplicate for original. . . . Fortune favored us. The Duke telephoned, informing us that he was leaving for an unanticipated holiday with friends. Pietro brightened at that news. Drawing a key from his key-ring, he explained that it was a duplicate of key to case in which the 'Borgia' was kept—a duplicate created from a wax impression he covertly obtained from the original. . . . He telephoned Francesca, telling her that it was our last night in Venice. . . . Radiant, he left the instrument, exclaiming, "Tonight I am to be admitted at the postern gate, which I shall manage to leave unlatched for you." . . . At ten o'clock Howard Ralston passed through that postern gate, leaving me on guard there. At eleven we had returned to our villa, the genuine 'Borgia' concealed in the hollow handle of my traveling bag. . . .

At 4 a.m., the villa telephone jangled. An unfamiliar voice purred into my ear the ominous words: "Signor Reni begs that Mr. Howard Ralston come to him at once." . . . Armed, we called a gondola and went directly to Reni's residence. The front door was ajar. Nevertheless, we pressed the buzzer. Repeated buzzings elicited no response. Donning gloves and gripping our revolvers, we slipped into Antona Reni's domicile, to find him sitting in his study chair, a sealed letter in his lifeless hand. There was no wound—no mark of violence on his body. . . . "Looks like a case of heart collapse," ventured Ralston. . . . Gingerly he slid the letter from between the dead man's fingers, for the missive was addressed to "Mr. Howard Ralston." Breaking the seal, he read:—

> *Mr. Howard Ralston—*
> *Behold, your agent has paid and the mark of death is not seen upon him. So will it be with you who do wrong so easily. We spare you until you return to your native land. You cannot make restitution now; but unless you make it then, the fleshless finger will still your heart. Be warned. Act if you would live.*
>
> *IMPERATOR*

Ralston bade us not to touch anything, warning that our visit to Reni's house must never be known.

"Uh-huh!" Denny was alert. "There you got something. Them Egyptians could of murdered Ralston."

"I saw the *ka* point its fleshless finger at his heart. Mr. Ralston collapsed then," I volunteered.

"Think that mummy drove the Chinese dagger into his back?" Ben queried—rather skeptically, I thought.

"Well, uh—," Denny's voice rumbled into nothingness.

Ben read on.

July 10. Vienna. Escaped Venice via plane. . . . Ralston consulted celebrated Dr. Koster here today. Great heart specialist advised R. take every precaution—beware exertion or sudden shock. R. refused to be convinced. . . .

Ben paused. When Denny glanced up, he said, "That last statement should tell us something."

"What, eh?" asked Denny.

"Could it be," Ben hinted, "that some one capitalized on that weakness of Ralston's heart?"

"If you ask me," Denny put it, "This murder was incubated before Mr. Ralston got home. Nobody had time to find out about his heart before then."

"You are mistaken, Denny," Ben told him. "For years it has been known that Ralston suffered from a mild functional disturbance—"

"But where does it fit in? I know you want me to consider that Seabury woman, but I ain't thinking the Italian told her about Ralston's heart."

"We wouldn't know," Ben murmured. "Well, there is but little more I wish to read."

"Thank the saints for that promise, me lad!"

July 20. Shanghai. Wah King today exchanged vengeance dagger of Scarlet Dragons for a tiny piece of green jade and a satchel of Mexican dollars. . . . Ralston, afraid to carry the dagger with him, wrapped it and took it to the American consulate, whence a trusted acquaintance will express it to Dr. Lao Wong in Minneapolis.

Again Denny interrupted, stating, "That heathen Chinee could of done it. Him or Mr. Cornier."

Ben had no comment to make, but read on.

Returning to our hotel and opening the door to our suite, we found ourselves confronted with a ghastly tableau. In a chair, facing us, sat the corpse of Wah King, grim horror on his leathery face. His two arms had been extended to rest, palms upward, upon the arms of that chair of death. In one palm lay the jade identification disc; in the other, a clipping from a Cairo newspaper:—

Syrian antiquarian found strangled. . . .

Ralston's face ashened when he looked upon the dagger hilt jammed to the flesh between Wah King's naked shoulders.

"Holy jumping Judas!" Denny leaped to his feet. "It was them Chinee what did it. Lao Wong, sure's I'm Irish. Him and that Mr. Cornier."

"Why, then, was the clipping about the strangling of Antona Reni's Syrian agent brought into the Shanghai murder?" Ben asked.

"Coincidence," Denny maintained. "Jeez! My whole case right in my hand."

"It must be some case," Ben murmured, closing my diary.

"That all—of the diary?" asked Denny.

"Only a small portion of it," Ben told him. "But there's no need to read more than is sufficient for present discussion."

"Discussion hell! What's there to discuss? It's an open and shut case."

"I'd like to exchange at least a few ideas with you," Ben urged.

"Okay, if you insist. I suppose you want me to start the ball rolling?"

"When you're through, I'll talk."

Nauseated by the stench of Denny's stogy, I brought out a box of first class cigars that I had been secretly cherishing. It was funny—and painful, too—to see Sleepy revive and aid Denny in scooping up the weeds.

"Now," Denny began, settling to enjoyment of his cigar, "let us look at this here case sanely and impartially."

Ben and I smoked our cigarettes, possessing our souls in patience.

"According to this here diary," Denny continued, after seemingly ponderous thought, "young Ralston give up the idea of marrying Miss Manning. The letter he wrote to West in Venice would indicate that. But—he said he was going to South America, huh?" He glanced sharply at Ben. "He could of changed his mind, yuh know."

"He could have," Ben agreed.

"I'll say he did change it!" blurted Denny. "After what we seen and heard last night and this morning—"

"I still believe he meant to clear out," Ben came back at Denny. "I hold that he was sincere in that letter to West, while at the same time I admit that perhaps all along he was kidding himself and that in the depths of his subconscious mind he clung tenaciously to the hope that he could marry Mildred—"

"Exactly!" Denny hitched his chair nearer Ben's. "Now listen, Bailey. Howard Ralston was profoundly loyal in his friendships. Under conditions deriving from Basil Manning's will, as we apprehend it, he considered himself bound to carry out his dead friend's request. Now, wouldn't he?"

"Sure. Ralston was a theosophist. He lived in the everlasting moment—in the Eternal Now, as he would have put it. To him, Basil Manning was not dead, but living along with him in the ever-enduring Present. Between such souls strange ties hold: ties that bind men like Howard Ralston steadfast to their supposed obligations."

"Well, I don't know nothing about this here Theoposy. Too deep for me; but if you say it's that-a-way, we'll let the matter rest as per mutual consent." He burned away at his cigar, taking 'time out' for reflection. Then, "Take young Ralston further. He falls in love with the girl. Being a red-blooded young American, he wants his woman. He thinks Basil Manning's will damned foolishness—thinks his old man's attitude all wet. So he determines to have his woman at any cost. That's the spirit of his father in him; and from what I gather, he's a chip off'n the old block, as you say yourself. See?"

"You imply," Ben asked, incredulously, "that you have come to the conclusion that Paul Ralston deliberately killed his father?"

"Oh, not quite that. They quarreled. There was probably another quarrel we don't know about down there in 'the tomb', and the deed was done on the impulse of the moment. Fact that it was done with the Chinee dagger, nearest weapon at hand, shows that likely's not it was unpremeditated and done under stress of emotion—"

"But—"

"Hold it! What about the intended blow yesterday morning? Only the fact that Martini appeared unexpectedly on the scene—"

"But there's Mildred Manning's testimony."

"Shucks, we've gone over that oncet. It's all right, young feller; but just the same, I've motivated Paul Ralston's possible crime."

"There remain to be considered the mummy of Serapion and the Borgia poison ring."

"All right, they're there—or they was. Look, Paul Ralston naturally would want to divert suspicion away from hisself. He knew everybody knew about them threats and all, so why wouldn't he drag in the mummy and the ring—'slong as he had used the Chinee dagger as lethal weapon? Huh?"

"You fail to take into consideration the similarities between the murder of the Syrian in Cairo and of Wah Sing in Shanghai."

"No I don't, and I don't think Paul Ralston did either. That boy's a smart lad."

"I won't believe that Paul killed his father."

"You don't have to. I'm not saying he did. I'm only telling what might have happened."

"Don't the incidents recorded in West's diary convince you that Howard Ralston was menaced by parties outside his household and that one of them might have done him to his death?"

"Not particularly so, youngster. When you've been at this game as long as I have—"

"I'll learn a lot!"

Unperturbed by Ben's sarcasm, Denny asked, "Now, what about the Italian?"

"You say," Ben challenged.

"Made up your mind, eh?"

"Pretty much so."

"Guilty?"

"No. However, I'd sooner suspect him than I would Paul Ralston."

"Your privilege to think that way. I'm suspecting everybody until he's proven innocent."

"And that's your privilege, Mr. Denny."

"This here Pietro knew a lot, and he had plenty reason to want Howard Ralston dead and Paul Ralston outen the way. His track clear, he'd inherit his share of the old man's estate and maybe get the girl. He'd get a heap of money by marrying her. Maybe Mr. Cornier's right when he says that Italian's a bad egg."

"What do you think of M. Cornier as a suspect?"

"I think he could of done it. He had his reasons. Him more'n anybody else, maybe. Privileged to come and go as he damned please in this here house, he could of staged just such a pretty murder as we have on our hands."

"And what about the strange disappearance of Ralston's body—along with that mummy?" Ben further challenged.

"Jeez, I don't know what to think!" Detective Denny frowned. "A minute ago your blamed diary had me ready to believe it was them there Egyptians done it, and then I thought it was them Chinks. Hell, what's a man to think?"

"If you'd use your head," affably suggested Ben, "you might get somewhere."

"You telling me, you young whipper-snapper, you?"

"Now, listen to me," Ben said, hitching his chair toward Denny's. "When West came to me in these early morning hours and told me his crazy story, an idea got me. I've read a great deal about the work of the Paris *Surete,* you know. Well, this bizarre murder—"

I was sorry that the entrance of Dr. Kelsey cut short Ben's promised explanation. But what Kelsey had to say compelled our forgetfulness of hypotheses for the time.

"I have the laboratory reports," he told Denny. "Poison. In the case of Martini, Mrs. Wilmorton, and Miss Manning, the dope was *sodium phenobarbital.* What it was in Paul Ralston's case remains to be determined. But it was poison for him, too. Some trace of either *belladonna* or *atropin,* the report suggests. If the young man could have been observed before being overcome, there might have been observable evidence of excitation and delusions; but since he was wholly unconscious when found—"

"Meaning there must have been another poison, huh?"

"Evidence of its presence is there, but our specialists are unable to identify it as yet. Whatever it was, it must have been deadly. Fortunately, the victim didn't get enough of it—"

"How was it took?"

"Worked into the toothpaste he used. It seems to have possessed rapid penetrating propensity, working quickly into the blood through his gums."

"He'll pull through?"

"That appears uncertain. He may and he may not. Conditions are not as favorable as they were a bit ago. He's still in rigid coma, stubbornly refusing to respond to treatment. The muscles of his throat appear constricted, the pupils of his eyes are dilated, and he doesn't respond to any of the standard antidotes."

"Leading you to suppose that the poison may be one of those for-eign importations?" Ben quietly asked.

"That is my supposition," Dr. Kelsey answered, regarding Ben ap-preciatively.

"How long before the others'll come round?" Denny wanted to know.

"Depends upon the dosage administered. They may snap out of it right away. Again, it may take twenty-four hours for the effects of the drug to wear off."

"I want 'em out quick," Denny snapped. "I want 'em to talk."

"Their testimony may not be worth much," Dr. Kelsey told him. "*Sodium phenobarbital* stimulates hallucinations."

Denny swung his eyes upon me. He said, "Maybe that's what was shot into you."

"No," Ben had it. "I know what was given West," To me, he added, "It tightens, this theory of mine. That *L*-file is moving nearer my *OP*-file."

"Huh! What's that?"

Ben ignored Hal Denny, while he kept smiling at me. I couldn't figure out what *L* could stand for, but I was positive that *OP* signified "oriental poison."

"Look," Denny said, "it's clear enough to me. My mind's made up. These others was gave a mild poison—a drug that wouldn't kill 'em. But young Ralston, he knows the jig's up. He gives hisself a dose that'll save him from hanging. Get it?"

6

Denny and Ben had it up and down, then and there, over that remark on the possible suicide of Paul Ralston. Detective Denny insisted that he was right in concluding that Paul was the murderer we sought. Paul knew chemistry, he pointed out. He had worked in the drug store of a pal's father one summer, and there had enjoyed every opportunity to know about available poisons. Ben wanted to know where Paul got the *sodium phenobarbital,* and Denny drily remarked that they'd be find-ing out "all right, all right."

"Paul Ralston got it, anyhow," Denny continued. "He could of got into Mrs. Wilmorton's bathroom and mixed it with the crazy water crystals in the white and green box she kept in the medicine cabinet on her bathroom wall, or he could have dropped it into the carafe when it was filled down in the kitchen."

Mrs. O'Grady and Deborah were thereupon quizzed about Paul's visits to and movements in the kitchen, but neither could be definite in their memory of Paul's activities. That he had visited the kitchen, they knew; but what he did, they could not say.

"Granting Paul obtained *sodium phenobarbital*," Ben argued on, "where would he get the poison that I suspect was worked into his toothpaste? That drug is rare in this country and obtainable only under extreme difficulties."

"Which proves, I suppose, that somebody else than Paul Ralston slung all these here poisons around so careless like. Huh!"

"Your deductions are most logical, Mr. Denny."

"Sure they are. I know my principles."

"Rot!" exclaimed Ben, mad through and through.

"Sure—rotten's what I call it," agreed Denny. "I know you think I'm haywire; but just the same, you'll be seeing. Remember that Paul hisself said right here in this room that if he killed the Italian, Martini would be getting his deserts. And all the time that poisoned milk was setting out on that funny table in the hall."

"But—"

"There ain't no 'buts' about it, Bailey. Mrs. O'Grady comes in here on her way to the Italian's room with the malted milk, and when we gets to hinting for a drink, she goes out and sets the tray with the malted milk in the hall. She came back in, didn't she, and we had our little fun—whispering and all that? And when Mrs. O'Grady goes to leave, who does she meet coming in?"

"Paul," Ben had to confess.

"There you have it. Paul Ralston was watching his chance; he took it when Mrs. O'Grady set that milk down out there in the deserted hall."

"I suppose you think that Paul deliberately mixed some stuff into his own toothpaste?"

"Who else was there to do it?"

"Why should Paul want to kill himself?"

"I already said, didn't I? He seen me closing in—knew I was getting him. Figured it would be easier to put hisself outen the way than to have the state do it."

"But why kill the others?"

"Well, with them dead, there'd be none to testify against him. He thought it a comfortable feeling, maybe, to die with the knowledge that his name wouldn't be smirched. None of us likes to die thinking the world is going to set in judgment on us."

"Think what you want to," said Ben. "As for myself, I stick to my original theory."

"Which is what?"

"That a party not of this household, but with the aid of a party or parties in this house, murdered Howard Ralston. The moment West told me how the murder was engineered, I knew the type of individual that did it. There isn't a single person of that type at *Windermere*."

"Piffle!" sneered Denny. "You're the guy what's haywire."

"You know, Denny," Ben irritatingly continued, "there's Pietro Martini's stranger. His appearance upon the scene certainly was not altogether accidental. Pietro not only lied about his adventure last night, but he also lied when he said that he did not know the identity of this stranger."

"Say, who is this Romeo, anyway?" Denny demanded.

For answer, Ben said, "See West's diary."

"I want to know who Romeo is!" Denny thundered.

"I know you do, Denny. So do I. But, unlike yourself, I have a clue and I've put one of my operatives on Romeo's trail."

"Yeah!" Denny eyed Ben with poorly concealed admiration. "That's fine—saves me the trouble."

"What I want to know," mumbled Sleepy Wallingford from the depths of his chair, "is how Howard Ralston made that lightning change of clothes out there in the hall last night—"

"Baloney!" said Denny, affecting a lofty air of superiority. "Brookes probably made a mistake and got a taste of that there—that there—"

"*Sodium phenobarbital*," Ben finished for him. "But don't pass up Mr. Wallingford's suggestion too lightly, Denny. There's something deucedly strange about that man on the roof and Ralston's lightning change from Tuxedo to business suit and back again—"

"Come in!" Hal Denny called, in response to a rap on my room door.

Miss Lutie, the nurse from police headquarters, who had come to look after the women, entered.

"Mrs. Wilmorton has rallied sufficiently to see you, Mr. Denny," Miss Lutie said. "She wants to tell you everything—"

"Fine. Tell her I'll be right across."

"I'll get her ready, then. Her maid went down to see if the laundry is ready, Mrs. Wilmorton wanting a fresh boudoir cap."

"We'll give her time," Denny assured Miss Lutie.

As the smiling nurse withdrew, Denny remarked to me, "Pretty little trick, ain't she?"

"Don't be making eyes at no woman now," Sleepy cautioned his superior. "You're on a case. So's she."

Before Denny could retort, my door flew open and Nurse Lutie confronted us with white face.

"Come quickly!" she cried. "Mrs. Wilmorton has had a sinking spell."

"How long has she been like this? Denny demanded, after we had trooped into the Wilmorton apartment and Denny had examined the woman on the bed.

"She was resting comfortably when I stepped across the hall to deliver you her message," Miss Lutie replied. "When I came back, I found her like this."

Fifi Burgoyne slipped into the room, a fancy boudoir cap in her hand.

"She has fainted!" Fifi exclaimed, regarding her unconscious mistress with wide eyes.

"Fainted nothing!" Ben sternly said, examining Mrs. Wilmorton's right arm. "Look here, West. It's like your arm was."

"Sure enough!" I agreed, observing the swollen, discolored spot.

"See, Denny," Ben continued. "The needle was jabbed in here."

"Huh?" grunted Denny, staring at the minute puncture and scratching his head. "Well, I'm a son-of-a-gun!"

"It couldn't have been a hypodermic needle," Nurse Lutie broke in. "There is no one that could have done it. Fifi was downstairs and I was across the hall, speaking to you. Mrs. Wilmorton was alone. No one could have entered these rooms without being seen."

"She could of done it herself," Denny opined.

"Where is the needle, then?" demanded Ben. "Mrs. Wilmorton was too weak to leave her bed—wasn't she, Nurse?"

"She was indeed, Mr. Bailey. I simply can't understand it."

"I can," Ben declared. "There's some one who doesn't want Mrs. Wilmorton to talk: some one who knew that Mrs. Wilmorton wanted to tell Denny everything."

He looked straight into the eyes of Fifi Burgoyne as he uttered the words, but her expression was as innocent as a babe's.

"There's a devil in this house!" swore Denny. "A devil that can come and go through walls and walk invisible through these here halls."

"Maybe it's Paul Ralston," Ben said—rather meanly, I thought. And yet I didn't blame him. Paul was his friend and Hal Denny had been nasty about Paul.

"Yeah? Maybe!" Denny snarled. "But a devil, just the same."

"A devil incarnate, I concede," said Ben. "Nurse, get either Dr. Kelsey or Dr. Howard."

Kelsey came and Ben advised him what had been shot into Mrs. Wilmorton's arm. He also advised a counter-actant, to be given immediately.

"I haven't any of the stuff," Dr. Kelsey deplored. "It can't be had this side of New York."

Ben dispatched me to my room for his bag, from which he took a vial of the stuff needed.

"Not much," he said, "but maybe it will serve."

Fifi brought a spirit lamp and a diminutive copper kettle, enabling Dr. Kelsey to sterilize his needle.

"Now," he said, "if—"

"If you ain't the clodhopper!" yelled Hal Denny, as in awkward moment Sleepy Wallingford and Fifi Burgoyne got in each other's way, colliding and inadvertently knocking the hypodermic needle from Dr. Kelsey's nervous hand.

"I couldn't help stepping on it," Sleepy muttered in self-defense. "There's too many of us in this here room," he added, glaring at the frightened maid.

"It's all I have of the counter-actant," Ben regretted.

"The poison will have to run its course," Dr. Kelsey hopelessly said. "Time we get the antidote here from New York, even by plane, it will be too late for our use." Hopefully he added, "Maybe Mrs. Wilmorton will come out from under the influence of the drug as quickly as Mr. West did."

Ben shook his head, saying, "Whoever shot that stuff into Mrs. Wilmorton's arm profited by his previous mistake and administered a larger dose than was given West."

"*Pardonnez-moi,*" murmured Fifi, "but I am sure that *madame ees* but fainted. She faint zat easily and often."

"In that case," said Ben, "maybe we better call in Mrs. Wilmorton's own physician."

"No need of that—," Dr. Kelsey began, bristling somewhat. But Ben cut him off with a warning look.

"Elsing is the name?" Ben asked Fifi.

"*Oui, M'sieu.*"

"What's his phone number?"

"I—I do not know zat, *M'sieu.*"

Ben found the number in the directory and dialed Mrs. Wilmorton's private telephone, while Fifi watched him through narrowed eyes.

"Damn!" exclaimed Ben, jamming the receiver upon its cradle, "No response."

"Say, you," Denny demanded of Fifi, "know anything about a hypo needle?"

"Fifi was downstairs," Nurse Lutie reminded Denny.

"Mrs. Wilmorton could of give it to herself," the detective said, turning to Ben. "She might of tucked the hypo under her pillow or something."

"Mrs. Wilmorton could have given herself the stuff if she were left-handed," Ben replied. "This shot was administered in the upper right arm, in a spot difficult to get at with the left hand. Some one else used that needle, Denny—some one who didn't want her to talk. Now, who knew that she was going to talk?"

"Huh?"

Ben counseled with Dr. Kelsey and Miss Lutie as to the care he considered it necessary for Mrs. Wilmorton to have. Then our party returned to my room.

"Bailey," Hal Denny said, "I want Paul Ralston's revolver."

Ben frowned, but requested that I go to Paul's room after it.

Dr. Howard was sitting beside Paul's bed, intently watching him. Like a corpse, Paul looked—his tall frame rigid under the sheet that had been laid over him. Still and stark his form—a form I had seen so vital in its beauty and strength. Do you recall an old poem that sang about the ferryman's son so slim and brown? Well, that was Paul Ralston: slim and muscular, brown from the golf links and the Minnesota lakes; alluringly masculine in the eyes of women and heartily companionable in the estimation of men. It was small wonder, I thought then, that Mildred Manning found him good to look upon. . . . Would she ever look upon him again as she had doubtless often looked, or would she in a day or two be yearning for a glimpse of the man forever laid beyond her mortal vision?

"I see no change," Dr. Howard said, as if answering my unspoken query.

"You are greatly concerned?" I ventured.

He nodded.

I stated my errand; took the revolver from Paul's dresser and went out.

Hal Denny examined the gun—a .32 Automatic Colt; then handed it to Ben, saying, "One shell missing."

"Well," Ben returned, "Paul said that he shot at the man outside 'the tomb.' That fact would account for the ejected shell."

"Maybe. . . . Look, Bailey, how do we know Paul Ralston didn't lie—same as Martini did? He could have put that bullet into his father—"

"What about the dagger found by West in Ralston's back?"

"We'll find the answer to that question, me lad."

"Now that you've possession of Paul's gun," Ben went on, "I suppose you'll send it to headquarters. And a lot of good that will do. What's your ballistics expert going to do with it?"

"He'll have it, won't he, when we find the bullet?"

"If we ever find it," murmured Sleepy.

Denny sent me to Mildred's room to inquire if she had revived sufficiently to talk; and if she had, to ask the time the previous night that Paul had secured the revolver from his room.

Mary Rose kept me at the door but forty seconds, promptly reporting that Mildred Manning recalled that when they heard the shot below in 'the tomb,' Paul dashed into his room to get his own gun.

"I told you so!" Ben crowed, when I carried them Mildred's answer.

"Yeah! Well, we're going down there right now and look for a bullet that fits this here gun."

Down we went, and Detective Denny found the bullet. It was deeply imbedded in the wall opposite the double doors and between the sarcophagus and the door to Pietro's shop. Laboriously Denny dug it out with his pocket-knife.

"A .32, I'd say," Ben had to admit.

"So what?" Denny triumphantly demanded.

"We'll first hear what your ballistics expert has to say," Ben replied. "And he'll have hard work with it. The bullet's deformed."

"Not so much so but it'll have some grooves showing. Anyhow, it'll be possible to determine the make."

"You're sure?"

"We're pretty well agreed about the caliber, ain't we?"

"We could be."

"The boys down there will soon tell us."

"Look here," Ben argued, "that could be the bullet Howard Ralston fired at the walking *ka!*"

I was again dispatched to Miss Manning's room, this time to ascertain if Howard Ralston carried a revolver when he left her and Paul to go down to "the tomb" the night before. Mildred's answer was that Ralston had no weapon, insofar as she knew. That left it looking as if I had dreamed seeing the boss fire that shot at the *ka*. Hal Denny was right ugly in the way in which he looked at me but I held my ground and looked back as defiantly as I knew how.

Brookes, when asked by Denny, replied that the master owned a .32 Automatic Colt, quite like Mr. Paul's. Search of the house, however, failed to locate Howard Ralston's revolver.

Paul's gun, together with the bullet dug from the wall, went to headquarters, with request for speedy report. Then we began going over "the tomb."

"I think," Denny said, "that we'll look at them French windows again—just to feel sure. That butler was too scared to draw them drapes last night."

Denny drew the drapes, beginning at the window next Pietro's shop and coming around the room toward my desk. At the third window in the long wall, he halted.

"The glass has been cut!" he exclaimed. "And from the outside." Opening the window, he examined the steel bars. "Them bars seem okay," he said.

"Just the same, the murderer came in through this window!" Sleepy maintained, down on his hands and knees. "Looky, Chief, here's his mud tracks."

One or two tracks were visible—heel toward the window; toe pointing toward the center of the room.

"But," Ben objected, "a man with a shoe to leave a track that size couldn't squeeze between the bars guarding that window."

"Unless," Sleepy began, testing the bars.

To his astonishment, one bar came loose.

"Jumping grandmother!" cried Denny. "Sawed off, is it?"

"With a steel saw," Ben declared. "Neatly done, too. See, here's what we might call the sawdust."

"Good Lord!" Denny muttered. "This room didn't enjoy no protection last night. Not with that window open, it didn't. And after all the precautions we took."

"We'd better open the safe and the cabinet," Ben advised.

"Who is there to open them?" I asked.

Ben's hand was on the door of the Chinese cabinet as I asked the question, and he whirled about—startled at the meaning in my question. In so doing, his fingers drew open the door of the cabinet. With an oath, he jerked the carved doors wide and peered inside the ugly monster. The secret compartment lay exposed. The Borgia was gone.

"The poison ring has been took," Denny said, "but I don't think it's went far."

"Ben," I faltered, "you don't think M. Cornier took it?"

"I wish I knew," Ben replied.

Ben sat down upon the Flemish bench—sat and stared at the Chinese cabinet. Watching him, I was convinced that he felt that his sleuthing had gone haywire sure enough.

With a gloating leer, Hal Denny said to Ben, "Maybe you won't think old man Denny so far wrong after all, huh?"

7

Under Ben's direction, Miss Lutie and Delia O'Grady went to work putting Julia Wilmorton's room in "apple-pie" order. Fifi, who practically had become Miss Lutie's prisoner, resented the ransacking of the rooms; but Ben wanted that hypodermic needle located. The search, however, proved fruitless.

Well, not quite; although I did not know it until later, when Ben called me aside and showed me a small black snap-case—but perhaps I shouldn't anticipate at this point. Ben wouldn't tell me what it was or just where he picked it up! It wasn't a needle case, however, but a small, almost square affair that could easily be concealed in a woman's closed hand. I say "almost square," because the side opposite the hinge was curved.

"Ever see one like it before?" Ben asked, grinning.

"No. Wish you'd tell me what it is."

"Merely a container—nothing more."

"Valuable?"

"Not in itself. But the things kept in it come rather high."

When Miss Lutie made report on the failure of the search she and Mrs. O'Grady had made, the Irish housekeeper supplemented with, "The Frinch hussy, bad cess to 'er, seemed that glad whin she sees our looks av despair. An' it made me that mad, that Oi remimbered av her carryin' th' wastebasket to th' furnace room this mornin'."

"Which reminds me," said Ben, "that Mary Rose Blodgett also was below stairs to dispose of trash."

And that took us to the basement of Windermere. The furnace room was large, and—like the other basement rooms—had a cement floor. Hal Denny led the way to the furnace and jerked open the door. Leaning forward, he sniffed.

"Poke your nose in," he said, stepping aside for Ben.

"Burned cloth," was Ben's verdict.

Denny nodded. He was about to shut the door, when Ben laid restraining hand upon his arm. Getting his blond head as far as possible into the furnace, Ben sniffed again—like a connoisseur seeking to distinguish some particular odor.

"Flesh!" he announced, straightening. "Burned flesh!"

"Blood!" was Denny's statement, after a closer sniff.

My flesh chilled. I found myself fearful of what we might discover.

It took considerable time to dig out the burned rags, to which clung shreds of meat—human tissue, Ben averred—badly burned, but not utterly destroyed. Denny wrapped them up and put them into a cardboard carton I found for him.

"There's enough blood," he remarked, "to let the boys find out if it's human or not."

The wall opposite the furnace doors drew Ben's attention. Opening a wooden door in the wall, he discovered a wood-lined closet—deeply recessed in the masonry. Stepping into that closet, Ben went over the three walls, ceiling, and floor, tapping and listening; but every sound indicated solid backing. He then stepped back into the furnace room and several feet away from the wall. Calling for a carpenter's rule, which I fetched him from the workroom, he took measurements of the walls right and left of the closet doors and of the width of the closet's interior. He jotted down figures in his yellow notebook.

He turned then to examine lime that lay scattered over the cement floor between the wall containing the closet and the furnace. This lime was splotched with color—bluing, I surmised. Here and there in the lime were tracks. A man had tramped there.

"Somebody dragged a body through this basement," Ben declared. "A lime trail has been tracked by the carrier's shoes, and his tracking is followed by parallel scratches made by the heels of the body dragged from the closet toward the outside wall yonder.'

"Where th' sam-hill did he drag the body to?" Denny wanted to know.

"Who can tell?" Ben answered. "The telltale signs end before the outer wall is reached. I venture to guess that the carrier was making for the coal chute."

"To pull the body up it, huh?"

"Well," Ben said, "that would be one way to get the body out of the house."

The two detectives examined the coal chute, but there was no evidence of its black dust having been disturbed.

We went up through Deborah's kitchen and out the back door to the terrace. Passing along to the coal chute, we looked for signs of the body's exit. If there had been signs, rain had obliterated them. Window itself was dusty, rain not having touched it. There were no indications that it had been opened.

Once, when I happened to glance toward *Fontainebleau,* I glimpsed an anxious face at one of the windows—the face of M. Cornier's man, Harry Patterson. And it was only a glimpse I had, for the fellow quickly vanished when he perceived himself discovered.

Denny suggested that while we were out, we might as well look about. We would be able to see better than we did on our earlier exploration, he advised. Well, we made several "finds." Outside that French window with the cut bar, we found a fragment of fingernail—long, ridged, yellowed with narcotic stain. This discovery the two detectives scrutinized minutely, after which Denny placed it in his carton. There were also numerous footprints outside that window. Whether made by more than one person, we could not fully determine, the pelting storm having disfigured them.

Scouting over the lawn between house and driveway, we found—near a clump of lilacs—blood on the grass the bushes had sheltered.

"Now what I want to know," Denny pondered aloud, "is this: was the body drug out here and bundled into a car?"

"If it were," Ben replied, "it'll be found in some roadside ditch. Better have the countryside scoured."

We turned toward the house, and it was then that I made an important discovery. How we had overlooked it, I cannot imagine; for there it lay, gleaming evilly in the morning sunlight. Picking it up, I handed it to Denny, he being the detective in charge.

"A thirty-two!" he exclaimed. "One shell missing. Well, I'll be damned!"

8

Mrs. O'Grady served our dinner in the upstairs sitting-room. Of our patients, all had, at least partially, revived from their attacks. Paul was the lone exception. He was still in a state of coma, and Ben was as glum as a puritan over his friend's condition. That circumstance naturally affected me, and as neither Denny nor Sleepy seemed inclined to conversation, we ate our meal in silence.

Mrs. O'Grady herself brought up dessert, a concoction prepared in compliment to her fellow-countryman. When he praised the dish, Delia thanked him sourly and set forth to express her indignation concerning Mademoiselle Fifi.

"Th' loikes av her," she fumed, "wanting two full trays sent up, an' me knowing that none av th' patients is to eat yet."

"You say that Fifi ordered two full trays?" Ben asked.

"Two it was, sir. Th' nerve av th' Frinch hussy!"

"You let her have them?"

"Oi did not. Oi sint up milk toast for Mrs. Wilmorton, just in case Miss Lutie would let her eat it."

"Mrs. Wilmorton is only semi-conscious," Ben said. "She won't eat."

"Oi'll be seeing whin th' trays is sint down," grumbled Delia.

"I'll be grateful if you will report to me, Mrs. O'Grady," Ben told her.

"An' glad Oi'll be to report, sir."

"What you figgering on now, Bailey?" Denny asked, as soon as Delia left us.

"Just what you should be figuring on, if—"

"If I'd study West's diary, eh?"

Further conversation was halted by clamorous ringing of the front door bell. Then we heard Mrs. Lucretia Lansing's strident voice.

"Don't have the temerity to tell me I can't see Mr. Ralston!" she shrilled, drowning Brookes' protest. "Don't tell me it's impossible."

We hurried down, just in time to see the towering lady sail into "the tomb" with the Duke of Vedena trotting at her heels.

"Mr. Denny is in charge here," Brookes explained, as Mrs. Lansing turned to face us.

At sight of the city detective, the flame of the majestic lady's spirit seemed to flicker uncertainly behind her green eyes.

"Mr. Howard Ralston was murdered in this room last night," Denny informed her.

The Duke uttered an odd gurgling sound, as he and the Lansing stared apprehensively at each other.

"I am sorry," the lady said, being first to regain her composure. "We didn't know. We haven't seen the papers. . . . Have you determined who—?"

"Only that he was stabbed in the back with a Chinee dagger," Denny answered.

"The sword of vengeance!" Mrs. Lansing murmured, her eyes swinging their glance toward the tabouret where the evil sword had lain. "Where is it?"

With a gesture Ben implored Denny to silence.

Himself answering Mrs. Lansing's question, he said, "It has been sent to police headquarters. We hope to find on it the fingerprints of Dr. Lao Wong, who—"

"Lao Wong!"

Mrs. Lansing's lips were colorless as she repeated the Oriental's name.

"Perhaps it would be better if we go at once," timidly suggested the Duke.

Ignoring her client's suggestion, Mrs. Lansing tartly inquired of Ben who he might be.

"I am a fraternity brother of Paul Ralston's," he replied. "I represent his interests."

"As private investigator?"

"If you wish to put it that way. I enjoy no official status."

I do not exaggerate when I say that the Duke's knees gave way under him and that he sank helplessly down upon the nearest chair.

"This strange crime," Ben continued, "seems to link up with the Borgia poison ring in which you and the Duke are so tremendously interested, Mrs. Lansing. So, if you will be seated, I should like to ask you and the Duke a few questions—with Mr. Denny's permission."

"Right!" said Hal Denny, swaggeringly magnanimous.

Mrs. Lansing glanced helplessly at the Duke; then selected a chair.

"May I ask where the ring is now?"

"Surely," Ben answered her. "Mr. Ralston locked it in that Chinese cabinet."

"We are glad the ring is safe," the lady murmured, her eyes falling before Ben's steady regard.

"If you will only give it to me," pled the Duke.

"Sorry, Duke," Ben replied, "but nothing can be done about the Borgia until this mystery is solved and the estate has been through the courts."

"Then I remain in these United States," the Duke affirmed "Right here in Minneapolis."

"That is what the police will insist that you do," Ben informed him.

"But," protested Mrs. Lansing, "the police cannot detain us. They dare not involve us in this terrible affair. Think of our reputations—"

"You should have thought of your reputations before making those rash statements last night, Mrs. Lansing."

"Just what do you mean, young man?"

"Have you so poor memory, Mrs. Lansing? You not only said that you would have the ring in the cabinet if you had to burn the house down to get it; but you also said, as the butler let you out, 'We'll show him a trick or two before the night is over!' I am afraid, Mrs. Lansing, that you permitted temper to override discretion. Now, my dear lady— and my dear Duke, up until the time of Mr. Ralston's death there were but three persons who knew how to open that cabinet. None of these opened it. In fact, some one came through that window—"

Ben paused, pointing at the window with cut glass and bar.

"Some one came through that window?" faltered the Duke.

"Obviously," Ben retorted. "And since no one in this house opened the Chinese cabinet, we conclude that whoever came through that window wished access to the cabinet."

"But you said that the ring—"

Ben interrupted Mrs. Lansing with, "You see, in the light of your threats and in the light of your subsequent actions, you do not show up favorably." He lighted a cigarette. "Talk now, if you wish."

"We left this house before dinner was served," Mrs. Lansing averred. "We have not been in it since—until now."

"I believe," Ben gave gentle assurance, "that we shall be able to prove the contrary. We know of your visit to the venerable Lao Wong, after you left here last night. If neither you nor the Duke visited this room, then your confederate did."

The Duke's lips formed soundless words.

"You make me laugh," Mrs. Lansing said—without laughter, however. "Why, we never heard of such a person as Lao Wong."

"You said, Mrs. Lansing, that you knew persons here in Minneapolis that could open the Chinese cabinet."

"But I did not say that they were Chinese, my shrewd young detective—or is it 'private investigator'?" She smiled—a deadly smile, calculated to damn the soul of Ben Bailey, if that were possible. "You college sleuth, you had better go back to your sorority porches and your cake and tea!"

"Have your little joke, Mrs. Lansing. But my advice to you is that you come clean. Did Lao Wong kill Howard Ralston?"

"Why don't you ask if I killed him? Or the Duke, for that matter?"

"Did you?"

"Certainly not!"

"Not directly," Ben agreed. "You are the type that murders by proxy."

"Mother of God!" breathed the Duke, shivering.

"The Duke and I have nothing further to say," Mrs. Lansing declared, rising. "We shall return to our hotel. It is there you will find us, if further contact with us be necessary."

She turned to go, but halted dead in her tracks as one of Denny's operatives appeared in the double doors with a slim, brown-skinned youth.

"Good work, Bowles," Denny said. "Bring the lad in." He surveyed the newcomer. "So you're Youssuf?"

The stranger made no reply, and Denny didn't seem to mind. He addressed Mrs. Lansing, asking, "It's possible you know this nice chap Mr. Bowles has brung along to join our little party, huh?"

"Yes," Mrs. Lansing answered, crisply, "we've talked to Youssuf. Why not? He and the Duke happened to meet at the hotel last night."

"Didn't talk about Howard Ralston, did yuh?" Denny asked of the diminutive Duke of Vedena.

"Is there any reason why not?" demanded the Duke, pugnaciously.

"None at all." Denny regarded the ember of his fragmentary cigar. "What did yuh say?"

"We've been interviewed, very much against our will, by one investigator," Mrs. Lansing piped. "I see no reason—"

"Hold it, lady! I ain't no private investigator. I'm official see? You and the Duke needn't talk to me now, 'less yuh want to but it might be unpleasant for yuh later, if yuh don't."

"Very well. What do you want to know?"

"I want to know what you folks and Youssuf said about Howard Ralston."

"We talked about the thievery of Mr. Ralston. Youssuf was interested in the mummy of Serapion."

Youssuf apparently didn't like having the spotlight turned upon himself; for he stepped back against Bowles, eyeing Mrs. Lansing reproachfully.

"The mummy, eh?" And to Youssuf, "You don't happen to be the lad that brung the funny letter last night, do yuh?"

Youssuf shook his head, but Brookes promptly identified him as the stranger who delivered the warning from the Brothers of Karnak.

"Now looky here, young feller," Denny sternly said, "if you try putting anything over on me, I'll have yuh locked away where dogs can't bite yuh! Understand?" And as Youssuf nodded, "All right. Now then, where'd yuh come from? How long yuh been in Minneapolis? What'd yuh come here for?"

"I come here from New York, and I have been een Minneapolis two weeks. I come to be near—"

Youssuf's tones melted into silence, as his gaze glued upon the sarcophagus of Serapion.

"You was here to kill Howard Ralston, huh?"

"I came only to warn and to take charge of the sacred mummy."

"You belong to that funny lodge over in Egypt?"

"I am of the Brothers of Karnak," the youth replied, with quiet dignity.

"Frisk 'im, Bowles."

The operative ran his hands with light, deft touch over the person of the Egyptian. "Nothing, Chief," he said.

"An' yuh didn't come to wreak vengeance on Howard Ralston? . . . Come on—out with the truth!"

"Meester Detecteef," Youssuf said, tone nicely modulated and lip curled in slightly disdainful smile, "if you have the leet'ry education, you will recall that the great Shakespeare put the vair wise word into mouth of the young Dane—"

"What Dane?"

"The Prince of Denmark, I refer to," Youssuf said. "He utter those superior word to hees friend: 'There are more thing een heaven and earth, Horatio, than are dream of een your pheelosphee!'"

"Meaning what?"

The Egyptian arched his brows and stared at Denny.

"Well?"

"Only thees, Meester Detecteef, that eet ess not necessary that any human hand wreak the vengeance upon Meester Howard Ralston."

"No?"

"The *ka* in that holy corpse has wreak the vengeance."

"Somebody got away with that mummy," Denny chuckled. He crossed the room to the ornate coffin. "See, it's empty."

He swung back the lid; as I live to tell it, the mummy case was not empty.

"Holy Mackeral!" gulped the burly Irishman, his face pale. "Where'd that there mummy come from, huh?"

"Did we smell cigar smoke in this room this morning?" Ben asked him.

9

"Now," proclaimed Denny, parading my room and burning up another of my cigars, "I don't put no stock in these here Chinamen and Egyptians; but, since you know Lao Wong, Bailey, I wish you'd call on him. However, we'll go first to see Howard Ralston's lawyers, and then pay our respects to our French neighbor, Mr. Henri Cornier."

Ben being agreeable, we drove to the offices of *Goodhue and Mayfair*. Ten minutes after Ben's card was sent in with a message scribbled on its back, we were summoned into the sanctum of Colonel Mayfair himself.

"What a mystery!" the Colonel muttered, after listening to the details of the crime as narrated by Ben. "We'll be glad to cooperate wherever possible, of course."

Then, in answer to Ben's query: "Julia Wilmorton! I should say that I do know Julia Wilmorton! Damned handsome woman. Twenty years ago she was quite a belle here in the twin cities. Admirers stormed her portals and strewed her path with roses. There were three suitors, however, that seemed to enjoy her particular favor—Basil Manning, Edward Wilmorton, and Henry Cornier. Cornier had not been one to notice women; but as Howard had married Anne Weatherford, the glamorous Julia's sister, Julia was often at *Windermere,* and Cornier was thrown in her company We all thought that Julia would marry him and live in the twin house."

"What kept 'em from marrying?" Denny asked.

"Cornier was bashful where women were concerned, and hovered in the background of Julia Wilmorton's flirtations. Everybody thought she inclined toward him more than to either Manning or Wilmorton; but Cornier was tongue-tied with timidity, and Julia had to make a satisfactory marriage. That left her to choose between Basil Manning and Edward Wilmorton. Basil loved her doggedly. I say 'doggedly,' because he was poor and could only hope that she would condescend to him."

"But she didn't, eh?"

"No. Julia chose to marry Eddie Wilmorton, who could in a measure give her the luxuries to which she had been accustomed. Manning went west, married, and settled in Long Beach, California. By chance he picked up a piece of property on Signal Hill. For some reason he hung on to it; and when they struck oil there, he was sitting pretty. His wife died soon after that, leaving him with one child—a girl, Mildred Manning, Ralston's ward."

"It was an unusual will Manning made, wasn't it, Colonel Mayfair?" Ben asked.

"Rather," replied the Colonel. "Manning was strongly attached to his friend, Howard Ralston. Took a freak notion that he would like to have his daughter marry Ralston, so he made his will with that in mind."

"Will you list the terms of that will for us?" Denny requested.

"The estate, which was considerable, was to be Mildred's dowry when she married Ralston. If she refused to make the marriage, the property and money were to go to Julia Wilmorton, with the exception of certain investments designed to yield Miss Manning twenty-five hundred a year. In event of Miss Manning's death, the annuity was to go to Mrs. Wilmorton and her heirs, forever. You see, Basil Manning never got over his romantic attachment for the fair Julia."

"And now, if Ralston be dead, how about the estate?" Ben inquired.

"In case of Howard's death before the marriage takes place—providing, of course, that the girl consented to marry him—Miss Manning will receive half the estate."

"And the other half?"

"Five hundred thousand of it is to go to Julia Wilmorton; the remainder will be put in trust for her heirs—she to enjoy income from it during her life."

"In either case," Denny observed, "Mrs. Wilmorton was to profit; that is, if Miss Manning refused to make this here marriage, or if Ralston died before the marriage took place?"

"You have it," Colonel Mayfair said. "But why, may I ask, this tremendous interest in Mrs. Wilmorton's affairs?"

"The lady in question, sir, has compromised herself most irregular. I'm building up a strong case against her and Mr. Cornier."

Colonel Mayfair looked to Ben, as if asking his denial of Denny's serious implication; but suave old Ben was noncommittal. "Well," the Colonel said, "I hope that Julia has not actually involved herself."

"Could she have had reason to do that?" Ben queried.

"I can only say that the crash of 1929 left her flat," the Colonel replied.

"Can you tell us anything about the financial status of her French sweetie?" Denny asked.

"M. Cornier," and there was ice on the tongue of Colonel Mayfair, "during the last month has suffered unhappy reverses. He is a poor man."

"Too poor to pay off a wager of fifty grand?"

"Too poor for that, Mr. Denny."

"So!"

"But," the Colonel protested, "you're not suspecting—"

"The case is as good as closed—or will be, when I have seen and talked to that bird."

Denny teetered foolishly on his toes, regarding Ben with that *now-what-yuh-going-to-say* look.

And I saw Ben meet Colonel Mayfair's interrogative glance with his tongue in his cheek.

On the way back to *Windermere,* Ben said to Denny, "You're on the wrong scent, if you suspect Mrs. Wilmorton."

"Oh, yeah! Well, what was Mr. Cornier heard to say to her when he carried her upstairs last night when she fainted?"

"Now, listen, Denny—"

"And don't say 'diary' again!"

10

Cornier's man, Harry Patterson, admitted us to *Fontainebleau* and led the way to the library and M. Cornier.

"I have been expecting you," M. Cornier said, closing the door upon the departing Patterson, who glanced back over his shoulder with troubled eyes. "I have waited anxiously since my man told me the terrible news. I was not at home last night, or I should have been over. Only this morning, after a late breakfast, did I learn from Patterson what had taken place. I feared to come over then, lest I intrude. I am so glad that my telephone was available last night."

I set it down right then that M. Cornier was talking too much. It has been my observation that a person who is voluble under such circumstances is endeavoring to mislead the other party. Trying to conceal something, or seeking to head off embarrassing questions.

"Considerate of you," Denny said, helping himself to M. Cornier's proffered cigars. "We was glad not to be interfered with. Huh, Bailey?"

"Quite."

M. Cornier smiled, evidently gratified that his thoughtfulness was appreciated. He offered us refreshments. It was then that I observed that this man, who was always one to be immaculately groomed, this afternoon carried appearance of being over-meticulous in his person. Something about him was not quite the same. I thought it might have been the fingernails, for they attracted my attention at once. They seemed too glossy.

"I have not been able to retire as yet," M. Cornier said (and his eyes indeed begged the ease of slumber), "for I have been most anxious to learn what has happened in my friend's house."

He sat down, careful to have a sunlit window behind him thus making it difficult for us to see his features clearly.

"Brookes told Patterson that Howard had been killed. Stabbed, he said. Is it indeed true?" He leaned anxiously toward Detective Denny. "Tell me the worst, Mr. Denny."

"It's true enough," was Denny's low reply.

M. Cornier seemed actually to grow smaller as he fell back in his chair and covered his face with his hands.

"God!" he muttered, hoarsely. "It is unbelievable! Killed by a stranger in his own house."

Said Detective Denny: "We think a stranger may have did it, Mr. Cornier; but we ain't certain."

The grey face emerged from the shield of masking hands. "You think—"

"As yet we don't know, but we are running down clues."

"God grant that you be successful!"

"You are a collector, Mr. Cornier?"

"A collector of long experience," he answered. "My friend and I have played the game together for more than a quarter of a century."

"You yourself was greatly interested in this Borgia poison ring, wasn't yuh, Mr. Cornier?"

"Naturally. It is a prize for any collector."

"And you said to your friend, didn't yuh, that you'd give twenty years of your life for that ring?"

"I made such a statement," M. Cornier reluctantly admitted. "Why are you questioning me so closely?"

"Well, there's a lot of funny angles to the case that baffle us. I thought as how you could throw light on 'em for us."

"I'm not sure that I can."

The two men eyed each other, with Detective Denny at a disadvantage, because M. Cornier's back was to the light."

"You and Mr. Ralston made a bet, didn't yuh?"

"We did."

"You allowed he won that bet, huh?"

"I did not. We were to discuss it this morning."

"H'm. . . . Is them checks still in possession of Mrs. Wilmorton?"

"I presume that they are."

"I see. . . . And you was with Mr. Ralston when that Duke and Mrs. Lansing called, wasn't yuh?"

"Ah, yes."

It was with obvious relief that M. Cornier answered that question. At Denny's request, he recounted the dramatic visit made by the foreign nobleman and his American agent the night before.

"What yuh think of Martini?" Denny next inquired.

"I warned my friend against him."

"Think he killed his employer?"

"I would not say that. However, he had considerable to gain by Howard's death—and there was opportunity to place the guilt elsewhere."

"You mean," Ben inquired, "that he would deliberately cast suspicion upon Paul?"

"May I ask you if he liked Paul?"

"Will you give us your idea of how the Italian might have did it?" Denny requested.

"It's easy, as I see it. My man, Patterson, gleaned facts from Brookes. These he imparted to me, like so many pieces in a jigsaw puzzle. I fitted them together."

"Please go ahead," Denny urged.

"Well, what I figured out is like this. Howard went down to the big room to challenge the menace of the Brothers of Karnak. Resolved not to be interfered with by members of his household, he locked the doors behind him. But Martini slipped into the room with that strange boy, a hired assassin. Howard, seeing that they were after him, shot at the stranger. Then Martini seized the Chinese dagger and plunged it into Howard's back as he turned to open the double doors and call for help."

"How do you account for West's experience?"

"Hallucinations induced by the dark and by the drug Martini shot into him."

"But why didn't Martini and this Romeo beat it after the murder?" Ben queried.

"Ah," M. Cornier replied, smiling knowingly, "there is where his clever devilishness comes in. He knew that Paul would come down, attracted by the shot. So he and the stranger hid in the shop. As soon as Paul was on his knees beside his father's body, the two entered, finding Paul with hand clutching the dagger. Simple, isn't it? Circumstantial evidence—accusation!"

Throwing out his hands in expressive gesture, M. Cornier sat there challenging us, as it were, to refute his theory.

"But Paul didn't clutch that dagger," Ben told M. Cornier, "for if he had, barbs on the dragon-spine would have left telltale punctures on the palm of his hand."

If Ben expected M. Cornier to throw a scared look into his own palm, he miscalculated. He did, however, slide the tips of his crookt fingers over the palm of his right hand. But the suggestion in Ben's words was so strong that I came near doing the same thing myself.

"Mr. Cornier," said Detective Denny, resuming the questioning, "do you know the secret of the Chinee cabinet?"

"I do not."

Denny's glance concentrated upon the strange ring gleaming on the antiquarian's finger.

"If you do not know how to open that cabinet, Mr. Cornier," he demanded, "how come you to be wearing that Borgia ring?"

"Are you accusing me of murdering my friend?"

"No."

M. Cornier continued, bitterly, "You come to me for aid, which I gladly render you. You reward my co-operation by asking me impertinent questions—by insulting me in my own house."

"Really, Mr. Cornier," Ben said, by way of oiling troubled waters, "Mr. Denny didn't mean his question to convey such implication; but he must leave no stone unturned in effort to solve this mystery. No personal offense was intended."

"This ring I wear," M. Cornier said, apparently mollified, "is not the genuine Borgia. This is Martini's clever imitation of the original. Mr. West will witness that my friend presented it to me."

He slipped his hand into a pocket, as if wishing to remove the ring from sight. Detective Denny pricked forward his ears as he heard a jingle of keys in that pocket.

"You got a key to Ralston's house, ain't yuh?" he asked.

"Yes. To the door over the *porte-cochere*."

"May I see that key?"

"But surely you will tell me why you want to see it?"

"I want to compare it with one the Italian has."

Lord, what a lie that was! But M. Cornier fell for it, and handed over his keyring. Denny scrutinized it thoroughly; then shook his head.

Still retaining the keys, he asked, "You ain't got another key to *Windermere?*"

"No."

"What about the key to that secret door at the front of the house?"

"I haven't the faintest idea to what you refer, Mr. Denny."

"No? . . . Well, let me tell yuh that Brookes has told us about that ten o'clock visit of yours."

Denny extended the keys toward M. Cornier; but instead of holding them by the ring, he held them suspended by an odd key that I could have sworn was a duplicate of the one Cornier had given Brookes the night before. M. Cornier took the keys, dropping them into his pocket with never a hint that he perceived the significance in Detective Denny's gesture. Witnessing the pantomime, I thought of the key that had been stolen from Paul's room.

"You left *Windermere* shortly after the departure of Mrs. Lansing and the Duke, didn't yuh?" Denny next asked. "By way of the second floor and the communicating passage over the *porty*—"

"That is correct," M. Cornier replied, with amused smile. "I returned to my own house by way of the passage over the *porte-cochere*."

"And you ain't been back since?"

Cornier regarded Denny with indulgent, long-suffering look.

"Mr. Cornier," and Denny's irritation was poorly concealed, "why stall? West here was in the big room, hiding behind a screen, when you stole through that secret door about ten o'clock. He can describe exactly what you did before you encountered the butler, and he can repeat the conversation you and Brookes had."

"Mr. Denny," Cornier replied, never batting an eyelid, "I will explain. I started on my trip to Faribault, but turned back. I was worried. I knew that the Borgia was in the Chinese cabinet. I had heard Mrs. Lansing's threat, and I suspected Martini. I went back to change the rings. If the thief should come, I thus would have saved my friend's prize for him."

"You're convinced that Mr. Ralston had the genuine Borgia, then?"

"I am. I couldn't afford to admit it to Howard, as I have reason to believe that I have lost everything I owned—excepting this house. Even my horses—"

"That's tough! I can see as how you was on the spot over there last night. But you didn't change the rings, did yuh?"

"No. After Brookes surprised me in my attempt to open the Chinese cabinet, I gave up the idea."

"And to throw Brookes off guard, gave him the key to the secret door—knowing all the time you had a duplicate?"

"*Monsieur,* you are clever. I knew when you returned my keys—"

"Okay. Now that we understand each other, suppose you shoot straight. Did yuh return later and exchange the rings?"

"I assure you that I did not."

"Where'd yuh spend the night?"

"At Faribault."

And there M. Cornier had Denny; for the Cornier chauffeur had days before been dismissed and Cornier's Faribault host that morning had departed for New York.

Thus ended the interview.

As we climbed into our car, Denny asked, "What think of Cornier?"

"I think he's a magnificent liar," Ben answered.

"Ready to admit he did it?"

"Not yet. We haven't heard what Dr. Lao Wong has to say."

11

We drove to Third Avenue South. Ben parked the roadster, and we walked half a block to an alley, into which we turned and came to a yellow door in a red brick wall.

"We are about to enter the House of the Narcissus," Ben informed us, "hoping for an interview with Dr. Lao Wong. Not a peep from either of you. I'll do the talking."

His fingernails clicked a sharp signal upon the wicket in the yellow door. The wicket slid back; a toothless Chinese doorkeeper peered out at us.

"Ah Ken, me got big business with Lao Wong," Ben urged. "Got to see him right away."

The saffron yellow mask that was the face of Ah Ken withdrew; the wicket closed. We waited. Ben was beginning profane mumblement, when the yellow door opened and the toothless one admitted us.

Evidently familiar with the place, Ben led the way down a long passage to a black paneled door. Here he rapped three times. An almond-eyed youth opened the door, pantomiming us to enter and be seated.

"Pretty much at home, ain't yuh?" Denny asked of Ben, as the servant boy slithered out of the room.

"Son of the house was a classmate of mine at the 'U'," Ben explained. "I've done business with Lao Wong. A number of my trails have run through the Oriental quarter, and both Lao Wong and his son have been of assistance to me."

The room in which we sat was typically Chinese. Teakwood furniture; tapestries of Hang-chin silk; josh sticks burning before a jade Buddha. Oppressive luxury; an atmosphere heavy with incense.

The almond-eyed servitor slithered back into the room and drew aside the black-and-scarlet-embroidered curtains that hung in Imperial yellow folds before a doorway in the wall opposite us. In the opening thus afforded appeared a majestic figure, clad in gorgeous robes of white satin, heavily overlaid with resplendent embroiderings in green, blue, gold, and vermillion. On his head he wore a white satin skullcap, artistically needled to match his robe. In his hand he carried a magnificent fan from which floated exotic scent of sandalwood. I knew at once that here was the man we sought—the venerable Lao Wong, herbalist, antiquarian, and underworld diplomat.

"Ah," he said, a smile hesitating about his thin lips, "it is my son's very dear friend, Mr. Ben Bailey."

Lao Wong took position opposite us in a huge black chair, gracing it as a potentate might a throne.

"How may I serve you, friend of my son?" he asked, slowly swaying the magnificent fan to and fro.

"You have heard of the Duke of Vedena's Borgia poison ring, have you not?" Ben asked.

An almost imperceptible tide of color washed the yellow cheeks of the venerable Chinese antiquarian.

"It has been stolen from the Duke," Ben announced.

The gray-violet incense curled lazily upward to lose itself in the shadows of the ceiling.

Ben went on: "It has been brought to Minneapolis by Mr. Howard Ralston."

The venerable one gazed dreamily before him.

"You have heard of the mummy of Serapion?" Ben asked next.

Lao Wong's hand had moved steadily and continuously during the interview, waving the exotic fan indolently to and fro; but now that fan came to rest against the breast of the satin robe.

"The mummy also was stolen, my honorable friend, and bought by Mr. Ralston, who shipped it into the United States—to *Windermere*."

Again the fan drifted lazily into motion.

"Howard Ralston secured and expressed to you from Shanghai the vengeance dagger of the Scarlet Dragons. You delivered that dagger to him upon his return to Minneapolis yesterday."

There was a slight slackening in the great fan's motion. The yellow lids drooped over the lacquer-colored eyes of the venerable one. The face of him looked suddenly very old. The thin lips molded unuttered syllables.

"Last night Mr. Ralston's house was broken into, and our friend was killed—slain with the vengeance dagger of the Scarlet Dragons."

The fan closed with brittle scraping of its sandalwood sticks. Through narrow slits the languorous eyes of the Chinese antiquarian regarded Ben suspiciously. Quickly the closed fan made upward gesture.

Almost immediately a dark-robed lieutenant appeared and took station behind the chair of Lao Wong, standing, arms folded, and regarding us with inscrutable eyes. I noticed that one of the beautifully shaped nails on the lieutenant's right hand had been filed down to the quick. Whether Ben and Hal Denny observed that fact, I could not determine.

"I came to you, honorable father of my friend," Ben explained, "because I know that Lucretia Lansing and the Duke of Vedena came here last night to hire you to extract the Borgia poison ring from Howard Ralston's Chinese cabinet."

Lao Wong drew in his breath with painfully sucking sound. His eyes contemplated the vermillion dragon that sprawled across the Imperial yellow of the tapestry opposite him, then closed wearily. His body shuddered beneath the ornate robe.

The dark-robed lieutenant behind him evinced no sign of comprehension, remaining stoically noncommittal.

"I would that I had ascended the dragon to the Chambers of the Dead ere this had come to pass," Lao Wong moaned, the words drifting all but inaudibly upon his breath.

Ben laid a hand on Lao Wong's knee, saying, "I am the friend of your son, your first born. I am your friend, honorable Lao Wong. Will you not enlighten me?"

The venerable one's knee trembled beneath Ben's touch.

"I have never done wrong, Mr. Ben Bailey," he said, his eyes opening to regard his young friend, "save when a wrong would right a wrong.
Mr. Howard Ralston, he was my honorable friend. Mrs. Lansing, she
is my friend. Mr. Ralston did great injustice to my friend's friend, so I
sent Soo Wang to aid them."

Urged to continue, Lao Wong told all that his lieutenant, Soo Wang,
had done and observed, and the inscrutable one confirmed the narrative in every item.

When he had finished, Ben said, "Dr. Lao Wong, you have given
me great help. I know that you are like unto your first born—good and
honorable. I shall strive to keep your honorable name clear."

Came then a knock upon the black door. Lao Wong gave a command in Chinese; Soo Wang opened the door. There stood Ah Ken, an
envelope in his hand. Soo Wang took the envelope, closed the door,
and delivered the missive to his captain. Lao Wong slit the envelope
and drew forth a dragon card. I gasped at sight of it.

"Chang Lee Hi, his eyes are everywhere! My honorable young
friend, my life is hanged on a flimsy thread because you are here; but I
do not fear the Scarlet Dragons."

"Chang Lee Hi," Ben queried. "Is it he who drops those cards about
so carelessly?"

"He is emissary of the Scarlet Dragons, seeking the sword of vengeance. He has been in Howard Ralston's house. He will enter it again."

"It must have been he on the boat," Ben said. "Some one crossed
the Pacific with Howard Ralston—some one who frequently left dragon cards to annoy our friend. One Mr. Ralston found slipped into his
laundry; another had been pushed under his plate in the dining salon."

"Undoubtedly it was Chang Lee Hi," murmured Lao Wong. "He is
everywhere; he sees everything. Even now he may not be far distant."

"Well," Hal Denny admitted, as we drove back to *Windermere,* "this
here interview knocks my case cockeyed!" And when Ben said nothing,
he continued, "But just the same, I'm going to prove that Mr. Cornier
killed Howard Ralston. And I'm going to prove that our beautiful Julia
Wilmorton is in it up to her eyes."

"What about your convictions concerning Paul Ralston?"

"Well—," and Denny's voice trailed away.

"I'm with you so far as Julia Wilmorton is concerned," Ben solaced him.

"Yeah! What about West's diary, huh?"

"Well—"

And Ben, in his turn, let his voice trail off into nothingness.

12

Back in "the tomb", Ben went to my desk telephone and called a physician friend of his.

"'Lo, Doc! Bailey speaking. . . . Say, I want the low-down on Dr. Adolphus Elsing, big nerve specialist on Pillsbury Avenue. . . . What? . . . Repeat that! . . . You're sure? . . . Good God! . . ."

"Don't tell me Elsing's been bumped off!" warned Denny, as Ben cradled the instrument. "I can't stand no more shocks."

"My friend informs me," Ben said, "that the medical profession regrets the untimely death of Dr. Elsing."

"When did it happen?" Denny irritably demanded.

"Death and cremation took place two months ago."

13

"How's the Wilmorton woman?" Denny none-too-pleasantly demanded of Nurse Lutie, who entered "the tomb" at that moment of our dumbfoundment.

"Still unconscious, Mr. Denny," the nurse replied. "But there are indications of improvement. However—"

"However what?"

"Fifi Burgoyne has disappeared."

Detective Denny took the stairs three at a time, Ben and I right behind him—Sleepy Wallingford lumbering along behind. Miss Lutie followed with dignity. She evidently didn't like being thundered at by detectives.

Julia Wilmorton lay unconscious upon her bed. In the maid's room beyond were several empty food trays—but no sign of Fifi.

"How'd she get out?" Denny demanded of Miss Lutie, rigid in her starched uniform.

"She'd kept to her room," Miss Lutie replied, "and had all that food brought up to her—soup, mostly. She never went past me and out that hall door, Mr. Denny."

"There's no exit to this room of hers except the door into the settin'-room," Denny fretted, "and that's locked on the settin'-room side. That maid would have to come through Mrs. Wilmorton's room."

"There's the window," Nurse Lutie, on the defensive, informed him.

Tied to the bedpost and thrown through the window, we found three sheets—knotted for someone's descent.

"So," Denny mused, leaning over the sill and peering down at the dangling white scarf.

"So my eye!" mocked Ben. "This improvised rope isn't long enough; no one has dropped into the loose soil down there."

"You can see for yourself she's gone," Denny argued.

"Not out of the house, my friend," Ben said.

"What d'yuh mean?"

"I mean that I've been expecting something like this to happen."

"Smart guy, you!"

"Thanks." Ben grinned at the irate gentleman from Erin. "And don't worry, Denny. Fifi can't get away. In the meantime, she's safe where she is. Also, in the meantime, you might profitably be reading West's diary."

"Hell! Where's Fifi?"

"You're the star detective. Why ask me?"

THE EVENING OF THE SECOND DAY

1

Upon Ben's suggestion, it was decided that Denny remain at *Winder-mere* to keep the Fifi Burgoyne situation under observation, while Ben and I visited the house on Pillsbury Avenue. Well armed, we took the roadster and started for Dr. Elsing's, little dreaming what we were to find.

"So Hal Denny's after Cornier's scalp?" I said.

"I'm after that of Dr. Elsing," Ben grunted.

"You think that he—"

"It's my psychic hunch," Ben laughed. "Remember last night when I consulted section *L* in my files. I had a hunch that I was right then. I've an even stronger hunch that I'm still right, and that despite Mr. Harrison Denny's expert sleuthing. If we find what I anticipate, I'll be going back to my files before we return to *Windermere.* Yep, Old Timer, it's a hunch I'm following—my ridiculed psychic hunch. Want to laugh?"

I didn't laugh, for I had come to entertain respect for that psychic hunch of Ben's. I was to entertain greater admiration for it before the case was solved. And so on to Pillsbury Avenue.

Fortune smiled on us. The chap living across the avenue from Elsing's place was in his driveway, washing a car. From him Ben elicited the following facts, scribbling them into his yellow notebook:—

Hedline family, living opposite Elsing establishment, knew of Dr. Elsing's death. . . . Have noticed Elsing house is occupied. . . . Physician's sign taken down. . . . Shades kept lowered; little

183

evidence of life. . . . Big cars visit place; large limousine comes frequently, bringing beautiful woman. . . . Description fits Wilmorton. . . . New occupant of Elsing place has car, driven by foreign-looking chauffeur; but rarely rides out days, away every evening. . . . No other servant than the chauffeur, who is taciturn when approached by neighborhood domestics. . . .

"I believe," said Ben, "that we shall call upon the doctor."

Repeated ringing of the front door bell brought no response. Our banging at the service entrance proved likewise futile.

"Well," opined Ben, "it looks as if we aren't wanted. This reincarnated Dr. Elsing is particular in selection of prospective patients."

The doctor's car stood in the garage, we discovered; but there was no way of getting at it. Completing circuit of the premises, we found a third door to the house. Here we rapped with increasing insistence.

A window in the house next door was thrown up and a woman shouted, "There hasn't been a soul about there all day!" Told that we wanted to see the doctor, she said, "Doctor or no doctor, he went away last night in a yellow cab. We haven't seen hide or hair of him since."

"Have you seen his man about?"

"No, we haven't. And that's awful strange, because there was a terrible commotion over there a while before the doctor, as you call him, went out. My husband and I heard an awful scream—"

"Man's cry?"

"Yes, it was. At first we were minded to call the police; but things quieted, and my husband said as it was none of our business."

"What sort of looking chap is this neighbor of yours?"

"Smallish and cadaverous looking."

"I thought he would look like that," Ben advised me. And to the loquacious lady, "Foreigner?"

"He and his servant, both."

"Again I'm right," Ben whispered to me.

We drove to police headquarters, where Ben contacted Denny by telephone. It took Denny sometime to arrange that Ben's request be met, so that it was dusk when we again drove up before the house on Pillsbury Avenue; but we were accompanied by the asked for brawny bluecoat and armed with a search warrant. Again our ringing and knocking went unanswered. Resolved to enter the house, Ben demonstrated what an excellent burglar he might have been, for we were soon inside that mysterious residence of the deceased Dr. Elsing.

It was dark and still in there—chilly, too. I felt my nerves tingling as we stood listening, not daring to turn on lights. Deciding that it was safe to begin operations, Ben and I ransacked the lower floor, with our bluecoat, Sven Svenson by name, acting as nervous rear guard. Reward *nil.*

"Upstairs next," Ben ordered.

About to ascend, Ben leading, we were startled by the shrilling of the telephone. In answer to that ringing, we heard the *slf, slf, slf* of bedroom slippers in the upper hall. Seizing Svenson and me, each by an arm, Ben drew us into a stuffy closet under the stairs. Safely hidden, we listened. The footsteps died away; the telephone did not ring again.

"Odd!" Ben muttered.

We waited something like twenty minutes. Then, led by Ben, automatics in hand, we ventured forth. No sooner had Ben set foot on the first of the stair treads than the telephone shrilled again, and again we heard the *slf, slf, slf* of bedroom slippers. Svenson and I bolted, but Ben stood his ground. Nothing happened, so the copper and I rejoined Ben.

"Must be an extension upstairs," I whispered.

"Listen," said Ben.

He stepped full upon the first stair tread. Immediately the telephone signaled and the ghostly footsteps—*slf, slf, slf*—chilled the marrow in my bones. Ben removed his foot from the stair tread, and shortly all was quiet.

"Now," he said.

Stepping again upon the stair tread, he stood there. Repeatedly the telephone shrilled and footsteps echoed.

"Clever, what!" exclaimed Ben. "Cute little gadget with an electric set-off for a fake telephone and a phonographic bedroom slipper."

"Ghostly steps," I murmured, appreciative of the ruse designed to frighten away intruders.

"Wal, I never look for no ghost ven I bane coom har," sighed Policeman Svenson, mopping perspiration from his brow.

"It's an ingenious ghost," said Ben, "but the gentleman that created it is a wizard. We wouldn't want to come face to face with him in this dark house."

"I tank ve better got reinforcement," cautioned Svenson.

"Come on," Ben urged. "The mechanical genius isn't at home."

"What dealings can Julia Wilmorton have been having with—" I began, as we started up the stairs, only to have my words halted by the echo of a thud—heavy and dull, like the dropping of a lifeless body.

We pulled up short, listening—breathless.

"That bane another ghost I tank," sighed Svenson.

"Don't get jittery, boys," Ben admonished. "Probably a branch of some tree blown against the side of the house."

We rummaged all the rooms, finding nothing, and coming at the end of our search to a locked door. As Ben twisted the knob, we heard a faint groan.

"There's somebody in that room!" Ben declared.

"He's hurt," I faltered. "Ben, remember what that woman said about a scream in the night."

We heard the moaning again. Ben tried to jimmy the door, unsuccessfully.

"There's an elm on this side the house that should be convenient to the window of this room. Hustle, fellows!"

Ben dashed down the stairs and out into the night. We caught up with him under the elm tree.

The woman next door threw up her window and yelled, "What you boys going to do?"

"Who wants to know?" Ben called back.

"Why—why, I'm Mrs. George Waterman."

"Okay, and thanks!"

Thrusting a glass cutter into my hands, Ben urged, "Up and cut a hole large enough to reach your hand through and turn the window lock, Win."

"I'm going to call the police," warned Mrs. Waterman.

"We *are* the police," replied Ben.

As Mrs. Waterman slammed down her window, Ben gave me a boost and up I shinnied—glass cutter insecurely gripped between chattering teeth. Gingerly I crawled along a branch, and, with none-too-secure foothold, managed to stand up and grasp the sill of the window we thought belonged to the room we desired to enter. It was no lark, cutting that glass; but cut it I did. Reaching through the hole I'd made, I turned the window's fastening.

Damned reluctantly, I crawled through. But I remained close to the window until the others joined me. All the time I could hear that pitiful moaning in the dark.

Ben's flash revealed—huddled on the floor beside the couch from which he had fallen—a man. His arms and legs were tightly bound; his mouth was gagged.

"Hey, fellow!" Ben called, prodding the prostrate man with his foot.

The chap groaned. Svenson turned him on his back. The man's shirt was blood-soaked. On the swollen right arm was a minute puncture.

We lifted the man to the couch. Further examination revealed an ugly knife wound in his left side. He had bled so profusely that it didn't look as if he could live. Svenson went down to call headquarters, while Ben and I did what we could in way of "first aid." When Svenson returned, we had removed the gag and induced the wounded man to talk.

Identifying himself, as Gaston Dupont, he told us that he had entered his master's service at Cherbourg, June 26, accompanying him to America. There had been a quarrel the night before, because Dupont resented being forced into questionable activities. There had been the flash of a knife. After that Dupont remembered nothing until he heard us in the house and tried to attract our attention.

"Dr. Elsing! Is that your master's name?" Ben asked him.

Dupont gasped. There was a rattle in his throat. The feeble pulse ceased to flutter.

2

Leaving the house on Pillsbury Avenue, we drove to Ben's apartment.

"File *L?*" I asked.

"That section has served its purpose, Win. What we unearthed tonight vindicates my original conjecture. The problem confronting us now is to identify—"

"Wait!" I caught him up. "Let me tell. You want to identify the gentleman directly connected with whatever this *L* is. Right?"

"You're warm. I have known all along who practiced *L* in this case. What I want now is confirmation—and identification of his accomplice."

"Whom you suspect of being at *Windermere?*"

"That's right."

"Mademoiselle Fifi?"

"Maybe. Can't say as yet."

"But you know that the so-called Dr. Elsing did it?"

"That's my idea, my lad."

"And I have him in my diary?"

"You have."

"What about Denny's case against M. Cornier and Mrs. Wilmorton?"

"That angle and several others puzzle me, Win. It doesn't all seem to tie up, somehow."

At his apartment, Ben looked over communications left by his operatives. From his files he extracted copies of a French newspaper and notes on celebrated cases solved by the Paris *Surete*. These he thrust into a brief case.

"Before returning to *Windermere,*" he next informed me, "we have another call to make."

"Nothing like our adventure on Pillsbury Avenue," I expressed hope.

"This call should prove a pleasant one, Win."

We drove to the Curtis Hotel. At the desk, Ben inquired for Signor Claudio Cesti. Informed that Signor Cesti had a few minutes before called for his key, Ben said that we would go on up—that Signor Cesti was expecting us.

"Cesti?" I queried, as the elevator shot upward.

"*Alias,*" was all that Ben would say.

On the tenth floor, Ben rapped lightly on No. 1063.

"Who is there?" called a musical voice in Italian.

"A friend of Pietro Martini's," Ben replied, using the same tongue.

"Go away," Cesti warned, "or I shall summon the house detective."

Cesti spoke now in English. I knew from the peculiarity of the accent that I had heard that voice. I was not left long in doubt, however, for Ben named the party on the other side of the door.

"You will not want us to go away when I tell you that Pietro is in danger, Signorina Francesca."

"*Miseri cordia di Dio!*"

The door opened, and she faced us in her roguish disguise.

"You!" she cried, staring at me. Then, shrugging her narrow, sloping shoulders, she muttered, "I might have known that I could not get away with it. Come in, gentlemen."

We entered, Ben closing the door behind us.

Francesca took a cigarette, gesturing us to do likewise. Ben offered her a light; but she declined the courtesy, producing a lighter, which she flinted in engagingly masculine manner.

"Tell me how I was discovered," she begged.

"Well," Ben answered, "I suspected last night that Romeo was the Duke of Vedena's daughter. I had one of my operatives radio Venice, and we received back word that you had departed that city with passport visaed by the American consul."

"But how did you locate me at this hotel?"

"I put one of my boys on the *check-up*. It didn't prove much of a task to find you."

"Does Pietro suspect me?"

"Now, now, *signorina,* let's not pretend. We must be serious. A man has been murdered. Pietro is suspected of killing him."

"Oh, Pietro did not do it!"

"I do not think that he did, *signorina*. But to eliminate him from the suspect list, we must know all that took place last night."

"Why should I tell you?"

"You love Pietro, do you not?"

"I once thought I did, *signor*—very much," she answered, eyes wistful. "But he deceived me cruelly, and he robbed my father. . . ."

Ben watched her narrowly as her words blurred into silence.

He asked, "You followed him to America to revenge yourself upon him, *signorina?*"

Pulling a long draft on her cigarette, she sat gazing out at the Minneapolis skyline.

"Yes," she finally said, "I came to kill him. He was Judas to me, *signor*."

"But when you saw him again, *signorina,* your heart forgave him?"

"I am not sure that I forgave him. But I did not kill him. Instead, I probably saved his life."

"Indeed!"

She pondered a moment, then continued. "I hired a car and found my way to the place you call 'Windermere.' I saw him leave there and followed him to that downtown hotel. From there I trailed him to the laboratory of Victor Martini. I waited."

"Revolver in hand?"

"Stilletto in my garter, *signor.*"

"Ahem! . . . Continue, *signorina.*"

"After some time, he came out. Getting into his car, he looked at a bottle he had in his hand. He seemed pleased, for he threw back his head and laughed. While he was trying to start the motor, a squat, dark man, with an ugly scar on his face, stole out of the laboratory. As Pietro moved away, the ugly man jumped upon the running-board. He held a revolver and made Pietro drive as he directed."

"You followed?"

"*Si, signor.* But shortly Pietro's car stopped, and although the evil-looking one pointed his revolver at him, Pietro could not again start the car."

"Was it then you saved his life?"

"I think it was, *signor.* I drove slowly by them, and the man on the running-board called to me to stop. With the evil one's gun pointed at my head, naturally I obeyed. The ugly one told me to lift the hood of Pietro's car and examine the engine." She smiled back into Ben's grin. "I told him I knew nothing about motors. He got down and did something to Pietro's motor. Then he got into my hired car and drove away."

Francesca continued her story, closely tallying with the facts as we knew them from Pietro's own account. She knew nothing further concerning the squat, dark man.

"This case will be solved before morning," Ben told her as we left. "Kindly be available—just in case we need you at *Windermere.*"

3

Returning to *Windermere,* we learned that the several patients were doing as well as could be expected. Only Paul gave us concern. He had regained consciousness, but was in a sort of paralysis-like condition and not able to talk much. Ben and I stood at the bedside and Ben strove to encourage Paul by telling him that everything was working out nicely, considering that not thirty-six hours had marched by since calamity overtook him. That the end was in sight, Ben confidently assured his friend.

Leaving Paul, we joined Hal Denny in my room, and the conference was on—with Sleepy Wallingford dozing comfortably in my student chair.

"So Fifi reappeared," mused Ben.

"Just like that!" answered Denny. "Mighty near scared the daylights outen Miss Lutie by opening the door of that funny inside room of hers and asking that the trays be sent down as it was luncheon time and she was hungry."

"I'll wager that she asked for hot soup again," Ben said.

"How'd yuh guess that?" demanded Denny.

"A maid in Fifi's condition requires soup."

"Yuh wouldn't be kidding me?" Denny asked, chewing hard on his cigar and quizzically regarding Ben.

"Far from it, Denny. I'm not surprised over Fifi's reappearance. She hadn't been out of the house."

"I don't see how yuh figgered that out. I asked her all kinds of questions, but all I got for my pains was *'no come pa'*."

Ben related our evening experiences.

"Good work!" exclaimed Denny. "But where does that put us?"

"On the goal line."

At that point, Brookes brought up Phil Strong, one of Ben's operatives.

"Dupont's dead," Strong reported. "Never regained consciousness."

"You tore Dupont's room apart?"

"Shredded it. Sewn up in the bloody pillow, we made our only find—other than the stuff you ordered carted from the doc's laboratory."

From the brown billfold which Strong handed him, Ben drew seven papers. He fingered through these, then read the name gold-stamped on the billfold.

"Dr. Adolphus Elsing," he read aloud. "And look at this. Recognize it, Win?"

I did. It was a police photograph clipped from a newspaper and showed the face of the blonde Gwendolyn Seabury.

"Broadcast by the New York police at the time she slipped into the United States," Ben informed Denny and me. "And now have a look at these, Denny."

'These' were six IOU's., all dated within the past six weeks. They totaled sixty thousand dollars and were signed *Julia Frances Wilmorton*.

"So that's why she killed Howard Ralston!" Denny exulted. "To get money to pay Dupont—our phony Dr. Elsing. . . . But," and he frowned over the newspaper clipping carrying the smiling features of Gwendolyn Seabury, "how does this dame fit into the Cornier-Wilmorton conspiracy?"

Ben grinned at Denny, his manner more pleasantly indolent than ever.

"Maybe she don't fit in," mumbled Sleepy, coming to and pulling an apple from his pocket. "Maybe Bailey's right and you're wrong, Chief."

Feigning not to hear the remark of his assistant, Denny dragged a chair to my desk. To Ben, he said, "Suppose we get down to brass tacks."

Ben being agreeable, the two seated themselves. I stood looking over their shoulders.

"Here's the fingerprint report," said Denny, initiating the discussion. "On the Chinee dagger was found the prints of young Ralston and West—also the prints of party unknown."

"Cornier's, obviously," murmured Ben.

"Why yuh say that?"

"You said that he killed Howard Ralston, didn't you?"

"Sure I did. But he might of been slick enough to wipe the weapon clean, mightn't he?"

"M. Cornier's nobody's fool." Ben dragged on his fag. "You recall, Denny, that West saw M. Cornier handle the weapon several times. We'd naturally expect to find his prints on the sword."

"H'm, yeah." Denny leaned back in his chair. "But those prints ain't his. I got Cornier's fingerprints this evening, and these don't correspond."

"Then," Ben said, "I suggest, in the light of what Lao Wong told us this afternoon, that the 'party unknown' may be Chang Lee Hi."

"Not a chance. That bird would of taken the dagger with him."

"Mr. Denny," said Ben, "that's one sensible remark. But let's see if the prints on the dragon cards are identical with those left on the dagger hilt by 'party unknown'."

Comparison revealed no similarities.

"There are still the prints of the Duke, Mrs. Lansing, and Dr. Elsing to be taken into consideration," Ben advised.

"Elsing, or Dupont, or whatever his name is, wasn't in this house last night," Denny began to argue.

"I quite agree with you that Dupont wasn't here," Ben said.

Laying out other charts, Denny informed Ben that they were photographs of fingerprints left about the wall safe. Ben identified them: Howard Ralston's, Paul's, Julia Wilmorton's, mine, and those of *party unknown.*

"But not same 'party unknown' as in the case of the dagger hilt," Ben pointed out.

"Here's the report on the prints found on the French window."

"Ah!" murmured Ben. "Chang Lee Hi's! That is, if those on the dragon cards be his."

They checked.

"So he *was* here!" Ben exclaimed.

"Here's more from that there window," Denny said, laying another chart down for Ben's inspection. "The boys at headquarters identified these."

"Whose?"

"One of the nastiest gangsters working out of Chicago. Luigi Donatello."

"Then Francesca was more nearly right than she knew when she said that she saved Pietro's life."

"Huh? Yeah. Sure. I get yuh."

That Denny was dubious, I felt reasonably certain.

"Look," he went on, "here's the prints from the gun found out yonder."

"Luigi Donatello again! Good Lord, Denny, are we never going to get to the bottom of this thing?"

"Sez you, Mr. Bailey? A few minutes ago you was going to have the murderer apprehended at dawn. Huh!" And to Sleepy Wallingford, he remarked, "Private Investigators!"

"Pretty punk lot," agreed Ben, winking at Phil Strong.

At eleven o'clock we adjourned to "the tomb", and Sleepy was sent to bring Fifi Burgoyne down for an interview. She came in with defiant look on her hard, pretty face.

"Evenin' to yuh, *madamzelly*," Denny greeted. "Have a chair. H'm, now, we don't believe that story yuh told about how yuh met this here Dr. Elsing. The boys in Chicago say there ain't never been no Mrs. Stanley Brown-Coppersmith III in that big town as you claimed you worked for. What yuh gotta say 'bout that?"

Fifi didn't seem to care whether he believed her or not.

"You said Dr. Elsing recommended yuh to Mrs. Wilmorton. Did yuh know Elsing's skipped out—vanished?"

Fifi shrugged, languidly patting her dark tresses.

"Been eating a great deal of soup today, *mademoiselle?*" Ben asked.

Fifi's dark eyes swung to his, but she said nothing.

Ben stared intently at her; then asked, "Why did you bother to knot those sheets you hung out of your window? Surely you didn't think that you could fool a clever detective like Mr. Denny." Denny swelled, pridefully. With a smile, Ben went on, asking, "Where'd you go when you disappeared?"

"That I mean for you to find out," was the impudent answer.

"I'm going to find out. Don't overlook that fact, *mademoiselle*. In truth, I already have a good notion."

Fifi merely studied the hands folded in her lap.

"Ever hear of Luigi Donatello when yuh was in Chicago? Huh?" Denny abruptly shot at her.

Fifi shook her head, unperturbed.

"You wouldn't be working with 'im—would yuh, now?"

Fifi sniffed, contemptuously. At Denny's request, she went to the Renaissance table, where the IOU's. of Mrs. Wilmorton had been laid.

"Ever see 'em before, huh?"

Fifi scrutinized the six bits of damaging evidence, but no look of betrayal crept into her dark eyes.

"Ever seen this before?" Ben suddenly demanded, thrusting the news photo of Gwendolyn Seabury under Fifi's pert nose.

Smiling faintly, Fifi again shook her head.

"That's all," Hal Denny said, as Ben laid the clipping down. "You can go back upstairs. Sleepy, you escort her."

A moment she hesitated—regarding Ben searchingly, then turned away toward the double doors.

As she was about to pass out into the hall, Ben said to her, "*Mademoiselle,* it sometimes pays to turn state's evidence."

Again she hesitated, for a moment only; then wearily preceded Sleepy across the hall and up the stairs. As I write this account, I wonder what might have been the outcome had Fifi obeyed that momentary impulse which must have been hers when Ben offered that suggestion. But then, it may be that things could not have been altered. One thing, however, is certain: we might have been spared further death and attempts at murder.

Fifi off our hands, Pietro was sent for. He came down, leaning on Brookes' arm and looking haggard and thin. His eyes burned feverishly.

"I have talked with Romeo," Ben told him.

Pietro jerked erect in the chair Ben had shoved under him.

"At the Curtis," Ben added.

Pietro settled back, grinning at Ben. "You cannot realize what a relief it is for me to have you know," he said.

"I can imagine. Now tell us about Luigi."

"Mother of God! You know about Luigi Donatello?"

Ben briefly outlined the findings. When the story was finished, Pietro began rocking back and forth, moaning piteously.

"He killed the *Master!* I know that it was he. Now he will kill me. He told me that he would kill me. If he fails, there are others to do it for him. Some day I shall be taken for a ride—" He broke off, hiding his face in his hands.

"Don't be foolish, Martini. He's on the *lam* now."

"You say that because you do not know Luigi. He will strike. . . . And my cousin Victor, him also will Luigi kill!"

"The police—"

"The police cannot save from Luigi!"

"He's been apprehended before; otherwise we wouldn't have his fingerprints."

Ben sent Brookes for a stiff three fingers of Scotch and handed it to Pietro, who downed it at a gulp. Then he told his story.

"I went to Victor and told him about the Borgia. I asked him for poison. He would not give it to me, so I overpowered him and tied him in his swivel chair. I secured the poison I wanted. Once I heard someone moving in the adjoining room. It must have been Luigi—in there spying on me. Victor did not dare warn me, for it would have meant being rubbed out. . . . I hurried to my car— but you know all that. Leaping onto the running-board, Luigi told me that he was going to have the Borgia, and that I was to get it for him."

"Then why did he leave you when your car stalled and Romeo came along?"

"I do not know, Mr. Bailey."

Unexpectedly he lurched forward, tearing at his hair and laughing hysterically—like a dog-gone woman.

"What difference does it make?" he screamed. "I killed him! I killed the Master!"

4

Ben handled Pietro roughly, slapping the hysterics out of him. "What do you mean, saying that you killed Howard Ralston?"

"I as good as killed him when I told Victor about the Borgia and Luigi overheard me."

Pietro sobbed uncontrollably. At Ben's suggestion, Sleepy and I carried him upstairs, stripped him, gave him a hot bath and rub-down, and put him to bed. Leaving him asleep, we returned to "the tomb," where we found Harry Patterson, M. Cornier's man, in conference with Detective Denny.

"I suppose M. Cornier told you my name," the fellow was saying. "Well, it's my own name, even if I have been in *stir*." Perceiving that Denny shot Ben a quick glance, he added, "I was framed. It's for fear I'll be caught in this mess that I'm here to tell you what I know. I don't want to do another stretch for a crime I'm not in on."

"What you want to tell us, Patterson?" Denny inquired with feline gentleness.

"Promise me protection. I don't want it known I squealed."

"We'll do our best. Shoot!"

"It's this way," Patterson began, nervously wetting his lips, "M. Cornier lied to you this afternoon."

"We know that."

"But you don't know everything. That's why I came to you gentlemen. . . . God, I've passed a terrible twenty-four hours!" Patterson glanced nervously about "the tomb."

"M. Cornier never went to Faribault last night," he said. "He was home a little after ten, and he never went to bed at all."

"Did you get that blue lime brushed out of the seams of his shoes?" Ben asked.

"You know *that?*" Patterson faltered.

"We know that he dragged a body out of this room," Ben replied, taking what I knew to be a long shot.

"What did he do with the body?" demanded Denny.

"It was upstairs in a nitric acid bath," Patterson mumbled. "I don't know what became of it—unless it was eaten up by the acid."

"Not time enough for that," Ben told him. "Takes a long time for that acid to consume a body. But how do you know all this, Patterson?"

"I inadvertently came upon M. Cornier. . . . My God, you'll have to protect me! He swore that he would kill me if—"

"We'll protect you," Denny promised.

"I advise that Patterson go back to *Fontainebleau* and carry on as if nothing had happened," Ben said.

"What think?" Denny wanted to know, when Patterson reluctantly left us.

"It looks," Ben admitted, grinning at the triumphant city detective, "as if you *might* be right."

"You know I'm right! Mr. Cornier did it."

"Patterson couldn't be diverting suspicion from himself, could he?" I asked.

Denny burned me down with the scorn of his glance.

Ben said, "Let's have this aspiring young architect in. Get Wayland, Win."

With the blueprints of *Windermere* spread out upon the Renaissance table, Ben studied them intently with Wayland Thomas.

"No sign of a secret passage," Wayland decided. "I fear that you are on the wrong track, Mr. Bailey."

"What!" Denny exclaimed, derisively. "No secret passage? No hidden room?"

"Odd, Wayland," Ben said, ignoring Denny's thrust. "These blueprints have been carefully preserved through the years so that anybody wishing to study the arrangement of the house might do so."

"*Tck! tck! tck!*"

Hal Denny was enjoying himself.

"You don't suppose," Ben asked him, "that Howard Ralston would keep a faked set of blueprints around just to deceive the curious, do you?"

Getting out his carpenter's rule, Ben set to measuring the walls about the fireplace, Wayland jotting down figures. From time to time these were compared with those on the blueprints. Denny grinned his appreciation of the performance.

"You're right, Mr. Bailey!" Wayland declared, when measurements inside and out of "the tomb" were completed. "The details of these blueprints do not check with details in the actual construction."

Denny was ready to protest, but Mary Rose Blodgett happily headed him off by coming down at that moment with a message from Miss Lutie to the effect that Mrs. Wilmorton was ready to be interviewed.

"This interview should prove interesting," Ben said, as we prepared for adjournment to the upper floor.

"Where yuh get that 'interesting'? You don't hold to my theory."

"But Mrs. Wilmorton is a vital angle in *my* theory," Ben replied, suavely.

"Aw, come on!"

"Half a minute," Ben urged. Turning to Wayland, he said, "While we're upstairs—"

"Say!" bawled Sleepy, who had squatted at the grate to strike a match. "Look-it!"

He pointed into the fireplace. There on the dusty cement behind the gas-logs was a footprint. It pointed toward the rear wall of the fireplace.

"Wayland," Ben said, "you and Sleepy find the gadget that releases that back wall."

"Come on!" growled Denny. "Quit playing with phony ideas."

We found Julia Wilmorton lying on her sitting-room couch, miserable semblance of her former self. She turned her face to the wall as we entered.

"How long have you been treating with this here Dr. Elsing?" Denny began.

"Since early in July."

"Saw him yesterday afternoon?"

"Yes."

"At his home on Pillsbury Avenue?"

"I did."

"Find his fees high, don't yuh?"

Mrs. Wilmorton began to cry; Nurse Lutie soothed her. "Lot of money yuh paid for them treatments. Sixty thousand dollars, huh?"

Julia Wilmorton's body stiffened.

"You devils!" cried Fifi, jumping up. "How can you torture her so?"

"Please," urged Miss Lutie. "We must all be calm, or I shall have to request that you withdraw."

Denny apologized, pleading urgency of the case. Cautioning him to be as considerate as possible, Miss Lutie consented to continuance of the questioning.

Denny sat looking down upon Mrs. Wilmorton. A moment her eyes held their gaze to his, then fluttering lids veiled them.

"Mrs. Wilmorton," Denny gently said, "we found your IOU's. Why'd yuh give 'em to this here Elsing?"

"Gambling debts," came the faint response.

Patient questioning brought out the facts. Mrs. Wilmorton had met Dr. Elsing at contract parties given by Maudie Lea Nelson in St. Paul. Broke, she had played for high stakes. Elsing proved friendly. He aided her in her bets at several places—lending her money to cover her losses, and generously accepting her IOU's.

"Ma'am," Denny informed her, "Dr. Elsing is dead. Now, you couldn't have killed him, could yuh?"

Julia Wilmorton sat bolt upright on her couch, staring at Hal Denny.

"Dead!" she whispered. "No, I didn't kill him. He—"

"His honest-to-God name was Dupont, wasn't it?" Denny queried.

"You can't mean that Gaston Dupont has been murdered?" cried the startled woman.

To Miss Lutie she said, "Steady me, please."

"*Madame!*" cried Fifi Burgoyne, as Julia Wilmorton turned fevered eyes upon her.

"Fifi Burgoyne," Julia Wilmorton reproached her maid, "you have deceived me. You and he promised—" She broke off, to point trembling finger at the French maid. "She killed Gaston Dupont when I sent her to Dr. Elsing's last night!" Her voice rose in shrilling crescendo. "She killed Howard Ralston!"

"She's crazy!" Fifi challenged.

"Fifi killed them both!" Mrs. Wilmorton hysterically screamed. "She tried to poison all of us!"

She collapsed in Nurse Lutie's arms, and we had to summon Dr. Kelsey. Angry at what we had done, he bawled us out plenty, chasing us out and across to my room.

"Can yuh beat that?" Denny wanted to be told. "Jeez, what a accusation!"

"Hysterics, doubtless," Ben cautioned. "We know that Dr. Elsing killed Dupont. That let's Fifi out."

"If she ain't guilty of Dupont's murder, then she probably ain't guilty of the other charges Mrs. Wilmorton slung against her," complained Denny, ruefully, as if reluctantly surrendering another clue.

5

In "the tomb," Wayland Thomas and Sleepy Wallingford excitedly awaited us.

"Show 'em kiddo," Sleepy urged.

Wayland pointed out the hidden spring that Ben had set them to find. Hal Denny pressed it; and, as we watched, the rear wall of the fireplace rolled ponderously out of sight. Letting Wayland lead, Ben motioned us to follow. We passed through the fireplace, to find ourselves in a long passage. In its left wall was an open panel. Squeezing through this, we descended a ladder into darkness. Ben found a section of thick wooden wall that slid upward. He moved it, revealing the basement closet we had previously explored.

"Ha!" cried Denny. "He drug the body down this way an' out into the basement, an' then changed his mind an' drug it back again."

"I surmise that you are right," Ben said. "He took the body back up into the passage and along it to his own house, where he placed it in that nitric acid bath."

We climbed back into the passage and followed it away from *Windermere's* fireplace to where it ended in a wall. Knowing that Cornier's mansion was built on practically the same plan as Howard Ralston's, Ben—concluding that we were now in *Fontainebleau*—had Wayland search for the spring that would release the rear wall of Cornier's fireplace. Wayland succeeded in locating it, and we stepped into M. Cornier's library.

Patterson, coming in with a cocktail service, almost let it fall when he discovered us. He explained that he had just served M. Cornier a stiff bracer in the music room and had come through the library to pick up whisky glasses that had been left there during the forenoon.

As we whispered with Patterson, we could hear the music of the organ. *Lieberstrum.* M. Cornier's dreaming of the woman that now he can never have, I speculated.

Denny's problem was how to get Cornier out of his house, in order that search might be made for the body of Howard Ralston. Ben had an idea, which Denny promptly acted upon. The plan was for Patterson to be ready for us in a quarter of an hour. Then we returned to *Windermere,* where it was arranged that Paul should have Brookes telephone M. Cornier Paul's request that he come over for confidential discussion of the case.

The scheme worked. As we stole down the stairs, we heard the click of the latch on the upper hall door admitting from the glassed-in hallway over the *porte-cochere.* Knowing that M. Cornier was safe for the time in Paul's room, with Phil Strong there in case of emergency, our party took the fireplace route to *Fontainebleau.*

From the library, Patterson conducted us to that upstairs bathroom where the body had been acid-soaked. The tub had been cleaned, but there lingered in the room the nauseating odor of the body-devouring fluid.

"That's that!" decided Denny. "Body's been et up."

"Hell's bells, no!" swore Ben. "There's no acid known that will consume a body in so short a time. Cornier has removed the partially eaten corpse and hidden it."

"Be a magician, wise boy. Pull the body outen a top-hat."

Ben carried on, serene under Denny's jibes. He led us through the house, prying into every nook and corner. Descending to the furnace room, we cleaned out the furnace. Disappointment confronted us at every turn.

"Begging pardon, gentlemen," Patterson then said, "but M. Cornier spent a portion of the forenoon in the stables. He was badly shaken when he came back to the house. It was then I served him whisky in the library."

Going upstairs and out through the kitchen, we passed an old-fash-
ioned icebox. For no reason at all, I lifted the lid.

As I did so, Patterson exclaimed, "That's funny! That refrigerator is
never used; now there's ice in the chamber."

Denny opened the box proper. It was empty and stale from disuse.
Then, while Ben kept his torch flashed upon the ice-chamber, Sleepy
and Patterson lifted out the ice. Below it was a piece of zinc, under
which had been placed a japanned tin box. Wayland broke the box
open.

The lifted lid revealed, neatly folded, the blood-soaked clothes of
Howard Ralston.

Silently we replaced the tin box, the sheet of zinc, and the block of
ice. The clothes we took with us. Hearts beating wild excitement, we
went out of the house, crossed the terrace, and entered the stables. M.
Cornier's blooded horses were champing restlessly in their stalls. The
distant clock boomed midnight.

Searching everywhere, we came finally to the hay room. Moving
the bales about, we came upon it. In a sort of grave, artfully arranged
among the heavy bales of hay, lay the gruesome thing—an acid-disfig-
ured body. In places the flesh was eaten away to the bone; in spots the
bone itself had been destroyed.

"It's him all right," Wayland Thomas replied to Denny's question.

Denny looked to me for further confirmation.

I could only nod my identification, too emotionally unstrung to
speak.

MIDNIGHT OF THE SECOND DAY

1

We took Patterson to *Windermere,* deeming it unsafe for him to remain at *Fontainebleau.* For some reason, too, Detective Denny didn't want M. Cornier's man out of his sight. Myself, I wondered about Harry Patterson. He had done time in Stillwater for a crime he claimed he didn't commit, and of which M. Cornier did not believe him guilty. M. Cornier had befriended him when he came out of stir a marked man, unable to find employment. Just what the situation obtaining between the two men? Was Cornier using Patterson, planning to make him a scapegoat; was Patterson the murderer of Howard Ralston, seeking to divert suspicion to his master? Frankly, I was puzzled.

As soon as we were back in Ralston's house, Hal Denny sent out calls for all who had been contacted in the course of the investigation, concluding his instructions in each case with the words: "Be at *Windermere* before 3 a.m." He said for them to come, and he meant them to be there—and on time. Ben had said that the mystery would be solved by dawn that morning of August 17, and Mr. Harrison Denny wanted to show Ben that he—official city investigator—would be the one to do that settling. Just his cussed contrariness, I thought at the time—and still so think.

Denny knew that Ben wasn't satisfied with the outcome of the investigation to date, even if that naked, acid-marred body had been found under bales of hay in Cornier's stables—even if every indication did point to Henri Cornier as the party who had knifed the life-blood out of that body; but he wasn't going to permit Ben to put anything over on him.

203

Alone with me, Ben threw himself down on my bed, saying, "Whichever way you look at it, Win, it's a mess."

"Denny says that the case is completed, Ben. He's going to make an arrest."

"And probably arrest the wrong man."

"But there's Patterson's story, Ben. Look at the queer things M. Cornier's done—and the lies he's told. . . . There's the body, Ben."

"Yes," he admitted, "there's the body. But things don't tie up as they should; there's a missing link somewhere."

"You mean between what Denny has uncovered and what you deduce from the pages of my diary?"

"That—and my psychic hunch. The spirit of truth within me is not satisfied." He dragged lazily, meditatively on his cigarette. "This crime isn't simply a Cornier-Wilmorton conspiracy. If it were, what about Chang Lee Hi, and Youssuf, and the Duke of Vedena? What about the Chicago gangster, Luigi Donatello? This murder is hooked up with those three menaces in too obvious a fashion."

"Don't overlook Paul and Mildred and Pietro—even myself, in listing your suspects," I reminded him.

"Sure. What about all of you? You have to admit, Win, that this case isn't as limpid as our Irish colleague would have us believe."

"He's got a pretty good case."

"Too damned good! But Denny's apt to switch suspects within the next ten minutes. That big boy doesn't know whether he's going or coming."

"What about the letter *L* in your files, eh?" I queried.

"You're the shrewd one," Ben complimented me, grinning. "That *L*-file is significant. In fact, it ties up nicely with a certain dossier I brought along with me on that last visit to my apartment."

He got up and opened his brief case, extracting several dossiers. One he laid out before me. It was labeled: *Case of the Baroness Mathilde*.

"Who was the Baroness Mathilde, and where does she come in?" I asked.

"That's a tale I may have to relate," Ben replied.

"I'd hate to see Hal Denny walk off and leave you holding the sack," I said, thumbing the leaves of *The Case of the Baroness Mathilde*.

"Don't worry, Old Timer. The big game isn't snared yet." He slipped his revolver from a pocket and examined it. "I'm going down to 'the tomb'," he informed me.

"Going to play your psychic hunch?"

"Right! Ever hear of psychometry? According to Webster, psychometry is an alleged faculty of divination through contact with, or proximity to, an object or person." He drew the little black box from the coin pocket of his trousers. "This little box, for instance, if we are to heed the wizards of the occult, has an aura of its own. All persons and things, the wizards believe, radiate a magnetic atmosphere peculiar to themselves. That aura absorbs the magnetism of the owner of this box, for example—making a permanent absorption. In every magnetic particle of that aura is permanently mirrored every emotion of the owner and every scene that has been reflected upon that box. . . . If I hold the box in my hand or place it against my forehead, I will catch the vibrations of the aura of the box—*tune in,* as it were, with the experiences of the box. As a result, one of several things may happen: I may clairvoyantly vision the owner of the box, or I may sense the personality of that owner and catch the recorded vibrations of his thoughts and emotions—even a cinema-like reproduction of his actions while he was carrying the box. Something like radio and television combined."

"That's all hooey!" I scoffed.

"Maybe. I'm not one to say. But I've read of some darned funny experiments and experiences. The annals of the Society for Psychical Research abound in them. A great many people who have given serious attention to psychometry testify to unusual results."

"Why don't you try it, then? You've got the little black box."

"I don't make the experiment, because my imagination has already wrapped itself about this little black box and fitted it into its place in the deductions I have made from facts gleaned from you and your invaluable diary."

Returning the box to his pocket and lighting a fresh cigarette, he said, "I've wired to the firm whose name is on the box. A telegram from them may arrive at any moment."

"What was in that box, Ben?"

"You've been looking at the contents for several days, my lad. Keep your shirt on: you'll soon be knowing."

"At dawn?"

"I shouldn't be surprised. Now, I'm going alone down into 'the tomb.' There's an experiment I want to try. You see, the wizards of the occult hold to another intriguing theory that whatever takes place in a room is photographed eradicably upon the walls of that room—each electric particle in the aura of the room mirroring all that has been enacted before it. If this theory be true, the murder of last night is recorded upon the four enclosing walls of Howard Ralston's 'tomb.' Pleasant thought, isn't it?"

"You're not going down there alone—and maybe read clairvoyantly that fearful record?"

"Sounds crazy, doesn't it? But that's my projected experiment. Seated in a comfortable chair, I shall induce psychometric trance and await developments. If possible, I shall clairvoyantly read the history of the crime. When I employ the word *clairvoyance,* I do not mean the actual seeing of things pictorially. A better term would be the word *clair-cognizance,* meaning mental clarity or acuteness. The whole process is but a matter of concentration and sensitive receptivity. In my psychometric condition there will come to me a purely intellectual perception."

"Sounds screwy to me."

"To me, too. But it's worth trying. I'm desperate enough to try anything. I know that I'm the guy who not so long ago warned you against things occult. I still warn you; but that's no guarantee that I fail to recognize the existence of stranger things than fiction in this world."

"Don't do it, Ben. There's no telling what might happen."

"Who knows what may happen if I don't do it? An innocent man may be arrested and convicted—a man I might otherwise save."

"Take me with you."

"No can do, Old Timer. You'll be busy anyway." He took from his inside coat pocket a sealed test tube. "This tube," he said, "contains a hair that I want you to analyze. In Pietro's shop are the necessary apparatus and chemicals. These notes I've made afford instructions as to procedure and objectives. Further, lock away those dossiers, and—if you want to do so—later on read the history of the Baroness Mathilde."

2

It was 2 a.m. when I returned to my room. Ben hadn't come up. To pass time, I read the *Case of the Baroness Mathilde*. Like a flash I got what Ben had been thinking all along. I understood, too, why he was down there alone in "the tomb." Lord, it was awful! A crime stupendous in its conception. I feared for Julia Wilmorton. But that acid-eaten body! For the life of me, I couldn't fit Henri Cornier into the crime.

I paced the floor, smoking savagely and imagining all kinds of things that could have happened to Ben. At 2:15 he came in.

"Good!" he said, pocketing the test tube and reading statement of my findings. "Just what I thought."

"What success with your clair-cognizance?" I asked.

"I didn't see any motion picture in an astral cinema, but I got results. Selecting my comfortable chair, I concentrated my mind on the murder of Howard Ralston, to the exclusion of every iota of interference. If you think that's an easy task, try it sometime, Big Boy."

"I'm listening."

"Holding my point of concentration steadily before what I am pleased to call my higher consciousness, I saturated myself with the atmosphere of the big room. With the entire case I had built up before me and associating with it the case of the Baroness Mathilde, I linked my suspect with the murder. I put myself in his place and sought to determine what I would do if I were out to murder Howard Ralston and had available to my hand all that the murderer found ready at his last night and in the weeks immediately preceding. . . . It must have been genuine clair-cognizance, Win; for, like the proverbial bolt out of a clear sky, the satisfactory solution illuminated my concentrated consciousness. . . . Of course, I may be wrong; but I think not. Anyway the pieces in my *Windermere* jig-saw puzzle fit. All I need now is that expected telegram concerning the little black box."

"And this hair in the test tube?"

"If I am correct in my deductions, that hair comes from the head of the murderer's accomplice, who is still in this house."

"Going to let Hal Denny in on this new solution?"

"Not on your life! Finders are keepers in this case."

"Going to let him make that arrest?"

"I can no more keep him from arresting Henri Cornier than I can halt the movement of an Alpine avalanche. . . . But we must be moving. Get Wayland!"

I found the chauffeur. He and Ben went down into "the tomb," locking the double doors against all intruders. Again I paced and smoked. I finally arrived at the stage where I could no longer bear to be alone, so I went down the hall to Paul's room.

About to knock on his door, I hesitated. Mildred Manning was in there with Paul, and they were talking. I listened, thinking that from what they were saying I could determine whether or not I would be *de trop*.

"The jig's up, Mildred," Paul was saying. "Detective Denny means to arrest me on charge of murdering my own father."

"Paul, he can't do that."

"Circumstantial evidence, Honey. He's got to nab somebody to save his face, and I'm as good a bet as the next one. The reporters have been playing ball with him and not spilling anything; but they want a story, and Denny has to let them have one. He's compelled to make an arrest."

"I'm as guilty as you are," Mildred said.

"Darling, they're not going to pin anything on you. If I find myself on the spot, I'll take the rap. You're not to be mixed up in this."

"Paul," she said, reproachful-like, "you know that I love you too well to let you keep me from sharing whatever fate overtakes you."

Judging from the manner in which the lovers seemed to react toward things, I decided it might be just as well for me to join them. I knocked.

I went in, when Mildred's voice bade me enter, to find Paul in a wheel chair, with Mildred on an ottoman beside him. Both looked relieved when they saw that I was their caller.

"Expecting the devil to walk in on you?" I laughed.

"In the semblance of an Irish policeman," Paul smiled. "Mildred and I have been talking the situation over, West, and—"

"I couldn't help hearing part of what you said," I confessed. "And I'm thinking you're all haywire. Denny has changed his mind about you."

Mildred's eyes lighted, but Paul looked glum.

"That's the trouble with that Irishman," he complained. "He doesn't know whether he thinks *this* or *that*. He can't make up his mind."

"He can't tag anything to you," I strove to assure him.

"Denny thinks I poisoned Martini. Denny's got my gun. Worst of all, there's the damning evidence Martini gave."

"Even I had to help things along," I complemented, ruefully.

"You *were* indiscreet in that diary of yours, West," Paul said.

"Yet Mr. Bailey maintains that Mr. West's journal has given him the key to the mystery," Mildred put in.

"Yeah!" Paul grunted. "What does Denny think of Ben and his deductions? What respect has he for West's diary? All he got out of it was my love for you and the fact that I quarreled with my father. Denny couldn't see beyond that."

"He's going to arrest M. Cornier," I told them.

"And who else?" Paul wanted to know. "He'll be arresting Deborah before he's through."

"Paul, dearest, you mustn't be pessimistic," Mildred counseled, her cheek against his hand.

Paul caught her to him. I discreetly turned away.

"That's all right, West," Paul laughed. "We may be successful in holding off the reporters, but I've found there's no need trying to have secrets from you. If Mildred and I escape this mess, we're going to be married."

"I'm thinking you have no cause to worry," I offered. "Ben has gone occult. He's been down in 'the tomb,' throwing a psychometric trance and reading astral photographs or something. Been warbling about clair-cognizance or some such fool stuff—"

"Ben's nobody's fool," Paul said. "If he's talked the occult, he's been stringing you or somebody through you. In this house the walls have ears."

"I ought to know," I said. "Anyway, Ben's down there in the big room, reviewing the entire set-up. He came back upstairs as radiant as a May morning. He's got something up his sleeve, Paul."

What I said seemed to cheer them; and I, hearing Ben's voice down the hall, left the lovers to themselves.

THE DAWNING OF THE THIRD DAY

1

At 3:15, while we were awaiting the arrival of Hal Denny's guests, Ben and I sat smoking on the seat in my chamber's oriel window.

"The skies overhead have cleared," I observed, "and the stars are unusually brilliant after the storm. It's as if peace had laid its benediction upon *Windermere*."

"There are ominous clouds in the east," Ben murmured, exhaling dreamily.

There were clouds in the east, dark and threatening, slowly mounting the heavens. Storm clouds in the east! Had peace come to *Windermere?* Or were ghosts forever to haunt that strange house? Was there symbolic implication in Ben's words when he said, *There are ominous clouds in the east?*

One by one the cars rolled in along the curved driveway, bringing the members of our oddly assorted house-party. There would be Colonel Mayfair, although I couldn't see why Denny should insist upon the old lawyer's corning, unless it were to give a certain aspect of legality to the proceedings. Also, Dr. Lao Wong, towered over by the protecting Soo Wang. There would be the mountainous Lucretia Lansing, trotted after by the feisty Duke of Vedena. There would be Pietro's cousin, Victor Martini, head chemist for *Maris and Maris*. Gaston Dupont lay naked on a slab in the city morgue; but where was his evil genius, the sinister Dr. Elsing, that we wanted so much to lay hands on? Where was Chang Lee Hi, emissary of the Scarlet Dragons? Dr. Lao Wong had said that Chang Lee Hi would come again to *Windermere*. But would he? And when? . . . Youssuf would be among our guests; and there would be present that *Romeo,* who had saved Pietro's life. But what of the Chicago gangster and blackmailer, Luigi Donatello? . . . With so many loose ends—each floating its question mark—could peace come to *Windermere?*

The distant bell boomed the half-hour. There was hint of dawn over the city. In the east the clouds continued to augment.

Suddenly my heart skipped a beat, for I saw a dark form stealthily making its way across the lawns towards *Fontainebleau.* From tree to tree it glided, never swerving from its course.

"Look, Ben!" I whispered.

"Excellent!" he chuckled, discovering the mysterious intruder.

"How come, excellent?"

"You'll be knowing presently."

2

Detective Denny came breezing in, and I forgot the incident of the shadowy figure on the dawn-caressed lawns until we burst frantically into "the tomb" and found—. But I must not anticipate.

"I got the report on Paul Ralston's gun and the bullet we dug outen the wall in the big room," Denny announced. "They don't match; and the markings on the bullet wasn't made in the barrel of Donatello's revolver neither."

"Now, isn't that too bad?" sighed Ben. "All this fuss about a bullet we know was fired by Howard Ralston from his own gun."

"Maybe!" snapped Denny. "Let's get going."

"Just a moment, Denny."

"Now what?"

"Are you going to arrest M. Cornier?"

"Any objection?"

"None that would mitigate your determination, Mr. Denny."

Denny wheeled and went out, mumbling imprecations upon the heads of all private investigators. Ben and I toddled after him. I couldn't interpret Ben's casual attitude—his almost jubilant mood; but then I didn't know what he and Wayland had been doing in "the tomb."

As for "the tomb" at that moment, the steel barriers were down and the doors all locked—with the key stowed in Hal Denny's pocket.

Some party awaited us in the drawing rooms. At least twenty people—including the members of Howard Ralston's "family," the Ralston
servants, and a pasty-faced Harry Patterson. M. Cornier wasn't present.

Facing the assembled company, Ben beside him, Denny said, "We
are awaiting the arrival of Mr. Cornier. To pass the time, I shall have
my friend and co-worker on this here case, Mr. Benjamin Butler Bailey,
give you a summary of the case as it now stands; after which I expect
to make an arrest."

Ben smiled upon Hal Denny, quite as if he were grateful for the opportunity thrust unexpectedly upon him—just as if he had been promised that opportunity. Me—I was dumbfounded! Why should Denny
spring that summarizing business upon Ben, knowing darned well that
he and Ben were miles apart in their conclusions? My resolution of the
situation was inevitable: maliciousness upon the part of Mr. Denny,
with purpose to embarrass Ben by making him appear ridiculous in the
eyes of that hyper-critical audience. But old Ben took it good-naturedly,
promptly agreeing to comply with Denny's request.

An apprehensive stir was noticeable among the jittery "guests" that
sat facing us.

"Ladies and gentlemen," Ben began, "it is with more pleasure than
Mr. Denny may ascribe to one so young and so inexperienced in the
gentle art of sleuthing that I assume this momentous task. Now, with
Mr. Denny's permission, I should like to tell you a story—a story that
comes to mind in connection with the case under present consideration."

"Now looky here," Denny began complaint.

"Five years ago this summer," Ben blithely went on, "a notorious
crime came to the attention of the Paris *Surete.* I refer to the case of
the Baroness Mathilde."

If Ben had abruptly planned a *coup de theatre,* he was then and
there disappointed in the reaction of that selected audience. If there
were parties present who grasped the significance of the case name,
they gave no sign. However, there showed no disappointment in Ben's
blue eyes as they swept the faces of his listeners. As if satisfied with
what he saw, he continued.

"There came to Paris, from Bavaria, a beautiful woman named
Mathilde Kronk. Having inherited a small fortune, she meant to utilize it

in making her way upward in the world. With her, the judicious spending of money must pave the way to security and happiness. Mathilde ravaged the Parision shops, blossoming forth as a magnificently gowned woman of the world.

"From Paris, Mathilde went to Saint-Moritz, ostensibly to enjoy the winter sports, but actually to make the catch of the season. She succeeded, for shortly continental newspapers blazed news that Baron de Longpres had eloped with the lady from Bavaria and was honeymooning with her on the Italian Riviera.

"Married to the baron, Mathilde became his principal heir. But the baron was miserly. To enjoy the gay and luxurious life she craved, Mathilde turned to gambling. She met Faustin Dufresne."

"Faustin Dufresne!" exclaimed Denny. "Seems I've heard of him."

"Very likely, Mr. Denny. He is wanted by the police of three continents. At one time he was a popular character actor in Parisian theatres. Retiring from that type of theatrical activity, he married Marietta Gale, a chic *mademoiselle* of French and English parentage. With her as assistant, Dufresne established his own theatre, making it a house of illusion. Again he attained fame and popularity, his expertness in the art of legerdemain ranking with that of Hermann and Houdini."

"Got into nasty scrapes, didn't he?" Denny questioned.

"Several," Ben replied. "Silly women pursued him. Capitalizing on their infatuations, he robbed them at roulette wheel and card table. The Baroness Mathilde was introduced to him at Deauville. First thing she knew, Dufresne was giving her tips at the gambling tables—then lending her money. Finally, at Monte Carlo, he was accepting her IOU's."

Apparently deaf to Julia Wilmorton's smothered exclamation, Ben hurried on.

"The baroness found herself on the spot. Faustin Dufresne pressed her for money; insisted that she buy up her notes. Fearing to reveal her predicament to her miserly husband, Baroness Mathilde found herself compelled to give ear to a scheme the designing Dufresne proposed. As a result, she became partner in wholesale murder—that is as 'accessory before and after the fact.'

"Along with his practice of legerdemain, Dufresne indulged in the art of hypnotism. It is the belief of the *Surete* that Dufresne had recourse to hypnotism in his control of the baroness. . . ."

"Hypnotism!" breathed Julia Wilmorton.

"Yes, Mrs. Wilmorton. Hypnotism—a dangerous power in the hands of an unscrupulous man like the criminal Dufresne."

"Who believes in hypnotism in this enlightened day?" sneered Lucretia Lansing.

"I shall be happy to furnish you a list of specified references, *madame,*" Ben replied. "It is an established fact that a victim under hypnotic influence cannot be urged into crime against his inclination. There must be something in that victim's psychological makeup that responds to the suggestion toward crime. Exhaustive inquiry into the past of the Baroness Mathilde unearthed information that as a child she was given to lying and deception and to sadistic practices on pets. In her youth, she was several times detected in petty thievery."

Covertly observing Mrs. Wilmorton, I saw her eyelids lower and a dull coloring mount her cheeks.

"The husband of the baroness died at his villa in Cannes, following a lingering illness," Ben continued. "Later, the other heirs sickened one by one and died—at discreet intervals and under seemingly natural circumstances, the baroness in each instance serving as compassionate nurse. She was assisted in her ministrations by a supposedly deaf-and-dumb boy, afterwards identified as Marietta Gale, actress-wife of Dufresne. The stomachs of the exhumed bodies were discovered to contain arsenic.

"Eventually finding herself sole surviving heir, the baroness went into seclusion for the traditional mourning period. That retirement ended, she married Dufresne—unaware that the deaf-mute was his wife, not his son. The luckless baroness was persuaded to make a will in favor of her new husband—a gentleman who was demonstrative in his affection, showering her with gifts and flowers.

"That will securely put away, the bridal couple went to Switzerland. There Dufresne, utilizing his mechanical skill, engineered an automobile accident in which the baroness was killed. Fortunately the gadget designed to fire the wrecked car did not work. Police discovery of that diabolical gadget led to exposure of the crime."

"They never caught up with them birds, I believe," commented Denny.

"Several times they were nearly caught," Ben said. "But Dufresne's experiences as a character actor enabled him to assume effective disguise. Taking the name of 'Chic Quayle,' and boasting himself 'king of international crooks,' he directed his gang's operations from a lair in the *Rue de Charenton*.

"Always on the alert for bigger and better game, Dufresne put his chic wife to voyaging on Atlantic liners. She served as finger woman for the gang. Imagine her delight when she met Pietro Martini and learned from him of the Josephine diamonds, of the unusual will left by Basil Manning, and of the widowed Julia Wilmorton. The information that Marietta Gale, *alias* Gwendolyn Seabury, carried to that den in the *Rue de Charenton* was as good meat as the wolf Dufresne, alias *Chic Quayle,* hungered for."

"What a fool I was!" muttered Pietro.

"Just an infatuated ass, Martini," was Ben's pointed rejoinder, "and lucky to escape with your life."

"How come you to tie up Chic Quayle, or Dufresne, or whatever his name is, with the Josephine diamonds?" Detective Denny indiscreetly insisted upon being told.

To my surprise, Ben had the red diary at hand. Opening it, he read:—

July 8. This morning Howard Ralston looked up from Paris edition of 'The Chicago Post' to stare at Pietro. "What—?" the Italian began. Howard Ralston read the following, which I afterwards clipped:—

The notorious international swindler, Chic Quayle, known as 'king of world crooks,' is believed to have entered the United States *via* Canada, New York police announced today. It is thought that he is accompanied by his clever partner in many crimes, who is known to the police of three continents as Marietta Gale, *alias* Riviera Fannie, *alias* Gwendolyn Seabury. . . .

"Bailey kept telling yuh to study that there diary," Sleepy Wallingford ungraciously reminded his chief.

"Look!" shrilled Mildred, her scream jumping every last one of us off our chairs. "There's a face at that window!"

A shot, accompanied by splintering of glass, and Pietro Martini fell to the floor.

The hurricane at that moment ripped loose. A long perpendicular line of jagged silver, accompanied the appalling report of crashing thunder. Outside the house, a man screamed. The lights went out.

"Lights!" cried Paul. "Brookes, lights!"

Paul's voice was crisp in the darkness. I could hear Brookes' murmuring reply and his movements as he sought the candelabrum. A moment later a match sputtered into flame, then a second, and a third. The candelabrum on the piano was lighted and after that several candles, until the wavering flames of a dozen wicks cast dancing shadows across the room.

"Pietro has been shot!" cried Mildred, dropping beside the beautiful Francesca, who was kneeling in dumb anguish beside the 'philanderer' she had crossed the ocean to kill.

Brookes and I lifted Pietro to a couch, while policemen came in from outside, supporting a bleeding, ape-like man between them.

"We caught him right outside that window," one of the officers said.

"He couldn't have gotten away," the other said. "Lightning must have struck him."

"Luigi Donatello!" exclaimed Francesca, echoing my thought that Donatello had come to join the other 'guests' beneath the roofs of *Windermere*.

I glanced apprehensively about the room as the policemen laid Luigi upon his back on the floor. Would Chang Lee Hi come? The heart in me trembled with fear of what might yet chance.

I looked at the face of Luigi. It was evil. One swarthy cheek bore a sickly-looking gash, resulting, evidently, from the slashing blow of some jagged instrument. Looked burned. The thick neck, too, must have been burned. Right shoulder and arm were seared.

"Only lightning could have done that," Paul declared. "The bolt that struck the light wires must have hit Donatello."

Luigi tried to move. He groaned.

Pietro's eyes opened as he heard the groan. Recognizing the man on the floor, he grasped the hands of his cousin, Victor Martini. "He won't let us escape," the boy sobbed.

Francesca patted Pietro's cheek and comforted him with endearing words.

Again Luigi groaned.

"I'm dying," he gasped, speaking with thickening tongue. "Get—a priest."

"And a surgeon," directed Hal Denny, dispatching me to the floor above for Dr. Kelsey.

When I got back into the thick of it again, Denny was kneeling beside Luigi, getting his story bit by bit. What Luigi told confirmed everything that Pietro and Francesca had related concerning their adventure the night of Howard Ralston's murder. Victor Martini, it seemed, had been innocently involved in the gang murder of a Chicago policeman. Luigi had the chemist buffaloed and was consistently bleeding him for "hush money." Thus the gangster accounted for his presence in Minneapolis. He was at the laboratories of *Maris and Maris* the night of the *Windermere* murder. Upon the arrival of Pietro, Luigi had gone into a room adjacent to Victor Martini's office and from there had overheard Pietro demand poison to place in the Borgia ring. Then and there he determined to get the ring for himself.

His further narrative implicated parties present, much to their discomfort, thus contributing greatly to the clarification of several elements in the baffling mystery.

"I came to this place," he said, struggling for breath, "and see people about. . . . Out by front of house . . . a cab with woman and two men. . . . I steal by them and come where tall man sawing bar of window. . . . That I think is luck for me. . . . I watch man cut bar and glass and get into house. . . . I follow after him. . . . That room—he is so big and almost dark that I do not see well. . . . Another come and squeeze through window. . . . I keep in shadow. See man standing by big doors with gun in his hand. . . . He shoot at ghost with green light on his finger. . . . Then he fall on his face. . . . Other people I see, but fright scare me away. . . ."

"Is he dead?" Pietro anxiously queried, as Luigi lapsed into silence.

Dr. Kelsey bathed the swarthy brow, while Hal Denny held Mrs. Wilmorton's smelling salts to Luigi's nostrils. Presently a sigh escaped the swollen lips; the eyelids fluttered.

"Better my man?" asked Dr. Kelsey.

"I am dying," Luigi gasped. "For the love of God, a priest!"

"A priest is coming."

A piteous moan answered that assurance.

"Can you finish what you was telling me?" Denny asked.

"*Si*—I talk."

"Did you see anyone kill the man who had the gun in his hand?"

"*Si*—"

Luigi paused. The rest of us held breath, as it were, fearful of not catching his next words.

"Who stabbed the man with the gun, Donatello?" Denny asked, his words caressingly spoken.

The dying man's lids fluttered again; he yielded Detective Denny a beseeching look.

"I do not know, *signor*. . . . He came from fireplace—with long, ugly knife. . . . I escape—"

"Did those men in the room with you escape?" Ben asked.

"*Si, signor*. . . . All . . . hiding. I see them—"

"Who shot you?"

"Man run from front of house and I run. . . . He shoot me . . . hit me . . . I fall in bushes and lie still. . . . He not see me and go away. . . ."

Luigi could scarcely make himself heard by then, but Denny kept at him. Luigi told how he crawled from bushes to find refuge in one of the tool houses. Only a short while before, he had regained consciousness. Thought of the Borgia was uppermost in his mind—together with desire to kill Pietro. He crawled to the house, finally getting to his feet and staggering to the window where he peered in at us. Sight of Pietro flamed the hatred in his heart. He blamed the artificer for his own failure to get the Borgia—for his injuries—for everything. He shot through the window at the boy. Then a blinding flash of lightning and a terrible burning on his face and arm. . . . Where did he get the revolver with which he shot Martini? Why, he explained, he always carried two weapons. . . .

There were other questions that both Denny and Ben wanted to ask, but Luigi, pleading for a priest, lapsed into unconsciousness and died in Dr. Kelsey's arms. Officers carried out the body, and Sleepy Wallingford put through a call for the morgue ambulance.

"Interesting testimony," Denny commented. "Don't make things no brighter for some folks. Heck, why doesn't Mr. Cornier come!"

"Doubtless he'll arrive presently," Ben said. "In the meantime, I should like to go on with my story. It needs to be fitted into the development of the crime—"

His words were cut short by the ear-splitting report of two shots, whipping out of the grim silence of the dawn in hard echo— the one upon the other.

"In 'the tomb'!" Paul cried.

I saw Denny and Ben at the double doors—saw those doors unlocked—jerked open. I saw the steel barriers slowly rising. At my side panted black Deborah; the others pushed behind us.

Before I quite realized it, the steel barriers were up and the candle-lighted "tomb" exposed to view. On the floor, the vengeance dagger of the Scarlet Dragons in one outstretched hand and a smoking automatic in the other, sprawled a dead Chinese man. Over against the mummy case leaned M. Cornier, a smoking revolver in his right hand— his left arm supporting a stiff something swathed in a horse blanket. In the fireplace crouched Wayland Thomas, covering Cornier with a policeman's special. Behind Wayland yawned a black hole—the rear wall of the fireplace having been rolled aside.

"Good work, Wayland," Ben commended. "Not exactly as we anticipated, but nevertheless satisfactory."

"I thought this here chauffeur was in yonder with the rest of 'em!" ejaculated Denny. "I never missed him." Then, swinging to confront M. Cornier, he demanded, "What you got to say for yourself?"

Staring at the prostrate Chinese, Cornier muttered, "He followed me, and I shot him. It was his life or mine."

Deborah, fascinated by the contorted features of the dead Oriental, wailed, "Gawd A'mighty, hit's him! Hit's de debbil what peer in mah kitchen windah!"

Turning, she fought her way through the jostling throng and fled to her room. Mrs. O'Grady later found her there, crawled in between her two feather beds, wet with sweat and chilled with terror.

Dr. Lao Wong, backed by the inscrutable Soo Wang, bent over the slain man. Drawing a long sigh, indicative of surcease from poignant anxiety, the venerable antiquarian looked up at Ben Bailey.

"Chang Lee Hi has indeed come again to this house, but his spirit will go no more out of it," he murmured.

A couple of policemen carried the body and laid it beside that of the dead Luigi, there to await arrival of the ambulance.

And I, knowing that Gaston Dupont was already dead, asked myself if Chic Quayle would join our company.

M. Cornier lifted his blanket-swathed burden and laid it upon the Renaissance table. Turning from there, he extended his wrists.

"Arrest me, Mr. Denny," he said brokenly. "I killed him, though God knows I did not mean to do it. It was a horrible mistake."

No one spoke. Only Julia Wilmorton made a futile gesture toward the man she loved. She sobbed a dry sob of deep hurt when Denny snapped the handcuffs upon M. Cornier's wrists.

The blood went cold in my veins as I saw Paul weakly wheeling his chair toward the Renaissance table.

"Don't, Paul!" Ben warned, sharply.

"But—it's my father," Paul reminded him.

"You mustn't look at him," I urged. "We've identified the body. No one must ever look at him."

Paul covered his face with his hands. Mildred wept beside him.

"Why did you bring the body here?" Ben queried.

"Finding that Patterson had walked out on me," M. Cornier replied, "I became alarmed. I brought Howard's body back when I discovered that his clothes had been taken from the icebox. I wanted to make a clean breast of it all, and—"

"Where'd this Chang Lee Hi come from?" Denny asked.

"He was out on the terrace when I carried the body from the stables. I couldn't prevent his following me. Once we were through the tunnel and in this room, he drew a gun on me. I was quicker on the draw than he anticipated. The rest you know—. Now, for God's sake, take me away! I'm guilty of the murder of my friend."

"How'd Chang Lee Hi come to be here, I want to know?" Denny demanded of Ben.

"My little ruse brought him," Ben admitted. "That's why I asked you to have the vengeance dagger returned tonight. I wanted Chang Lee Hi. It wasn't difficult to lure him here. I merely asked Dr. Lao Wong to pass word to Chang Lee Hi that the dagger had been brought back—"

"So that's your game? All right, that clinches everything. Call in the reporters, boys!" Denny called jubilantly. "Tell 'em the case is busted wide open. An' send for the wagon!"

"Hold everything!"

Ben's voice rang out above the pandemonium that reigned in "the tomb," his command halting the policemen hell-bent on doing Denny's bidding.

"Looky here, Bailey," Denny angrily protested, "you been messing things long enough!"

"Not quite long enough, Denny. You're going to see this thing through."

Their argument was interrupted by entrance of a plain-clothes man.

"Telegram for Mr. Bailey," that gentleman said.

Swiftly Ben's eyes swept across the message. From the typed strips on that yellow sheet he lifted his eyes to mine, a triumphant grin on his handsome face.

3

Nevertheless, Detective Denny was for sending everybody home and for hauling M. Cornier to jail.

"You told these people," Ben coolly reminded him, "that I was going to sum up this case. I insist upon doing that right now, before the papers get this story and make you the jest of Hennepin county."

"What yuh mean by that crack?"

"I mean, Mr. Denny, that you are not yet at the bottom of this mystery."

"I suppose that you are, Mr. Private Investigator!"

"My feet have just touched bottom, Mr. City Investigator. All that remains now is for us to find the murderer of Howard Ralston and apprehend his accomplice."

"What you talking 'bout?" sneered Denny. "Ain't the murderer here in my hands with confession fresh on his lips?"

"I don't think so."

"You said *accomplice*. Explain yourself."

"There has to be an accomplice," Ben replied. "Chic Quayle couldn't have worked alone. For one thing—"

"So, in spite of Mr. Cornier's confession, you going to insist that this here mysterious Chic Quayle murdered Howard Ralston. Next thing I know, you'll be saying that the Baroness Mathilde is haunting this house."

"Right, Denny. There is a Baroness Mathilde at *Windermere.*"

Detective Denny snorted contempt of Ben and viciously twisted the link of the handcuffs upon Cornier's wrists, saying, bull-doggedly, "You did kill him, didn't yuh?"

"For the love of heaven, take me away and end this torture!"

"M. Cornier honestly believes that he has killed his friend," said Ben. "But he is wrong. He couldn't have done that. In fact, I am so dead sure he didn't that I'm willing to bet as much on the accuracy of my statement as M. Cornier himself bet with Mr. Ralston in that fatal wager on the Borgia poison ring."

"Now I know you're screwy," Denny mocked.

"M. Cornier," Ben suggested, "suppose you tell us exactly what happened here in 'the tomb' last night."

Reluctantly the handcuffed friend and partner of Howard Ralston told of his resolution to substitute for the genuine Borgia the counterfeit that Ralston had given him. Praying that the Duke of Vedena would break into "the tomb" and retrieve that which he regarded as his property, M. Cornier saw in that possible burglary an escape from obligation to pay his lost wager.

Briefly he outlined the attempt he had been caught making, and then went on to his midnight effort. He came to "the tomb" *via* the fireplace route, puzzling over means of opening the Chinese cabinet. He didn't know its secrets; but he felt reasonably sure that with ample time at his disposal, he might get the hang of the contraption.

As he entered "the tomb," he saw Ralston shoot. Horrified, he recognized the mummy of Serapion standing not ten feet from his friend, its fleshless finger pointing at him and discharging a ray of greenish light against his heart. Rooted to the spot by numbing terror, tongue-frozen, M. Cornier knew his senses reeling. He closed his eyes against the fearful spectacle, but the crash of the falling body of Ralston caused him to jerk them open. He saw Ralston lying face down upon the floor, his left arm folded under him—his right outflung, with the hand gripping a smoking revolver.

Then he saw me, staggering dizzily—my eyes fixed upon the form of the master of *Windermere.* To his amazement, I, too, crumpled to the floor. Before he could command his own motion, a third form glided from the shadows beyond the teetering mummy and knelt beside me.

In the hands of that third individual something glittered evilly in the light from the gas-logs. I jerked, M. Cornier said, as the glittering thing struck my arm, and groaned. From me the stranger glided to the prostrate Ralston.

"Did you see the face of the intruder?" Ben interrupted to ask.

"His back was toward me before I was aware of his presence and intention," replied Cornier.

"Okay. Go on."

Rapid thinking on the part of M. Cornier convinced him that Ralston had only fainted from sudden faltering of the afflicted heart. The stranger, whatever he might be, evidently intended to kill. Fear for the life of his friend galvanized Cornier into action. Snatching up the vengeance dagger of the Scarlet Dragons, he plunged it into the back of the would-be assassin. Then, suddenly aware of other forms moving in "the tomb," M. Cornier lost nerve and fled.

Later, drawn by compelling inquisitiveness, he returned to that chamber of horror. He found "the tomb" still dimly lighted. Howard Ralston's body was gone.

The sound of movement beyond the door of Pietro's shop and of Paul's anxious voice in the hall accentuated his alarm. He moved to make his getaway, but curiosity drove him back to look upon the face of the man he had slain. Drawing the dagger from that bloody back, he turned the body over. What he saw like to have killed him. How, he wondered, could Howard Ralston and the man who had been about to attack him have changed places so quickly that the dagger, impelled by his, Cornier's hand, entered the back of Ralston instead of the back of the attacking assassin? And where was the body of the slain man?

A single urge obsessed him: he must take Ralston's body away. He lifted the body and escaped with it into the fireplace tunnel. The rest was as Patterson had told us and as we had figured it out.

"He's said enough to hang hisself higher'n a kite!" declared Hal Denny. "There's no use prolonging this affair."

"Let the young fellar alone," grumbled Sleepy Wallingford. "He's got brains. Better listen to 'im."

"I ain't listening to nobody."

Denny's ire was up—the Irish blood in him fighting hot. He jerked at the handcuff link, as he started dragging M. Cornier toward the double doors.

"Please be patient, Mr. Denny," Paul pled. "Let's hear what Ben has to say."

"There ain't no sense in it."

But the flame of determination had flared inside Paul as well as inside Mr. Denny. He had his way.

Given free rein, Ben took position over against the wainscoting between the fireplace and the Chinese cabinet, not far from where Mademoiselle Fifi sat. He didn't take notice of her, but I saw her measuring him from the corner of her right eye—all the while her hands toying nervously with an odd locket she had elected to wear. It was the one and only time I ever saw jewelry upon her person.

"It is now time to reconstruct this crime," Ben informed us. "You have heard the story Luigi Donatello told. You've heard M. Cornier's story. Neither man heard the other, yet their narratives dovetail. However, they haven't told everything. Nor have they held anything back, for each man told all that he himself knew; but there was more taking place in and about 'the tomb' that night than either of them knew. Let us get the entire set-up before us.

"We have done a lot of talking about three menaces: the Borgia poison ring, the vengeance dagger of the Scarlet Dragons, and the mummy of Serapion; but we have been inclined to ignore the fourth and most vicious menace. I refer to the Josephine diamonds.

"The night of August 15, this house was the destined scene of crime. Murder was inevitable. Why? Because Mr. Howard Ralston had inadvisedly—and not altogether honestly—brought into 'the tomb' four objects that actually were dynamite in his hands. Repeatedly he had been warned; but characteristically he ignored the warnings, even to the extent of recklessly exposing himself to the death blow.

"First came the Duke of Vedena and Mrs. Lansing, demanding return of the Borgia and threatening to burn the house down to regain possession of the jewel."

"But," Mrs. Lansing serenely interposed, "we didn't do that."

"Mrs. Lansing, we have the admission of Dr. Lao Wong that you requested him to burglarize *Windermere* and get the Borgia for you. How's that for a college sleuth, *madame?*"

Did you ever see a toy balloon deflate? Well, the towering lady's reaction to Ben's question reminded me of that.

"The Duke and Mrs. Lansing, accompanied by Dr. Wong's lieutenant, Soo Wang, drove in a hired cab to this house night before last.
We located the taxi driver, *madame,* and dragged the facts out of him.
While you sat there in that cab, Soo Wang came to the house, bent
upon obtaining the Borgia. He left a broken fingernail in testimony
of his nocturnal visit. Soo Wang found, however, that someone had
preceded him; for as he approached the windows of this room, he perceived a kneeling figure—a gaunt Chinese man, busy with a steel saw.
That man with the saw was Chang Lee Hi, who had just descended
from the cornice above this room, where he had cut light and telephone
wires. Soo Wang waited in the shadows. Chang Lee Hi cut through the
bar of the window yonder, cut the glass about the window lock, and
crept into this room. Soo Wang followed.

"That gives us two men inside the supposedly locked 'tomb.'

"Also seeking the Borgia, came Luigi Donatello. Fortunately for
him, he found the convenient window and entered 'the tomb.' That
gave *Windermere* three uninvited guests that night. . . . But there were
more than three men in this room. . . .

"How many more men were present, you ask me? Four others,
ladies and gentlemen. Seven in all." (I knew that Ben was counting me
among the seven, and shivers raced the length of my spine.) Ben went
on, "Mr. West sat there at his desk. Hidden in the shadows of the sarcophagus was Chic Quayle—known as Dr. Adolphus Elsing—"

Julia Wilmorton clutched the arms of her chair, every vestige of
color drained from her beautiful face. Fifi Burgoyne looked mighty
sick, I thought.

Ben continued: "Over there before the double doors stood Howard
Ralston, he having come to 'the tomb' to challenge the *ka* of Serapion.
And—there was M. Cornier, standing there before the fireplace. Every-
body in this room—if we may except Chic Quayle—was horrified; for
the *ka* of old Serapion had stepped forth from that ornate sarcophagus.
It had paced half the length of the room. It had pointed its fleshless
finger and shot an eerie beam of green light upon the heart of Howard
Ralston."

Awful! That's the only word to describe the tenseness of "the
tomb's" atmosphere as Ben dramatically paused to let us visualize the
dangerous situation.

"Suppose you let us have your solution," Denny insisted.

And Ben let us have it—with results that even he had not anticipated. It worked out in greater part as he and Phil Strong and Wayland had planned. But the horror of it, they had not dreamed of.

"The crime perpetrated in this room that night was designed to be the greatest scare in the annals of crime," Ben said, smoothly.

"Scare?"

"Scare is what I said, Mr. Denny. Chic Quayle didn't want to kill Howard Ralston with his own hands. Knowing the legend of the *ka* of Serapion and knowing also of the threat of the Brothers of Karnak, he decided that he might as well kill Mr. Ralston by scaring him to death. You see, Pietro had communicated to the gentle Gwendolyn Seabury the fact that Howard Ralston had a bad heart.

"By making it appear that Mr. Ralston died of heart failure, Quayle would divert suspicion from himself and his accomplice, thus permitting them to move easily along the line of their future action without fear of detection. Positive that he had planned skillfully enough to cover his trail, Quayle worked confidently. In fact, audacity has characterized every movement made by Chic Quayle and his pretty Marietta Gale, *alias* Gwendolyn Seabury. But Quayle's love for the bizarre proved his undoing."

"You mean to imply," Paul asked, "that Gwendolyn Seabury was in this house?"

"She is in this room right now, Paul."

If respiration hung suspended before that statement was made, it now seemed to cease altogether. Gwendolyn Seabury! Ben had said that she was at that moment in "the tomb," seated there with the rest of us. She had to be either Rose Marie Blodgett or Fifi Burgoyne. Which? I reasoned that she could be no other than Fifi Burgoyne. But Fifi was a brunette, whereas Gwendolyn Seabury had been a demure little blonde. Same size and build, I argued—striving to convince myself. Hair could be dyed. And there it was! Ben had sent me to analyze a hair. My findings indicated that the hair had originally been blonde. . . . But, again, Gwendolyn Seabury had blue eyes. No, a person couldn't change the color of the eyes. There was a catch somewhere. I hoped that Ben wasn't slipping.

The French maid sat there tugging at that odd locket she had strung about her neck. Her eyes kept seeking those of Julia Wilmorton.

As we sat there spellbound by Ben's narrative, a blinding streak of lightning shot weird illumination athwart the room. Women screamed; men cursed. Without warning, Mildred Manning slipped to the floor.

"Stand back, all of you," commanded Nurse Lutie. "Give her air."

Brookes opened the mystery window. A draft of cold air swept in upon us, extinguishing every candle. All as swiftly, there followed a lull in the storm.

"Don't anybody move!" Denny's voice crackled in the dark. "Brookes, light the candles."

More than one sprang to execute that order, despite Denny's imperative warning. Matches sputtered into fire in various sections of "the tomb"; candle flames flickered uncertainly in a faintly stirring breeze.

"Where's Ben?" Paul cried in sudden alarm.

"Where's Fifi Burgoyne?" my cry echoed.

Uniformed officers had been on duty at every door and also without the house. Neither Ben nor Fifi could have crossed the room and escaped through the window Brookes had opened. Amazement marked the candle-lighted features of every occupant of "the tomb."

Pointing to the wainscoting against which Ben had been standing, Julia Wilmorton whispered, "They're behind that wall. There's a hidden room there."

"Just as Mr. Bailey and I figured," Wayland Thomas exulted. "Only we couldn't figure out an entrance to it, other than the ladder going down behind the paneling in Fifi's clothes closet."

"You've been down that ladder?" snapped Denny.

"No, sir. We just knew it was there, that's all. It had to be there, Mr. Bailey said. We couldn't find the entrance from the closet, however. Howard Ralston planned too cleverly—and to his tragic undoing, if you want my opinion."

Gripping his gun firmly, Detective Denny advanced to the wainscoting and rapped sharply upon one of the panels. For answer, a bullet splintered the wood not an inch from his hand.

"Better get back, all of you," Denny warned us. "We're dealing with a desperate woman." Himself stepping to a position of safety, he shouted, "Come out, Fifi, or I'll shoot you out!"

There was no response. Hal Denny plugged the paneling once—twice. In quick return there came answering shots.

"Wait!" Paul urged, leaning forward frantically in his wheel chair. "Ben's in there!"

Ignoring that request, Denny fired three shots more, each time bringing return fire from the barricaded woman.

"She's got one shot left," murmured Sleepy Wallingford. "How's she going to use it?"

We waited; but there was no sound from beyond the punctured wainscoting.

"Come out!" commanded Denny. "Come out, or we'll bust through and get yuh!"

The sixth shot came through, nearly getting Denny, who for the moment had forgotten his caution and moved within range of fire.

"That's her last," pronounced Sleepy. "She ain't got no more."

"Brookes, get an axe! Smash in the panels!" Paul gave order.

Unmindful of his wound, Pietro bounded across the room, calling Brookes to follow. He seized up two paleolithic hammers, tossing one to the butler. Together the two men crushed out the panels.

Cowering in the farthest corner of that secret room, they found Fifi Burgoyne. They dragged her out into "the tomb." Denny took handcuffs from one of the policemen and had Fifi fast bound. Her lips tight together, the French maid sat in her former chair, glaring murderously at Hal Denny. She still enjoyed sufficient freedom in the use of arms and hands to continue fumbling with that odd locket of hers.

"Find Ben!" Paul kept calling.

As if in answer to his anxious calling, the double doors were opened, revealing a disheveled and scratched Ben Bailey, who grinned at us from just across the threshold.

"Where'd you come from?" demanded amazed Hal Denny.

"From successful checking up on my deductions and from making an interesting discovery."

If ever I saw Ben nonchalant, it was then. He lighted a cigarette with all the studied technique of William Gillette playing Sherlock Holmes. Inhaling a couple of easeful *drags,* he serenely surveyed his expectant audience.

"You *was* in that secret room yonder, wasn't yuh? Huh?"

"I was indeed, Mr. Denny; but I climbed a ladder to freedom and complete vindication of my theory. I have just descended from Fifi Burgoyne's room, which is right above the two hidden rooms—into one of which you have smashed your way."

"You know?" faltered Julia Wilmorton.

"Everything, Mrs. Wilmorton." He saw Fifi then. "So," he said, "you've got her?"

"You're darn tootin' right we got her!" gloated Denny.

"I was afraid," Ben went on, "after she jammed me into that second chamber that she might kill herself with her last bullet. Decided to live and face it, have you, *mademoiselle?*"

Fifi regarded him defiantly, her scarlet lips a thin, tight line across her white face.

"I hate to tell you this, *mademoiselle,*" Ben continued, "but Faustin Dufresne is dead."

Like a creature frozen into marble, Fifi sat staring silently at Ben—her dark eyes registering unbelief.

Ben crossed to the Renaissance table and uncovered the face of the dead man lying there. The crowd gasped as it recognized the features of Howard Ralston.

Ben smiled, remarking, "Good make-up."

"What?" from Hal Denny.

"Yes," said Ben. "A make-up worthy the artist creating it. When the boys down to the homicide bureau clean up that map of his and scrape away nose putty and grease paint, the resemblance to Howard Ralston will disappear."

"You're telling me," gasped Denny, "that the dead man on the table—"

"Is Faustin Dufresne, *alias* Chic Quayle, *alias* Dr. Adolphus Elsing."

An anguished cry broke from the painted lips of Fifi Burgoyne as she pressed that odd locket against them. She fell to the floor—dead. Quickly Ben was on his knees beside her, the curious locket in his hands. Two little white sticks fell from it.

"*Cyanide of potassium,*" he murmured. "Quickest way out. After all, it is perhaps best."

Ben straightened the limbs of the body; then rose and faced Denny.

"There lies Gwendolyn Seabury," he said. "The little blonde who intrigued Pietro Martini once upon a time during an Atlantic crossing."

"But—I thought that there diary said that the Seabury woman was a blonde?"

"*Was* is right, Denny. But blondes have been known to become brunettes."

"Their hair," scoffed Denny. "But never their eyes."

From his pocket Ben pulled the yellow sheet of that telegram. "This wire from *Hoyt, Incorporated* of New York City says that they do."

"You got some explaining to do, Big Boy."

"Right now," Ben evaded, "you must rescue a man from that second mystery chamber. I don't know where the trap door is through which Fifi pushed me, so you'll have to smash your way in. But be careful; the man is in a small place—alone in the dark and ill."

A saw and knives from Pietro's shop did the trick.

"Follow me, you guys!" Denny ordered Sleepy and Phil Strong.

The three of them disappeared through the aperture. Shortly they emerged, carrying a wounded man. They brought him into the candle-lighted "tomb" and placed him upon the Spanish sofa.

Anxiously I bent over that supine figure. Pietro was at my elbow; and, as my heart almost died within me, I felt his iron grip nigh to breaking my arm.

"It *is* the Master," he sobbed, brokenly. "He's not dead! *He's not dead!*"

He fell to his knees beside the sofa, fondling one of the *Master's* hot hands and weeping his joy.

Slowly Paul wheeled his chair to the sofa. There he sat, his own eyes dim with tears as he looked upon his father's face. Impulsively he reached out a hand, placing it gently upon Pietro's bowed head.

4

Howard Ralston, vaguely conscious, was carried up to his own room and placed in care of Dr. Kelsey and Nurse Lutie. Thanks to the soup Fifi had fed him, he was not so weak as we had apprehended. His greatest suffering resulted from the drug Chic Quayle had shot into him and from a cut in his temple where he injured himself when he fell. The bandages from that wound were the blood-stained rags we had found in the furnace the day before.

And who unlocked the handcuffs for Henri Cornier? Why, the woman he loved, of course.

"I calculate it'll be all right," Denny hesitated.

"Naturally," affirmed Ben. "We know he didn't kill Howard Ralston."

"Sure not," Sleepy Wallingford chimed in. "All along, I didn't think Mr. Ralston was murdered."

"Smart guy, you are!" growled Denny.

"Well," murmured Sleepy, "there's some smarter, an' some not so smart."

"Maybe Mr. Cornier didn't kill Howard Ralston," Denny flared. "But he killed two other guys, didn't he? This here Chic Quayle and Chang Lee Hi."

"Surely," Ben affably agreed. "He killed two master criminals that were wanted by police of several countries. New York has a dead-or-alive reward posted for Quayle, and I reckon Chang Lee Hi won't embarrass M. Cornier in difficulties with the law—not when he's proved himself a benefactor to society."

"There's technicalities," Denny demurred. "Mr. Cornier will have to stay put, just in case—"

"All that can be arranged," Ben caught him up.

M. Cornier sat on the arm of Julia Wilmorton's chair, his protecting arm about her shoulders.

Denny searched for a stogy, but I had a fragrant weed handy.

"Now, Bailey," he said, spreading himself like a turkey cock, "finish your talk to these here folks and tell 'em how we got at the truth in this here case."

"I'll be happy to tell them," Ben said, "if they want to linger."

No one took advantage of opportunity to escape, so Ben let them have it.

"When West stumbled into my study with cry that murder had been done at *Windermere* and outlined the horrible experiences he had undergone in witnessing the emergence of the so-called *ka* of Serapion from that sarcophagus, I immediately thought of the black arts—legerdemain, the craft of stage magicians."

"Ha!" I involuntarily ejaculated. "That accounts for the cards from the *L*-file."

"Right, Win! I knew that there is no *ka*—that there had to be magic in that stunt pulled here in 'the tomb.' I realized that the crime was too bizarre to have been conceived by an American—let alone the average type murderer. The engineer of the *ka*-walking exhibition had to be a European—a Frenchman, likely. The *Surete* has on file records of numerous such queer crimes.

"A foreigner, then, I reasoned. But who? Because of the outlandish drug* administered to West—a drug scarcely known to medical practitioners in this country, and only slightly abroad, for that matter—our murderer, therefore, had not only to be one versed in the art of illusion as demonstrated in the *theatre de legerdemain* but also one who knew considerable about Oriental drugs.

"From what West told me, I decided that such an unusual crime could not have been perpetrated by one person alone—there had to be an accomplice. That confederate would of necessity have to be a party in the Ralston household who knew everything about the house and the people in it, and who—"

"And so we picked the French maid, huh?"

"She seemed the most likely suspect in the line-up you had awaiting me when I arrived," Ben replied.

"That's the way I figgered it," Denny said. "Couldn't have been nobody else."

I thought that I detected a smothered snort from Sleepy.

"Then I read West's diary," Ben went on. "There it appeared that the blonde Seabury woman should be accomplice to my master of legerdemain and that her husband, who robbed and beat Pietro Martini, should be the magician sought. Unfortunately, I couldn't recall any French magician who had been involved in criminal activities.

"My suspicion of Fifi Burgoyne mounted. I watched her closely, but she proved wary. Further, there were certain contradictions that baffled me. There was Fifi's dark hair. I asked Miss Lutie to watch for combings from Fifi's pretty head, but Fifi was too neat to leave any about. Only last night did Miss Lutie succeed in getting one lone hair

---

* *Mahamaya,* a drug jealously guarded by the *Dugpas,* red-capped necromancers in the fastnesses of Tibet.

for me. This West analyzed in Pietro's shop and found to be dyed. Microscopic examination of the shaft close to the root revealed that the hair had originally been golden.

"Fifi's eyes bothered me most. Gwendolyn Seabury had blue eyes; Fifi's eyes were dark—a sort of deep hazel color. Hair could be dyed; but as Mr. Denny has sagely informed us, the color of the human eye cannot be changed.

"Nevertheless, the conviction that Fifi Burgoyne and Gwendolyn Seabury were identical grew on me. The ransacking of West's room added further evidence that the murderer or his accomplice was in this house. It wasn't likely that the murderer would tarry here, so it had to be the accomplice—some one left to keep watchful eye on proceedings here and signal when the hour was ripe for the getaway.

"The fragrant odor of the cigar smoke left in West's room and in 'the tomb' was convincing evidence. No woman at *Windermere* smoked. The criminal figured that we would take that fact into consideration and conclude that only a man could have been after the diary. But as West said, women sometimes smoke cigars. In Europe he had seen women smoking little black cigars. So had I. Again the finger of detection pointed to Europe and to European capitals. Fifi Burgoyne was admittedly foreign born.

"Take that attack upon West in his own room. Recourse was had to *la savate* in attempt to knock West out. Who at *Windermere* knew the art of *la savate?* Pietro Martini, yes; but Pietro was not on hand for such playfulness. Not M. Cornier, for he was in his own house. Again the finger of suspicion pointed to the French maid. She had but to step across the hall from West's room to secure haven. Still I wasn't positive—hadn't sufficient evidence.

"Followed rapidly the series of poisonings. Mr. Denny's suspicions ran wild—as whose wouldn't? Elimination left only Fifi Burgoyne.

"Then she foolishly staged a disappearing act. The knotted sheet didn't fool us, for we knew that it was impossible for her to leave either house or grounds. But where did she go? We already knew there was a secret passage and a secret closet in the house. Why not other such rooms? Why not one to which Fifi had access from that tiny room of hers? Wayland and I studied the blueprints of the house and decided that the undiscovered secret room should be just where we found it tonight. But there was no sign of ingress. Again Mr. Denny and I were baffled.

"But, returning to Fifi and the main thread of my—*our* deductions. The simple item of Fifi's disappearance and the impossibility of her being outside the house was tremendously damning in her case.

"Dr. Elsing, absent and mysterious, fascinated my cogitations. The discovery that the real Dr. Elsing was dead and that some one was impersonating him gave me food for considerable reflection. You know the results of our visit to the Elsing establishment.

"A sudden expansion of my consciousness, if I may so term it, threw light upon the problem. Those IOU's. of Mrs. Wilmorton's tipped me off mentally. Memory of the *Case of the Baroness Mathilde* flashed upon my memory.

"From the Elsing house I drove to my own apartment. While in Paris, I had made notes at the *Surete*. Fortunately the celebrated case involving the Baroness Mathilde intrigued me. I had taken down a complete dossier on it. I had newspaper clippings on it. I had in my files photographs of Faustine Dufresne and Marietta Gale. That of Marietta Gale resembled Gwendolyn Seabury as pictured in the photo found with the news story and the IOU's. I knew that we had the case in our hands. I knew that Dufresne was, or had been, impersonating Dr. Adolphus Elsing, and that his wife, Marietta Gale of the numerous *aliases,* must be the French maid he had recommended to Mrs. Wilmorton.

"What brought them to *Windermere?* I next asked myself. The answer was in West's diary—"

"Mr. Bailey kept urging you to study that there diary, Chief—"

"Shut up and listen, will yuh?"

"West, in his diary, recorded how Pietro told Gwendolyn Seabury about the Josephine diamonds—recorded how Howard Ralston in Venice read of how Quayle and his wife slipped by emigration officials—recorded, too, how he had been concerned for the safety of his million and a half dollar jewels. Clearly, *we* told ourselves, Quayle was after the Josephine diamonds."

"But why drag Aunt Julia in?" Paul asked.

"Recall how the Baroness Mathilde had been more or less innocently used by Quayle. Mrs. Wilmorton knew the combination of the diamond safe—she was heiress in Manning's estate in event of the death of Miss Manning; in fact, she was key to the entire situation insofar as Quayle's plans were concerned."

"What about the other menaces and the people that wanted them?" I asked.

"None of them worried us after we began concentrating upon the diamond clue," Ben replied.

"That's right," Denny concurred, pleasantly puffing at his cigar.

Ben talked on: "Having identified Quayle, my next problem was to locate him. I conceived the idea of his engineering the mummy illusion. Materials located in Dr. Elsing's laboratory clearly revealed that part of the plot to me. But where was our adept in legerdemain? Elsing had to be Quayle; Fifi had to be Gwendolyn Seabury. But was she?

"It became increasingly clear that I could locate Quayle only through spotting his accomplice. Luckily, I found this little black box." Ben displayed it. "This case, Mr. Denny, is stamped with the name of an international optical firm—*Hoyt, Inc.,* of New York City. It is made to contain contact glasses. Recently I had been sent circulars from *Hoyt, Inc.* I wired that firm. At opportune moment, the reply came—came to clinch my identification of Gwendolyn Seabury. . . . But still I couldn't account for the whereabouts of Chic Quayle.

"During the night I came down here, alone into 'the tomb,' to ponder my problem. Gwendolyn Seabury was in the house. Why couldn't Chic Quayle also be here? There was a secret room. And, Mr. Denny, there was that legion of soup bowls. . . . Suddenly it came to me. The man on the roof. Howard Ralston, in business suit, seen by Brookes going into Mrs. Wilmorton's suite. That was Chic Quayle. He had to be in the house. And there was no place for him to hide save in that secret room yonder under Fifi's room. We had found the body of Howard Ralston. Quayle was therefore in hiding, and Fifi was feeding him. When the excitement subsided, she planned to sneak him out of the house. We know that he was clever at getaways.

"But there were the bloody bandages that had come from the furnace. They set me thinking along a new line. Somehow I perceived that there had been a mistake in identity—that Fifi had spirited away the body of Howard Ralston, thinking it that of her husband. The darkness of that hidden sanctuary and the fact that Fifi carried only a faint torch enabled Mr. Ralston to escape recognition and possible death at her hands. Had Mr. Ralston regained consciousness, there is little guessing what might have happened.

"Mr. Cornier, returning to 'the tomb' shortly after that secret performance by Fifi, found the dead Quayle. Because of the excellent make-up Quayle had created, M. Cornier mistook the body for that of his friend and did those things of which he has told us."

"And maybe you folks don't think I felt like a dirty so-and-so when we found that out," Denny assured our audience.

I believe that Sleepy wanted to grunt again, but a warning look from Denny inhibited the attempt.

"I sent for Wayland then, because he knows a lot about houses, being a student of architecture," Ben resumed. "In vain we searched for an entrance to that secret chamber. We did find the practically invisible wiring laid by Quayle for his bizarre performance. . . . Well, it was a lucky break when we frightened Fifi to the point where she pushed me through the panel into the first of the secret rooms. And—well, that's all."

"And damned clever work, I'm saying," was Denny's comment. "Mr. Bailey has been indispensable to me in this here case. I doubt if I could of handled it without him."

"He surely is to be appreciated," was Mrs. Lansing's acrid remark. "Now, may the Duke have his ring?"

"That is up to Howard Ralston," Ben replied.

"Ben has done superior work," Paul cut in. "He'll never know how much it is appreciated. There are, however, some questions I still wish answered."

"Sure!" was Hal Denny's magnanimous response.

"I should like first to know," Paul began, "why Chic Quayle was so slow about getting the diamonds. He could have taken them long ago, so why the delay and this crazy performance of his?"

"You tell him, Bailey," said Denny.

"Compare this case with that of the Baroness Mathilde," Ben said. "Quayle, or Dufresne, was caught up with in that plot. He wasn't taking chances again. Having learned of the threats of the Brothers of Karnak, he seized upon the *ka* idea as happy means of covering his tracks. The Karnak threat and the walking *ka* would divert suspicion from himself. He knew of Mr. Ralston's weak heart, and figured that the magical appearance of the ka—at which Ralston scoffed—would undoubtedly scare his victim to death, the shock of surprise being too great. The police would concentrate on the *ka* mystery, overlooking the diamond angle entirely, thus leaving Quayle free to carry on for even greater game. Luckily for all of us, the program worked out only in part."

"Right here," Denny said, "I want to know your part in this conspiracy, Mrs. Wilmorton."

"I have that figured out, Denny," Bailey spoke, to the relief of Julia Wilmorton. "Quayle planned to take Mrs. Wilmorton to France with Fifi and himself when the estate was settled and Mrs. Wilmorton had taken over Basil Manning's property. You see, Quayle not only wanted the Josephine diamonds, but also the millions left by Manning. In time, he would probably have gotten Mr. Ralston's entire property, just as he did that of the Baron de Longpres. Mrs. Wilmorton, you are indeed a lucky woman to have escaped the snares laid for you."

"I think the man must have hypnotised me, just as he did the baroness you told about," Julia Wilmorton murmured. "He had strange eyes, with penetrating, compelling stare. . . . Oh, he and Fifi threatened and tortured me! The mental agony I have been through cannot be described."

The pathetic story came out piece by piece. The night of the crime, the pseudo Elsing compelled Julia Wilmorton to send Fifi to him with a business suit belonging to Ralston. Accustomed as he had been to easy access to *Windermere,* Quayle realized that he must no longer be seen about the place in his impersonation of Elsing. He had to get into the house, however. To facilitate the gaining of such entrance, he decided to be seen, if seen at all, as Howard Ralston. Made-up and dressed as Ralston, Quayle came to *Windermere,* climbed a rose trellis to the top of the house and descended to the roof of the *porte-cochere.* His imitation of the screech of the owl signaled Mrs. Wilmorton that he had come.

"I let him in at the *porte-cochere* window," Julia Wilmorton continued, the hand on which she wore an emerald ring brushing in slow gesture across her forehead. "I was afraid not to, for Fifi was standing in the door of my suite with a gun in her hand. He changed to a Tuxedo in Fifi's room and descended by the ladder from her clothes closet to the secret chamber below, carrying that fearful bundle with him—"

"The 'grave clothes' he had forced you to smuggle into the house that night?" Ben queried.

Julia Wilmorton nodded, shudderingly.

"He had been down that ladder many times before, I take it?" Ben asked next.

"Every time he called—professionally, Mr. Bailey. That gave him the secrecy and the time he needed for—"

"Hold it!" Ben stopped her. "We aren't ready for that revelation yet."

"I think, Bailey," Denny had to say at this point, "that these here folks would like to know how Fifi managed about her eyes."

"Think we ought to tell them, Mr. Denny?"

"Well—why not?"

"They might be tempted at some time—"

"Shucks, now," chortled Denny, with a sort of swagger, "I calculate none of these respectable folks is going to try anything like that—that there disguise."

"Very well, Denny. I'll tell; but the consequences be on your head. Had Chic Quayle been able to keep Gwendolyn Seabury entirely out of Pietro's sight, the disguise would not have been necessary. The fact that when she came to *Windermere* she must not be recognized as Gwendolyn Seabury, drove Fifi to an optician, who gladly ordered her contact glasses from *Hoyt, Inc.* Contact glasses are saucer-shaped shells of optical glass which are worn under the eyelid in direct contact with the eye itself. Fitted snugly over the cornea, they are designed as a substitute for ordinary eye glasses. They are being worn by millions of people in this country and abroad. Practically invisible, they move freely with the eyeball in every direction. The apparatus with which to remove them will probably be located when a thorough ransacking is made of Fifi's effects."

"Wouldn't contact glasses be transparent?" Paul challenged. "Fifi's eyes would still show blue."

"You will find that her lenses have been tinted a yellow-brown against sun glare, Paul. That color superimposed upon the natural blue gave her eyes a hazel tone."

"Ain't that the damn trick for yuh?" Denny asked of the interested audience in "the tomb."

"What I want to know next," Paul said, "is how Quayle made the *ka* walk out of that sarcophagus."

"Simple," Ben laughed. "He didn't. He put the genuine mummy back there in the hidden room while you folks were upstairs, replacing it with the duplicate he had fashioned and which Mrs. Wilmorton smuggled into *Windermere* for him. The duplicate now lies hidden in the innermost secret chamber. It is the thing that walked. To a master of the art of legerdemain, such a stunt as making the *ka* of old Serapion walk was comparatively easy in accomplishment."

"But how'd he do it?" Sleepy Wallingford's interest compelled him to ask.

"I puzzled a lot over the phenomena of the walking *ka*, Mr. Wallingford, but a satisfactory answer eluded me. I had it all figured out—that is, how it could be done; but I could lay hand upon no tangible evidence to substantiate my theory. If Faustin Dufresne, who had once managed a theatre devoted to illusions, engineered that weird phenomenon, it had to be legerdemain; for there was no way of manipulating that fragile mummy and making it act as West declared that it did. When we ransacked the Elsing house yesterday, I ran across the concrete evidence I needed. You see, Quayle prepared the whole thing there and made Mrs. Wilmorton bring it to *Windermere*—"

"Ha! I get yuh!" exclaimed Denny, momentarily forgetting his pose of omniscience. "Quayle dressed up in a mummy suit."

"Quayle wasn't taking chances like that, Mr. Denny. The shot that West saw Mr. Ralston put through that floating mummy would have killed Quayle and spared M. Cornier the trouble."

"But you just said Quayle couldn't manipulate the real mummy."

"Quayle didn't." Then with mocking smile for the city investigator, Ben added, "If you will all adjourn to the drawing-rooms and remain there until I call you, Strong, Wayland, and I will stage the apparition for you—that is, if you want to linger longer."

There wasn't one in that crowd that didn't want to see Ben's show.

5

In about three-quarters of an hour, when Ben summoned us back to "the tomb," we found him with Phil Strong. Wayland had vanished. Ben placed us where we could observe the things he wanted us to see, at the same time reserving space for his floor show.

Looking at his watch, he said, "It is exactly six o'clock. A storm is with us, as it was the night the *ka* walked toward Howard Ralston. We shall imagine, however, that it is midnight—the menaceful hour at which Howard Ralston was to die if he failed to promise return of the corpse of Serapion to Egypt. In re-enacting the drama of night before last, Strong will play Howard Ralston, Wayland will be Fifi, and I shall impersonate Chic Quayle. . . . Strong, as Ralston, is armed with an automatic. It carries genuine bullets, and he is a dead shot; I want everybody to keep out of line of fire—to stay right where you are placed."

Phil Strong went out into the entrance hall, locking the double doors as he went. The drapes were tightly drawn at all windows and the tapers of the huge candelabrum extinguished. The gas-logs were lighted and turned to burn so uncertainly that "the tomb" enjoyed faintest illumination.

"Now," cautioned Ben, "don't anybody move until I give word." He disappeared into the shadows of the sarcophagus. A pause. We waited.

Then Ben called, "Let her go!"

The storm crackled fearfully. My own heart contracted in agony of apprehension. I knew that Howard Ralston lay upstairs, alive and in capable hands; but somehow it seemed to me then in "the tomb" that I was again to see him struck down. . . . Then we heard a key turning in the lock of the double doors. Those doors opened, disclosing Phil Strong, gun in hand. He stepped into "the tomb"; shut the double doors and locked them. Again an almost total darkness—just light enough to outline things in ghostly indistinctness. Then Strong's exclamation as he pretended to find the light switch failing response to his touch.

Hard upon his ejaculation, a creaking sound smote our ears. I knew that every pair of eyes in that chamber of horror—impelled like my own—focused upon the spot whence the sound emanated. We saw the lid of the sarcophagus slowly swinging outward. Looking more ghoulish than ever I imagined it could, the mummy of Serapion faced us. I sensed the shiver that stirred the company of nervous spectators. I heard the gasp of amazement as the mummy began to move.

Majestically it stepped from the sarcophagus, moving slowly, seeming to float rather than to walk—yet I noted that its feet touched the floor. It advanced straight toward Phil Strong. Within ten feet of him it halted. Its right arm lifted. The weirdest light I have ever seen suddenly emanated from its pointing index finger to fall upon a spot below Strong's heart.

Phil Strong raised his automatic, coolly took aim, and fired. The bullet passed through the hateful mummy, trembling it slightly. A moment Phil Strong stared, horrified, at that swaying apparition. Then, with a little gasp, he clutched at his heart and fell to the floor.

Ben, impersonating Chic Quayle, glided swiftly from hiding. Before we quite grasped the meaning of his action, he was kneeling beside Strong, affecting—pantomimically—to shoot that *mahamaya* into Strong's arm.

A cry of consternation echoed through "the tomb" as the electric lights blazed into brilliance. One of the plain-clothes men, unaware of what was being performed in "the tomb," had at that moment succeeded in adjusting the lightning-injured system. Blinking in the dazzle of that startling illumination, we all stood staring at the *thing* hovering there in our midst—the abominable *ka* of Serapion. It indeed looked the cheap contraption that it was, the atmosphere necessary for its effect of hideousness being removed.

This time Ben insisted that Julia Wilmorton tell the story. Chic Quayle, she said, impersonating Dr. Elsing, had called often at *Windermere*. At such times, he worked unmolested in "the tomb," where he carefully laid his mechanism in place. He photographed the genuine mummy upon its arrival and rapidly noted its dimensions.

"Fit rival to Pietro—that Chic Quayle," I remarked.

"He did give Pietro a race for honor in being prize artificer," Ben laughed. "But he proved himself the greater genius by breaking and re-sealing the sarcophagus so that Mr. Ralston never suspected it had been tampered with. And what a craftsman he proved himself in constructing the fake mummy. Look at the thing. Built on a wire frame and covered with bakerlite to make it as weightless as possible. It is fashioned and painted in exact duplication of the aged corpse.

"Quayle installed inside his mummy a direct current motor to operate the simple mechanism of the thing. Artfully contrived wires and a nicely adjusted system of weights and pulleys caused the thing to simulate a walking movement. The electric light flashed through its finger is an ingenious contrivance, I think. . . . Just a robot, that's all. A time clock was placed within it, set for the hour, when, according to the warning, the Brothers of Karnak would draw the *ka* out of the sacred corpse to point the finger of death at Howard Ralston's heart.

"The invisible wiring that Wayland and I discovered led to the hidden room there—one proof that there was such a room. Wayland is in there now, doing as Fifi did. She pulled a tiny switch that set in operation an electric current that swung open the sarcophagus lid. The time clock inside the bakerlite mummy did the rest—and the terrifying corpse walked forth to meet its victim."

Continuing her story, Julia Wilmorton told how, after she brought the fake mummy to the house that night, Quayle had inflated it with helium gas to facilitate its semblance of a floating movement as the weights inside it made it walk. Mrs. Wilmorton had been forced down the ladder into the secret room with Fifi, the maid being afraid that her mistress, left alone, might become panicky and give the alarm. Mrs. Wilmorton had been compelled to aid Fifi in dragging the body, which Fifi mistook for Quayle's, into the second of the secret chambers. She had seen Fifi lower the steel barriers. Then the two of them had climbed the ladder to Fifi's room—after Fifi, usually mindful of every detail, had failed to return the mummy to the sarcophagus after concealing the robot. She had also been forced to descend into "the tomb" with Fifi the next morning to replace the genuine mummy in the sarcophagus. At that time, Fifi had smoked a cigar to suggest that a man had visited the big room.

"Thereby aiding us in our deductions. Eh, Mr. Denny?"

"Right, Mr. Bailey."

"Heigh-ho, Mr. Denny," yawned Ben, "what a find we made, eh what?—locating the ingenious robot in the hidden room, along with the semi-conscious Howard Ralston? We have Fifi and la *savate* to thank for that discovery."

"La *savate?*" queried Paul.

"You see," Ben explained, "I figured this way. If Fifi resorted to *la savate* to knock out one victim, she would employ it on another in case emergency demanded. I provided that emergency by standing over there against that particular spot in the wainscoting—beyond which I was certain lay the room I sought. I played her for a goal, and she followed the lead. I admit that it was a risky gamble, but it worked. Whatever the chance to be taken, I had to gain access to that secret room."

NOON OF THE THIRD DAY

1

It was noon of that day when the oddly assorted company assembled for the last time in "the tomb." Everybody there had a copy of the *extras* that shouted the story of the *Windermere Mystery* with banner heads and a picture of smiling Harrison Denny—a photograph snapped with one of my cigars in his wide, Irish mouth. He was lauded by the press. A promotion was promised him.

Good old Ben Bailey—whom the reporters forgot to mention, along with Sleepy Wallingford—grinned when he was shown the news sheets.

"Denny's a good scout," he said.

And that was that.

When we were all assembled for the last time in "the tomb," Howard Ralston, in a wheel chair, was pushed in by Nurse Lutie. Paul walked at one side of that chair, holding his father's hand; Mildred, *ditto,* on the other.

"Youssuf shall carry his mummy back to Egypt," Mr. Ralston murmured. "I hope never to see it again."

"May I have the robot?" was Ben's request.

"That—and more. I can never repay you—"

"I am repaid in seeing you safe and sound, Mr. Ralston."

"Henri," the boss continued, "draw that Borgia from your finger and surrender it to the Duke."

"But you said—"

"I know I did, Henri. A little sleight-of-hand. I substituted rings on you, wishing to guarantee safety of my prize. You understand, I was afraid that some party might break in and steal it."

245

"Then it was the counterfeit ring that disappeared!" I exclaimed.

"Disappeared?"

"Yes, Mr. Ralston. We found the little compartment empty."

It was Pietro's turn to confess. He, afraid to leave the prize where Mr. Ralston had put it, removed it to his own person. He produced it now, and, after M. Cornier had delivered the genuine Borgia to the tearful Duke, gave it to M. Cornier as Howard Ralston directed that he should. But—well, I'm still wondering. . . .

"In as much as Henri has acknowledged that I won the wager, I am satisfied," the boss said. "Further, Julia, get those wager checks from your safety box this afternoon and we'll burn both of them."

As if impelled by some inward urge to rid himself of all the menaces, he next said, "The vengeance sword of the Scarlet Dragons I give to you, Lao Wong, to return to the Scarlet Dragons."

"It shall be as my honorable friend wishes," murmured the Chinese antiquarian. "It is pleasing to me that my friend lives."

"As for the Josephine diamonds," the master of *Windermere* continued, "Well, if Mildred doesn't mind letting Julia have the oil millions, I'd like my son's wife to have those jewels—"

"Dad!"

Howard Ralston joined the hands of Paul and Mildred, placing his own in benediction upon that lovers' clasp, while M. Cornier beamed his approval.

Diffidently, M. Cornier suggested to Paul that there be a double wedding at *Windermere*.

"There shall be," Julia Wilmorton assented. "Mildred and I will divide the 'oil millions'!"

"I don't know about no double wedding," interposed Detective Denny. "Yuh see, Mrs. Wilmorton, you'll have to be held as 'accessory' to this here crime. The courts may even call it 'collusion,' and—"

But Howard Ralston refused to prefer charges and Bailey got in his explanation on hypnotic influence in the two parallel cases, so that the grand jury never even had a chance to bring in an indictment.

There was a double wedding, with Ben and Howard Ralston acting as best men.

And again, that was that.

Oh, yes! Up in my room, after that last general meeting in "the tomb," Hal Denny wrung Ben's hand, saying, "Fine piece of work we've did, Bailey. You been a lot of help."

"Thanks," said Ben, giving Denny a good-natured blow on the chest. "I hope you get that promotion. If ever a man deserved it, you do."

Whereupon Sleepy Wallingford gave the last snort that I shall record.

And me—I thrilled happily when Ben commended me on the way I kept that diary.

"Without it," he said, "I should have had a heck of a time!"

And finally—that was that!

THE CASTLEFORD CONUNDRUM

COACHWHIP PUBLICATIONS
COACHWHIPBOOKS.COM

THE DARTMOUTH MURDERS /
THE WAILING ROCK MURDERS

COACHWHIP PUBLICATIONS
COACHWHIPBOOKS.COM

THE WINE ROOM MURDER

MURDER IN A WALLED TOWN

www.ingramcontent.com/pod-product-compliance
Lightning Source LLC
Chambersburg PA
CBHW020635260626
47157CB00008B/2760

* 9 7 8 1 6 1 6 4 6 3 9 8 4 *